THE HOUSE OF
ELAH

LAUREN STINTON

A NOVEL

The House of Elah
Copyright © 2012
Lauren Stinton

For more information on this book and others by Lauren Stinton, visit www.facebook.com/laurenstintonbooks or write to lestinton@gmail.com.

Cover design by Trace Chiodo
trace@chiododesign.com

For Mom and Dad,
who love me well.

For Donna Sparks,
who invested in me.
It was a big deal, and
I wanted to be sure you knew.

acknowledgments

Many thanks to my mother, Susan Stinton, for all the time she put into editing this manuscript and listening to me go on and on about the plot. I appreciate you.

I want to thank Brooke Ewers and Cherish Brunner, who haven't actually "read" this book...They had it read to them, which I loved doing. Your insights and encouragement were wonderful.

I also want to thank Ashley Van Winkle, who read the manuscript, gave feedback, and squealed in excitement at all the important parts. You are the reader every writer wants to have.

And finally, thanks to Trace Chiodo, who made this book a work of art. Well done. The cover's extraordinary, and I'm still digging that leaf.

part one

The Chosen Son

$\mathcal{A}$lashar Vereen never had difficulty selling slaves until he tried to sell the Furmorean. The man was well built and muscled, with hands used to labor. Most of the merchants in this city owned mines. The land was not for farming; it was filled with granite. They would need men like this—ones who were used to hard work and lifting. But no one would touch him because of the scar on his chest.

It was shaped like a half-moon, and whoever had marked him like this had done it with a steady hand and a sharp blade. The scar was precise. Alashar had, of course, noticed the mark right away, but never would he have considered that the silly, superstitious minds of Blue Mountain would be afraid of it and avoid the slave as they would a diseased dog. Half a dozen men had suggested Alashar drown him. Another half-dozen suggested he burn him as an offering to the gods.

Alashar had no intention of doing either of those things. He had purchased the man to sell him at a profit, and it would be ridiculous to kill him because of people's inane fear. If he couldn't sell him in Blue Mountain, he would take him north into Paxa and sell him for their blood games. Let him die there, *after* Alashar had collected the profit he intended.

Within six days' time, Alashar unexpectedly emptied all four of his wagons of wares. He had anticipated spending two weeks in Blue Mountain and then continuing his journey north with a brief stop at Footbridge, some three days' distance around the mountain. But what Blue Mountain lacked in civilization and wisdom, it possessed in coin. The city had grown since Alashar's last visit three years before, and his profits were double what he had expected. His purses were filled to overflowing. He could return to his family in the desert much sooner than anticipated, with ease and plenty of pride, bearing many gifts for his wives and children.

The one item he could not sell at a profit, no matter how hard he tried, was the scarred Furmorean. Alashar could not travel north for the sake of selling one man. However, by the time his pre-planned two weeks were over, only one offer had come in for the Furmorean. A rather sordid offer.

As he made up his mind to accept it and sent his assistant running for the gamer, Alashar stared heavily at the Furmorean, considering the possibilities one last time. The man had to go. This was the only way, but Alashar was sorry to assign any man an end such as this one.

The Furmorean sat in the back of the wagon, his ankles and wrists manacled with bands and chains of black iron. He had not caused him any trouble. In all likelihood, he had been a farmer's son—an innocent man, until war had fallen upon his town and destroyed it, killing and enslaving those around him. He was built like a fighter, but he did not look like a fighter as he sat there in silence, head bowed, his chained hands in his lap.

Alashar approached him. "Which gods do you serve?" he quietly asked him.

The head rose quickly, as if the man were surprised to be addressed.

"I serve Abalel," the Furmorean answered, eventually adding, "my lord."

It was the first set of words he had said in Alashar's hearing. Alashar had not asked him his name or how he had acquired the half-moon scar on his chest.

It is a sign of the gods, the other vendors had whispered. *You should kill him now, before he brings a curse on your family.*

"A Furmorean who serves the god of the sun?" Alashar asked. He looked at the slave with suspicion in his eyes. "Don't your people prefer the gods of the woods? Of rock and stone?"

"I serve Abalel," the Furmorean answered simply.

The simplicity did not make sense to Alashar, and he preferred things to make sense—to line up and form something that could be added and subtracted and multiplied logically. He frowned at the man and said snidely, "Do you not see where you are? Do you not know the offer I have received for you? Don't put your trust in the god of the sun, who can be distilled by shadow. Put your trust in one who responds to a man's service. You are going to need a god's help where you're going."

Something flickered through the man's dark eyes. A line of uncertainty appeared between his brows, but then he released a short sigh and said, "Abalel."

A simple farmer. That was the issue here. Alashar shook his head, putting aside his slight sting of conscience. The man was not his responsibility. His life did not matter.

The merchant who had made an offer for the Furmorean served one of the many gods of death. Alashar did not know which one, but it likely was not one of the more pleasant ones. The man ran a public gaming enterprise involving high bets, flowing wine, and wild beasts in an arena. In Alashar's opinion, the local games proved what he knew about this city—dirty, low class, possessing a general lack of sanity. Who would ever want to watch such a frightening sport? His decision to sell the slave to Erthus Bolare brought him a level of misgiving, but he wanted to go home.

As he saw the merchant approaching, weaving his way through the crowded market, Alashar looked at the Furmorean one last time, and his condescension ebbed. He was giving this man up for death. The men of this town would make bets on the number of wounds he received, the time of his death, and which animal struck the killing blow.

"May your god protect you," he muttered.

The slave had lowered his head again. Ever since his purchase, he had showed uncommon submission for a man who had been free only two months ago. Alashar did not expect a reply from him, but he received one.

"I hope he will, my lord," the Furmorean answered softly.

The sale was made, and Alashar walked away from it with only half of his original investment. But never mind that. It had been a good lesson for him. The next time he came to trade in Blue Mountain, he would plan for their superstitions. He could make a fortune here, with only a little bit of study.

The new fighter caused something of a stir when the master's private guard walked him through the court and the southern garden to deposit him underground with the others. The man was handsome. There was no denying that. The kitchen girls twittered until Majda developed a headache—a fierce one, right behind her left eye.

"Enough!" she shouted, and the girls dropped into trembling silence. She did not often yell at them, so when she did, they contemplated her orders with a severe sort of seriousness. She had been the housekeeper of Erthus Bolare, merchant and gamer, for seventeen years. Though not a free woman, she had authority here, and the master listened to her. Every so often, it was important to remind the girls of such things.

"Did you not see the mark on him? It is the sign of death, made by a sacred priest. The fighter will meet his time here this very night. Do not *giggle* over a man who bears such a mark. You could find yourself dying alongside him."

For one blessed moment, the kitchen was quiet. Majda could hear the kettle hissing over the fire.

"My lady," one of the girls whispered. Her name was Alena, and she was the worst offender of them all. It did not matter the age or the lack of talent; if he had a pleasing face, she immediately and thoroughly dropped on her head in fluttery passion.

Majda scowled at her, but the child remained undeterred.

"Tonight, my lady? He will send him into the arena *tonight*?"

"Aye."

"Without any preparation or training?" Her bottom lip trembled, and she observed in a whiny voice, "Paying customers will not like that."

The attempt at manipulation was so obvious that Majda considered slapping her.

"The master did not buy him to prepare him! He bought him to appease the priest whose work remains unfinished. The new fighter shall be the first man through the gates."

chapter 2

As evening fell, the milling sounds of the mountain town suddenly split with a roar. It was loud enough to echo off the peaks, and it drove residents out into the streets.

Marcus Elah spent a few moments outside the inn with the others and then returned with a full report. "Erthus Bolare has captured a dragon."

Myles Hileshand saw the excitement in the young man's eyes and knew the request that would soon be following. Feigning disinterest, he said, "A dragon, you say?"

"He told the town he had a surprise for them—no one had any idea he meant a *dragon*. He's showing it in the arena tonight."

The question Hileshand expected immediately appeared, but not in the way he had anticipated. The younger man did nothing to hide his glee.

"A *dragon*, Myles! You will go see it with me?"

Hileshand smiled in spite of himself. "My dear Lord Elah, do you have any knowledge of this man Erthus Bolare?

He kills men for sport. He has no understanding of the value of a life. You would have us contribute to a vile practice."

"'Tis a dragon."

"I know it—a dragon who will eat his fill tonight."

"We could leave beforehand."

"We would still be lining the foul man's purse."

"Two farthings could hardly be called a *lining*." Marcus had already discovered the arena's pricing. He lifted his hands, beseeching. "A dragon, Myles. This is the sort of thing one remembers and talks about. No one has seen a dragon in this province in decades."

Marcus, at twenty-one, was more than capable of doing whatever he wished and he knew it. But every time he sought out Hileshand's counsel like this, willing to align himself with it, Hileshand felt appeased. The young man had been his charge for ten years now after being turned out of his house by his father. Hileshand had loved him before the father's rejection of him, and that love had done nothing but grow, despite the difficulties of the road set before them both. The young man supplied him with something his heart had long desired: family. He had never married, but he now had a son.

His brows rose. "I do not approve of supporting this man."

"Have *you* seen a dragon?"

Attempting a stern expression, Hileshand demanded, "You would attempt to manipulate me into this?"

"I manipulate nothing. You pretend disinterest, but I know you want to see this as much as I do. You contain more stories than a king's library—I know you. You will want this story as well."

Two hours later, Hileshand and Marcus filed into the

arena with a thousand others. The air smelled heavily of scented oil and incense. Hileshand grimaced and wondered what other smells Erthus Bolare was so intent on concealing.

Hacked into the side of the mountain beneath the town, the arena was an open-air building with rows of tiered seating surrounding a yawning pit in the center. The pit was wide enough to be visible from every seat in the building yet deep enough to prevent any of the gamer's pets from escaping. From what Hileshand had been able to gather, Erthus Bolare was particularly fond of several varieties of large cats, including the sielkis, a horned lion that lived on the southern plains.

They chose seats near the main door in preparation for their departure. The crowd immediately began shouting for the creature they had come to see. The roar of voices filled the evening.

Hileshand drew near boredom waiting for the large iron doors at the opposite side of the ring to open. The place felt dirty to him, as if he had entered an old tomb. He sensed that something unfriendly lived here, hidden on the other side of the laughter. He had been to similar places before—in Paxa and Ruthane, many years ago. They all felt the same.

The sky began to grow dark. The stars came out, and thousands of lamps lit up the stands. The arena floor revealed itself clearly, despite the retreating light of day and the appearance of the half-moon in the eastern sky.

Finally, a trumpet blew. The crowd screamed until the trumpet blew again, and the doors began to grind open.

The dragon appeared to be young. It was significantly smaller than the subjects of the dozen or so stories Hileshand had heard. This one was similar in size to a draft horse. It skittered out of the doors and filled the pit with fire and smoke as the crowd gave in to its craze even louder. Erthus Bolare had apparently clipped the creature's wings, for it nearly beat itself senseless in its wild flapping but was unable to rise off the ground. It shrieked again and again. Hileshand's ears began to ring.

As the smoke cleared, he leaned forward and studied the creature, rather fascinated. It was a beautiful but ferocious thing, full of mystery and a sense of danger that he could almost tangibly feel. The scales were gray and opaque, the wings a shade of green similar to the underbelly of a crasa leaf. Flat blades protruded from the back of its head all the way down the tail.

The man next to Hileshand jumped to his feet and shouted, "Fighter!"

The rest of the crowd joined in. "Send in the fighter!"

"We want the fighter!"

Hileshand dropped his hand on Marcus' shoulder. They needed to go.

As they stood up, the doors opened again and a man was shoved into the arena. He stumbled forward and caught his balance as the door thundered shut behind him. He wore a suit of armor that did not fit him. The helmet covered his entire face and hair, and only a wide strip of his throat was visible. It was impossible to tell his nationality.

Hileshand looked for the man's weapon and paused as he realized the fighter did not carry one. Full armor, without a weapon. What was this? They sent a man without a weapon into the ring against a dragon? The beast was young, yes, but it appeared fully capable of making short work of this fight.

Seeing the fighter, the dragon roared. The floor beneath

Hileshand's feet trembled. The crowd screamed as the creature turned on the man.

Hileshand's grip tightened on Marcus' shoulder. "Let's go—" he began and tried to draw his eyes away from the despicable scene about to be played out before him.

His command faded as the fighter started running. Not away from the dragon, but toward it. The creature released a fiery blaze, and the man slid away from it, spinning out of reach as he continued his run. The dragon directed its flame. It connected briefly with the armor that was too big, charring it, but the fighter spun again and the brunt of the force carried beyond him. Coming up to the creature, he slammed his metal-gloved fist into its snout.

The crowd screamed as the dragon reeled back, shaking its head from side to side.

"Did you see that? Did you see that?" the man beside Hileshand hollered at his companions. "He struck a dragon with his fist!"

"Sit down!" someone commanded behind Hileshand, and a moment later, rough hands helped him and Marcus find their seats again.

Grabbing two of the flat horns that extended from the back of the creature's neck, the fighter used his weight to jerk the neck down. In a fluid motion, he slammed the head to the ground and dropped his full weight on top of it, his knee to the neck. He reached for his helmet, but before he could complete the movement, the dragon screamed and shoved him away with clawed hands.

The man landed on the hard-packed dirt several paces away. He staggered to his feet again, and the crowd yelled encouragement to him—to the man fighting a dragon without a weapon.

He removed his helmet.

They screamed louder.

The same dance was followed a second time. The dragon attempted to incinerate him. The man avoided the fire as best he could, swerving as he ran. As the dragon pulled in breath to bellow again, the man dove beneath the creature's head, rolled up to his feet, and connected his helmet against the wide jaw, his full momentum behind his swing. The metallic thud could be heard through the entire stadium, despite the crowd.

The dragon was not as swift to respond this time as the man again forced its head to the ground. He dropped his weight on top of the neck, holding it down, and bashed the creature's head in until dark blood flowed.

The crowd cheered his success.

The man beside Hileshand kept repeating, "Did you see that? Did you see that?"

The arena fell silent as the man ignored them all, continuing his work.

He shifted position on the dragon's neck and pried open its mouth, bracing himself with a knee to the ground. He strained with the helmet in his hands.

"What is he doing?" Marcus asked, leaning to the side, trying to see.

The fighter had his back to them. They could not see his face and could barely see his task. The dragon's claws had ripped open the back of his armor. He was bleeding extensively, but he didn't seem to notice.

His arms moved in rhythmic motions. Powerful. Purposeful. He looked like a smithy at work over his anvil. A sharp sound grated through the stands from the arena floor. Adjusting his position, he pulled upward with all his strength, forcing something to bend in his grip.

When he stood again, he held a weapon in each hand. He had slit the helmet into two pieces. The edges were thin, and Hileshand wagered they were sharp.

"Resourceful fellow," he murmured, his heart sprinting behind his ribs. He had no desire to sit here and watch the continuation of this story, yet he could not make himself move. What sort of man was capable of defending himself in such a fashion? He had smoothly removed one impossibility and had now prepared himself for the second. He faced the doors in a crouch, hands extended to either side, ready for whatever came for him. His strength would not be able to sustain him for much longer. The dragon had shredded his back with its claws.

"Is it not over?" Marcus asked stiffly. They had both seen more than they had come to see. It needed to be over.

"Doubtful," Hileshand replied. Feeling the rush of the battle and the crowd, he silently cursed his choices this evening. Erthus Bolare knew what he had here with his arena on the mountain—Hileshand had to stay and see this. He had to know if the man survived.

The iron doors began to open again. The crowd screamed.

Hileshand looked at the fighter standing alone, the slain dragon beside him.

"Live," he commanded.

chapter 3

A streak of red fur bolted like lightning out from between the doors. The fighter ran back a few steps, putting the dragon carcass between himself and what came at him. But the horned cat, a sielkis, was not interested in the beast that lay dead. They never were. It leapt over the body and tackled the man to the ground, rolling him across the soil.

The fighter's full armor greatly hindered his mobility. Hileshand had sudden understanding that that detail had been planned on purpose. Someone was set on seeing this man's death tonight. Where was the fairness in such a fight? But the crowd didn't seem to agree with his assessment. They roared with excitement as the lion pinned the fighter to the ground.

The man attempted to block his face and throat with one metal-wrapped arm, and with the other hand, he slammed the shard of his broken helmet against the cat's torso. The creature ignored him, intent on stilling his struggles. But he kept at it, his hand moving almost rhythmically—*boom,*

boom, again—until the cat finally flipped away from him and retreated a few snarling paces, its fur drenched with blood.

As the man climbed to his feet, he lost his balance and staggered to keep it, for the first time revealing his face to Hileshand's side of the stadium. He was covered in blood, his features indistinguishable. The cat had torn him in several places—but it somehow had missed the vital areas of his throat. He transferred his helmet shard to the other hand and reached up with his glove to feel his skin. The movement seemed to be one of surprise—he had not fully expected to be standing now. Satisfied, he returned his weapon to his hand and watched the cat, waiting for another attack.

The cat tensed as the crowd screamed. The doors were opening again.

Marcus dropped an angry hand around Hileshand's arm. "What nonsense is this?" he shouted into Hileshand's ear. The roar of voices nearly swallowed his words.

"Erthus Bolare wants him to die," Hileshand shouted in reply.

A second sielkis raced across the pit. They fell into position on either side of the man, stalking their prey with care, bodies held low to the ground. He circled as they circled, his arms out, tense, weapons gripped. But his steps began to wobble, as if the ground were uneven, when it was perfectly flat. He had lost much blood.

He realized now he was going to die. No other thought could be racing through his head.

Hileshand did not wish this image to be ingrained in his mind. Many years had passed since he had seen so violent a death.

He grimaced. *Make it swift. We've stayed too long.*

As if he had heard Hileshand's thoughts, the fighter drew

himself up. A moment passed in which Hileshand held his breath. Then the man spun on his heel and hurled one helmet piece like a knife at the first cat and whirled around to face the second as it rushed him. The other lion joined the first, and in only a few moments, it was over. The man went down, and he stayed down.

Servants ran out onto the open ground and captured the lions with large nets and spears, herding and sometimes dragging them back through the iron doors. Other servants carted off the dragon's body, and eventually, as if they had momentarily forgotten about it, they swung around and returned for the fighter's body. They tossed him on top of the dragon and pulled the cart through the doors.

Hileshand stared after them. The sight of the man lying still and discarded on the dragon's corpse horrified him in a unique way, one he could not explain.

Buy the body. The words walked through Hileshand's mind, and without a single thought in question of them, he agreed. He would buy the body, and he would give the man a decent burial. He had killed a dragon with his helmet. He had been utterly fearless in the face of certain death. He deserved an actual burial, where someone cared what happened to him, that he was placed securely.

As the arena prepared for the next event, Hileshand grabbed Marcus' arm and pulled him from his seat. "Let's go."

Majda watched every game, without fail. She had done this since her promotion to housekeeper and viewed it as an extension of her weekly chores. As housekeeper, it was part of her job to know every single thing that happened within, or concerning, the house of Erthus Bolare. Never in her seventeen years of observing fights had she seen anything re-sembling the fight that had just concluded.

Yes, she had seen brave men die. Yes, some of them had even been gallant about it and put on a show for the crowd. But there had been something different about this man, and it frightened her. Even now, as the cart pulled into the tun-nel and she fell into step behind it, she trembled, hoping her master knew what he was doing. What if the slave was not supposed to die? What if the priest who had carved the moon into his chest had let him live on purpose? To kill the wrong man would bring certain death! To kill him without a means of defense, in humiliation before a crowd, would be even worse.

They carted the bodies into the back room where they would be dissolved in the furnace and then buried, all mem-ory of them forgotten from the surface of the earth. Majda wondered if she would be able to do that this time—to forget this one, the slave who had been marked to die and yet had fought in incredible ways to keep death away from him.

As the others prepared the furnace, she reached out a trembling hand and laid it on the bent, bloodstained breast-plate.

At the lightness of her touch, the dead man opened his eyes, and she started screaming.

He was *alive*? How could he be alive?

Fellis, a tall Ansan who had served Erthus Bolare for nearly as long as she, jumped toward her and slammed his hand down on her mouth. She screamed against his grip, terror pumping through her blood, until he bent down and hissed into her ear, "Yes, he's alive. Silence, you old fool. Do you want to bring the master in here?"

Her gaze jumped to his.

He pulled his hand from her mouth cautiously, and she sputtered, "How is that man alive?"

"The cat must have scruffed him and that was all." Fellis released her and stepped over to the wagon, grabbing the man's blood-covered jaw. He jerked the head up and inspected the throat. The Furmorean groaned. "Didn't touch the artery."

"B-but I saw him fall! They tore at him!"

Fellis gave her a cocky grin. "'Course they did. That's what hungry cats will do. Not every man dragged through the dirt here is dead, Majda. The master wants them to *look* dead for the crowd, but not everything we pull up off the ground has lost its soul yet. Some of them are still alive until we alleviate their pain back here." He looked purposefully toward the furnace.

Then he returned his gaze to the fighter lying immobile on the dead dragon, and his smiled faded. "And some of them we let live, to go off and die on their own somewhere else. He should be not one of them, marked as he is."

She shuddered. "Does the master know about this—that you let some of them go?"

Fellis grabbed the collar of her dress and hauled her close to him. "No. And if you tell him, it would mean the head of every man in this room. Including yours." He reached over and slapped the metal boot sticking out of the back of the cart. "I do not wish to kill this one. But I do not see how I can let him live. At the mere whisper of a man with this mark, the master would know of our actions and think us unfaithful."

The slave lived. Marked for death, he had fought a dragon and two sielkis, and he lived.

By the gods, Majda thought, running a trembling hand

across her face.

A little girl named Foca ran into the room. "Majda! Fellis!" Her blonde braids bounced up and down. She saw death and gore every time the iron doors opened and a man was thrust into the pit; neither of them turned her head. "Two men in the corridor want to see you. They want the body."

Majda shook. She put her hand on the girl's shoulder and forced the fear into a state of calm. "They won't be the last. Tell them the dragon has already been sold. For a very high price."

"But they don't want the dragon."

The room quieted, the servants turning to stare at Majda and Fellis.

To be certain, Majda pointed at the Furmorean's boot. "They want *this* one?" she demanded of the girl.

Foca nodded. "They want the fighter."

Majda looked up at Fellis. "What do we do?" she whispered.

His face grim, he grunted, "We'll have to kill him."

"We *can't* kill him! Not now!"

"Have you lost your mind, Majda?"

She rambled unsteadily, "The gods want him left alone! He's lived thus far! We cannot kill a man the gods want to live."

There was a clatter of commotion outside the door to the hall.

"The master!" Majda gasped, her hand springing to her chest. She nearly fainted.

Fellis jogged to the door, prepared to delay Lord Erthus' entrance. One of the other men stepped forward with a knife to slit the groaning man's throat. He paused there, the blade pressed against the Furmorean's skin, and waited for Fellis' signal.

Fellis stopped in front of the door. He stood there and stared and did not move. He gave no signal to kill the slave.

"You..." He began and swallowed, the muscles working in his throat. "You have come to claim the fighter's body?"

"We want to purchase it, yes."

A moment passed in silence.

"Why?" Fellis asked simply.

"I saw the man fight. He was impressive."

Fellis' eyes narrowed. "Is that the only reason?"

The man's tone grew impatient. "Let me bury him. I will pay you in gold."

Fellis glanced at Majda, then back at the man in the hallway. "Are you...are you his father?"

Why all the questions? Ridiculous questions at that. Majda marched across the room. Fellis put his hands on her, blocking her path. She saw what he had seen and started screaming again. He responded as he had before and clamped his hand roughly across her mouth.

The man frowned at both of them and repeated, "I will pay you in gold."

chapter 4

When Hileshand saw that the fighter was still alive, he realized who had spoken to him in the stands. He realized whose voice that had been. *Buy the body.* It was not to bury him.

There would be no burying today.

You give mercy, he thought, surprised by this turn of events. *Mercy.*

Without a word, he counted ten gold pieces into the tall Ansan's hand. The man's eyes widened. It was an exorbitant sum, especially for an injured slave, but Hileshand hoped for his silence as well. He looked through the room. Ten faces stared back at him. A coin per servant.

"I intend this to be a private matter," he said.

The Ansan gripped the gold pieces to his chest and agreed. "Very private."

Standing in the back of the cart, their feet positioned in various places around the dragon's carcass, Marcus and two others wrestled the man out of his crushed and mutilated armor. He wore nothing on the other side of the metal pieces, not even a loincloth, and the interior of the armor had been rubbed down with some sort of oil that made Hileshand's eyes water. Where it had connected with the metal, the man's skin was raw and covered with blisters. He had groaned and passed out the moment Marcus had crawled up beside him.

"What is that?" Hileshand demanded, blinking the water from his eyes and glaring as the last of the armor was tossed aside.

"Red oil, sir. It is used for the dogs. Most of the time."

"What did this man do to earn such a heinous punishment?"

The room became silent.

It was the woman who finally answered. "He has been marked by a priest's hand."

"By what?"

"Look at his chest, my lord."

Hileshand leaned forward and saw the half-moon that had been carved cock-eyed into the fighter's raised, blotchy skin. The scar was old. It had been healed for a long time.

Many years had passed since Hileshand had seen a wound such as this one. It had been another lifetime, one that he treasured and despised both at once. His gaze moved from the scar on the fighter's chest to the man he had raised as his son. Marcus was not of his blood, yet every day, it seemed that he became more and more all the things Hileshand would desire a son of his blood to be. The man was not perfect, by any feat of the imagination—and yet he was perfect, by all accounts. Hileshand could not love him more than he already did.

And this pleasure in his heart, this opportunity for deep loyalty and a father's affections, had come about because of a scar like this. A half-moon carved into the chest of a squalling infant. The mark was everything this woman declared it to be—a sentence of death, drawn into the skin by a priest's hand.

Hileshand's gaze flickered back to the fighter, a thought playing along the outskirts of his mind. He was about the right age, wasn't he? The right build. The right coloring. Blood obscured the man's features.

No, he thought. The man was a slave.

"No one else in the market wanted him. Clearly, a priest intended his death, and the master bought him to finish his work and bring a blessing on his house."

Hileshand frowned at her, and she winced as the sentence trailed away. "'A blessing on the house,'" he repeated and could hear the mockery in his voice. "Is that what this is?" With an exasperated sigh, he asked, "How do we get him out of here?"

From the back of the cart, Marcus said warily, "Myles…?" He had a hand wrapped around one of the flat spikes sticking out of the dragon's back and was leaning forward, studying the fighter's blood-covered face.

The man opened his eyes as Marcus spoke. His clouded gaze focused on the young man for a moment, held there, then glazed over and closed as he fell asleep again.

"Myles, you will want to see this," Marcus said.

Hileshand stepped closer to the cart. "What is it?"

chapter 5

Myles Rosure didn't know where he was or what was happening around him for two weeks. He remembered being in the back of a cart, tree limbs passing overhead. He remembered sunlight and birdsong, divided by long periods of blackness and pain in his back and chest. Sometimes his whole body felt like it was on fire, and at other times, the pain lessened so he could actually sleep. He remembered being carried up some stairs and deposited on a bed near a window. Someone had poured wine down his throat and spooned warm broth into his mouth.

Eventually the fog lifted, and this morning when he opened his eyes, he managed to keep them open.

He was lying in what appeared to be a room in an inn. He could hear the quiet murmur of voices coming up through the floor. There were two beds along the wall and a third bed, a pallet, made up on the floor in front of the fire. Sunlight spilled inside through the open window, and sitting in front of it, sound asleep with his chin in his hand, was a middle-aged man.

Myles remembered him—vaguely. He had been at the arena.

He lifted his hands from the bed. When that motion did not cause him pain, he made a slow, cautious move to sit up. The skin tightened severely across his back, as if it were about to crack and begin to bleed again. Nausea washed through him, but he ignored it. When he had achieved his goal, he sat there, hands in his lap, head down, and waited for the room to stop churning around him.

"Morning," his companion said.

Myles had not noticed he had awakened. He glanced at him, then grimaced and closed his eyes again. Why did he feel so ill?

"It's the rhusa bark," the man told him without being asked. "Not pleasant on the stomach, but it has done an excellent job repairing your back. You developed an infection, but it has passed now."

Briefly, Myles wondered about respect and protocol. This man had, in some way or another, aided him after the arena. If he intended more than that, to lord it over him and make him a slave again, no doubt it would quickly become apparent. "Where am I?"

"Still in Edimane," the man assured him. "Specifically, you are in the unique little village of Sasha, about a hundred miles north of where we found you."

Myles knew little of the geography of Edimane, and he frowned, bothered that he had no idea where Sasha, or Blue Mountain, would be placed on a map of this land. Never in his life had he expected to be this far east. In his head, all maps ended at the distant border of Tarek and ventured no farther.

"What's your name, son?"

"Rosure," he said after a moment of quick contemplation. "Myles Rosure."

The man did not return the favor and Myles looked at him slowly. His stomach did not respond in offense if the movement was slow enough. The man watched him, a line between his brows.

"Who are you?" Myles asked.

"Myles Hileshand," he answered and then waited, as if that name should mean something to him.

It did not. *Myles* was not a common first name, but overall, it was fairly unremarkable. Myles had not heard the surname of *Hileshand* before this day.

Hileshand hesitated. He leaned forward in the chair and studied Myles, his frown growing more pronounced. Cautiously, he asked, "Your mother's name is Hana—isn't it?"

Myles stared at him. At least eight hundred miles separated him from his homeland—the Galatian soldiers had brought them quite a distance. The muscles tightened in his jaw as he remembered how they had exclaimed over her. Their remarks had sickened him. Even now, two months later, he could not seem to uproot them from his head.

Do not fear for me, she had whispered, her hand on his cheek. Then she had been ripped away from him, and he had not seen her again.

"How do you know that?" he asked gruffly.

The man closed his eyes, apparently relieved. He opened them again. "She still lives?"

Myles blinked and said, "I don't know. Answer my question."

"I knew your mother in Gereskow."

The port city of Ruthane. *A heathen city,* his mother had

told him. *They worship strange gods and make strange sacrifices.* Not once had she mentioned she had *lived* there. Even though this man did somehow know his mother's name, Myles had no reason to trust the rest of his words.

Hileshand smirked at him. "I cannot tell you how many times I have seen that exact expression before. A perfect resemblance."

Resemblance?

The bolt slid in the door, and as the panel opened, a second man stepped into the room. Myles remembered him from the arena as well—a speaking shadow that had somehow seemed familiar to him.

"Oh," the man said, mildly surprised to see Myles sitting up. "He's awake."

Myles gave him only a cursory glance at first. Then the headache between his eyes seemed to part, allowing a faint light of clarity. He realized something, something that could be important, and his head came around again. *What?*

The man smiled. "Yes," he agreed, though Myles' exclamation of surprise had remained inaudible. He shut the door and approached the bed. "That was my exact thought as well. A bit unexpected. Not what I intended to see under a mask of blood." He glanced at Hileshand with affection. "What none of us intended, I think."

Myles stared at him, not yet able to see what humored him about this. He despised this feeling of helplessness within him. *What is this?*

The man looked just like him—or, at least, what he used to look like before the arena. He had no idea what he looked like now. His head ached in such a way as to suggest that not everything was the same as he remembered it.

Hileshand stood to his feet. "This," he said, coming

around the bed and putting his hand on the man's shoulder, "is my son, Marcus." He looked at Myles. His brows rose and he stated the obvious. "He is your brother."

chapter 6

Twin sons were born to the House of Elah in the city of Gereskow in Ruthane. Twins were considered a sign of the gods' favor. The infants would be placed side by side, and a priest would divine the child of the gods' choosing. That child would be marked with the symbol of the current moon and offered as a sacrifice in the holy temple. Hana Rosure, a slave in the house, had assisted in the birth.

The mother began to experience complications, and the bleeding, squalling child of favor was thrust into Hana's arms to be taken to the temple and sacrificed. Usually, the procession to the temple included an accompaniment of guards, musicians, and several others, but that night, Hana was sent alone. The mother died as Hana stepped out of the house, and in the uproar and sorrow, no one considered a slave girl sent out on an errand.

The father did not know of his son's disappearance until the next morning, when the temple heard that twins had been born and sent words of caution to the family. The chosen son needed to be handed over to them. Where was the chosen son?

Hana was sixteen at the time—a beautiful girl, with eyes the color of spring grass. Lord Elah was incensed when he discovered her betrayal, and among those he sent in search of her, he included his trusted friend Myles Hileshand, captain of his personal guard.

"None of you found her," Myles Rosure said, an undeniable smirk in his dark eyes.

He was proud of his mother, a young girl who had escaped a death sentence just as strong and determined as the one assigned to him. Hileshand, with a slight smile, found no reason to contest him.

The young man's Furmorean upbringing was more than apparent. Furmorea was a harsh land filled with dangerous things and dangerous people, who did what needed to be done and did not balk at the effort. Most were farmers. Some were tree fellers. Without exception, every Furmorean Hileshand had ever met appeared as this one appeared—brawny and *big*, used to an unhealthy amount of labor out in the sun. Hileshand remembered the sturdy thud of the helmet smashing against the dragon's jawbone and smiled, impressed yet again with the man sitting on the bed before him.

It was said that Furmoreans possessed a morality as strong as their arms, that they would not lie, steal, or commit murder. Hileshand observed the claw and tooth marks on the man's forehead and across his jaw—these had been jagged wounds—and wondered if those statements were true. What had happened to his mother? What had happened to enslave him and bring him so far from home?

He continued, "When you were ten years old, the priest who had presided at your birth began to lose his mental faculties. Rumors began to spread that he had marked the wrong son—on purpose, to bring a curse upon the House of Elah. Elah serves the king quite closely. He has made many enemies, so when these rumors appeared, he believed them, as did many others. The priest was eventually executed, and Elah, at the temple's urging, renounced Marcus as his son and turned him out of his house. He did not kill him; however, with such a renouncement, he proclaimed him as such."

At one point in time, the telling of this story would have bothered Marcus, as it would bother any man whose trust in his father had been viciously betrayed. But as Hileshand watched Marcus now, he saw very little of the previous sorrow wash through his expression. Marcus had finally found his peace, but the journey had been long for him.

The man was leaning up against the windowsill and collecting sunlight with the back of his tunic. He picked up the story where Hileshand had left it. "When Myles learned what had happened, he sent men throughout the city to find me. I was hiding under a bridge, for it was raining, and I had nowhere to go. None of my friends' families would receive me because they did not want to be condemned by the court. King Habeine is *highly* religious and full of superstition—because of that, he has allowed the priesthood far more power than is safe, and much of Gereskow lives in fear of the Temple."

After his brief summation, Marcus shrugged. "For what it's worth, that scar on your chest is a symbol of our father's ambition—and nothing more. He did not *have* to obey Temple Law, but he chose to do so because he had plans for his future. Those plans would have ended if he had not obeyed the full ordinance of the king's religious beliefs." Marcus shrugged a second time. "You were named the chosen son at birth, and I was the chosen son eleven years later. In the process, Elah showed his full loyalty and commitment to the king, and he was made governor. He achieved what he wanted."

Hileshand watched Myles' expression as he listened to his brother. The man frowned deeply, but he did not ask questions. He seemed to treat this story as if it were the biography of another man's life.

With a sigh, Hileshand waited for the weight of Marcus' words to settle before he continued. "I resigned from Lord Elah's service and left for the inland country, far from those who would potentially make Marcus' life more difficult than it already was. We were passing through Blue Mountain on business, Myles. That was all. We arrived that morning and intended to leave the morning following. It was the purpose of God that we found you."

"Which god?"

"Abalel, the god of the sun."

Something flickered through the young man's eyes. "Is not the god of the sun considered...slightly *dim* in Ruthane?"

He knew that because his mother had told him. Hileshand had no doubt of that, but he kept that understanding to himself, for he did not want to take space from the man, to force him into familiarity with a stranger. He had seen the suspicion in his eyes at the mention of his mother and Gereskow; perhaps certain topics should be approached with care.

Hana had defied the sacred fears and protocol of the king in order to save a newborn's life, and eleven years later, Hileshand had followed her example, in a way. He had thought of her as he had resigned his commission, and he had thought of her every time little Marcus had broken down in tears, missing his home and not understanding why his father did not love him anymore.

Hileshand had fathered one son, while Hana had mothered the other—in Furmorea, where he would grow up familiar with soil and seed and strong principles.

And, somewhere along the way, Myles had developed the courage to run down a dragon and slay the very thing that was meant to be his death. She had been successful in her instruction.

Hileshand leaned forward. "If you are willing...tell me your history. Tell me the part of the story I do not know."

chapter 7

$\mathcal{M}$yles' story required a few days in the telling, for his strength returned to him slowly, and the mixture that upset his stomach did not readily allow him to converse with ease. Apparently, Hileshand and Marcus did not consider him a very good storyteller, for they asked many questions and consistently pressed him for additional details.

He had grown up in a small farming community called Nan. His mother married before he was old enough to remember, and her husband did not allow Myles to assume his last name, declaring that it wasn't fitting. Myles was not his son.

Myles told them about his schooling, what little there was; he told them how he was the best archer in ten villages and that he, like many of the men from Furmorea, preferred the ustrian metal bow of Tarek over the traditional bows of other lands. Some details he gave when they asked for them, and some he withheld.

Myles thought about all the stories his mother had told

him of his father—how he had upset an entire company of highwaymen and they had eventually disbanded because they feared him. Once, he had fought five men at a time with only a broken staff, yet he had still managed to beat them soundly, though they came at him with swords. Another time, he caught an arrow in the arm. He pushed it through his flesh and shot it back at the offender, killing him instantly. She had made him sound like a hero of war, a mighty man.

But according to Hileshand and Marcus, his actual father, the one who had given him life, was bound by ambition and the laws of a dark god of death. The more Hileshand spoke, the more apt Myles was to believe his words. He did not think the man was lying to him—but why would his mother have told him such stories? He did not wish to think this way, to look at his life with unexpected doubt. Yet that was what happened now. He did not know how to focus his thoughts anymore.

"What did she tell you of your father?" Hileshand asked on the morning of the third day.

Myles did not know how to answer that question. He could not tell him what she had actually said, not now. "It's difficult to say," he finally replied. Even if he could no longer trust them, he preferred her stories of the man to Hileshand's stories.

The room fell quiet as Hileshand and Marcus watched him. He knew the story they wanted to hear now.

Pulling in a deep breath, Myles began, "About six months ago...men started to talk of war with Galatia. There were many stories—rumors—of villages destroyed and dismantled near the border. Rand, my mother's husband, claimed they were rumors and that was all. Nan is deep in the hill country—what army would march so far for so little return? We have nothing of true value. Most of the town runs on barter and trade; there is very little coin on hand and no gold to be had. But Rand was mistaken in his assumptions."

Myles paused. This memory was different than every other memory he possessed. It was like a platform in his head, a foundation for every other thought. He remembered these details. He remembered all of them. "I was out in the fields with Rand when we saw the smoke rising from the house through the trees. We returned in secret through the woods and killed several of their men. Eight, at least. I can't fully remember. My sisters escaped into the woods behind the house. One of the soldiers gave chase but returned empty-handed. My mother they had tied into the bed of a wagon. They put a knife to her throat and threatened to kill her if I fought them any longer. So I had to stand there while they chained me hand and foot. And once they had me bound so I could barely move, they took revenge for killing their men. I woke up two days later with my head in my mother's lap, everything else strapped down to the wagon boards."

Hileshand nodded. Myles could not read his expression.

"The husband?" Hileshand asked.

He did not refer to the man as Myles' father, though he had, smoothly and seemingly without thought, referred to Hana as his mother. Had Myles somehow revealed with his words that Rand's last name was not the only thing the man had not given him? He didn't think so, for he had learned to speak with care about such things. Rand had not been an evil man; he simply had not wished to father what he had not fathered. *Isn't fitting. Don't you want to honor the boy's father? We must honor him.* And so he had. With distance.

His attitude had been different toward his two daughters, who were of his blood.

"My mother refused to tell me how he died, just that he did. They killed him with vengeance. But me they spared."

He considered his next words carefully, and nausea twisted through his abdomen. Myles frowned, took another breath. *Steady.* "The last time I saw my mother, she was standing before a man from Paxa, a wealthy man who worked for a wealthy master. He was commenting on her age and making remarks that should not be made, about any woman. The man saw me looking at him and laughed at me. When they told him I was her son, he pretended he had not said those things and that he had not mocked me."

Afterward, one of the soldiers had come near to Myles and said, *You want to kill him, man? You should. Hold on to that hate, and you will see yourself a free man again.*

They had intended to sell him as an arena slave in Paxa. Then, for some reason, they had changed their minds, and he had been shipped south instead, where he would battle beasts in the place of men.

That evening after supper, Hileshand took his pipe and went downstairs to the common porch. Much to his satisfaction, he found it empty and pulled a chair closer to the railing so he could smoke with his boots up. He sighed as his body relaxed.

Several minutes passed with him in this position. His boots propped on the railing, he watched the comings and goings on the street through the posts before him, and eventually, his many thoughts came together into a single form: *a door.*

A door had been opened here, with Marcus' brother—

one Hileshand could take, if he so desired. And he did desire. He thought of Hana, and with another sigh, he pulled his pipe from his lips and frowned at the street before him.

Marcus found him. He pulled up one of the nearby chairs and sat down beside him, also propping his boots up on the rail.

"I know what you are considering," the young man said at last.

Hileshand glanced at him.

Marcus pulled in a deep breath and said, "I would like to propose something to you. Two items, actually, now that I think of it."

"What would be the first?"

"Honor the mother."

Hileshand lowered his pipe hand to his thigh, turning to look at his son fully. "Do you realize the difficulty of trying to find a woman who has been sold at market in a foreign country? You would have much better luck finding one particular stalk of wheat in a field ten miles long."

Calmly, the young man asked, "Is it a wheat field?"

Hileshand scowled at him. "Of course it's a wheat field. The metaphor does not work unless it is a wheat field."

The corners of Marcus' mouth twitched. "I just wanted to be certain before I made my commitment. Do you know what he has, Myles? Something I have never had. He is my brother—that much is certain, yet I have never known what he has known. Did you see the strength in his eyes when he spoke of his mother? He was willing to lose his freedom to spare her life, and I am certain that he would be willing to lose much more than that, if it meant sparing her again. Such a bond is worthy of honor."

Marcus dropped his boots off the rail and leaned forward, putting his elbows to his thighs. Intently, he asked, "Is there a possibility that we could locate her and recover her?"

"It would require time. Much time. It would require Abalel's favor and the movement of forces we cannot control. It could be a hard, difficult road that may or may not possess the ending we desire. Any number of things could have befallen her since her sale in Tarek—look at the number of things that befell your brother."

"Yet it is a road you were considering before I suggested it. Weren't you?"

It was a road he would take. He had already decided this. He simply toyed with the details now—the bits and pieces of the past. "Aye."

"You desire to search out and find Hana Rosure."

Hileshand twiddled the pipe in his fingers. "Aye," he said at last.

"What remains your principle hesitation?"

Hileshand looked at the street and returned the pipe to his lips. For several reasons, the words were difficult for him to speak. He was unsure if the young man would be able to understand them. "I have not been a soldier in ten years, son. I fear I am out of practice. And…I fear I have grown old."

Those had been Hana's last words to him. With exquisite clarity, he remembered everything she had said that day. It had not been true then—but it since had become true. *Or truer,* he thought. Twenty years was a long time. He was fifty years old now.

He could feel the young man's gaze on the side of his face, studying what could be studied there. The lines of another life. The signs of time. Hileshand allowed him as long a look as he required, wishing him to have all the details before both of them committed to something that could potentially carry a high cost.

Eventually, Marcus said, "I have one other proposition."

Hileshand's brows rose. He looked at him.

The man was all seriousness now. "Honor the father," he said, his voice rough.

Hileshand did not understand.

"I do not know why I have withheld this from you. Seeing Myles…" Marcus shook his head. "It has helped me to order my thoughts afresh, to consider what is truly important and what is not. Do you remember the night we were camped outside the Wasdil Mountains and we were beset by thieves? They intended to strip us of everything we owned and then do to us what the soldiers did with Myles and his family. We would have had a similar story."

Of course Hileshand remembered that night. Marcus had been a boy of thirteen.

"You fought like a madman. I have never seen anyone fight like that. You would not let them touch me." Marcus paused in his narration. A line appeared between his brows. "I realized that night that you were not my father."

He what? Concerned, Hileshand watched him.

"Elah never would have done what you did. I used to lie awake at night and fear that one day, you would do to me what he had done to me, that you would send me away. But that night, watching you fight my enemies for me—it helped me realize what you were and what you were not." His voice caught. He cleared his throat. "So, from this day forth, I will do what I should have done starting that night at the campfire."

Marcus stood up and left, without any further explanation.

Hileshand had no idea what he was talking about until later that evening when Marcus called him *Father.* Marcus never called him *Myles* again.

chapter 8

The road between Sasha and the border of Tarek required four weeks to traverse. Every night during those four weeks, Hileshand and the sons of Elah made camp some distance from the road itself, concealed by trees or the stones that jutted up from the soil quite liberally in that area. Marcus would take the first watch, leaving Myles and Hileshand alone at the fire.

Hileshand slowly learned details from Myles that the young man had withheld when questioned the first time. Myles could speak three languages: Furmorean, of course, followed by Ruthanian and Terikbah, the language of Tarek, which bordered his homeland. His Ruthanian was flawless, thanks to his mother's tutoring. His Terikbah was decent.

Myles possessed the understanding and strength of thought to give Hileshand an answer to almost every question he asked, yet over time, Hileshand began to suspect that Myles did not consider himself all that intelligent. Most of the time, he seemed surprised whenever Hileshand complimented him, and some of the time, Hileshand's compliments earned what appeared to be full-bodied suspicion.

Myles and Marcus shared many of the same expressions, and on several occasions, Hileshand had to look away quickly before he chuckled at an inappropriate time. Never had he suspected that one day, he would be here, in the presence of both of them.

Myles had learned of Abalel from his mother, but that, too, somehow became an awkward topic. Hileshand asked him questions, attempting to gauge the man's thoughts and assumptions, but after the first several nights, Myles visibly began to withdraw whenever Hileshand ventured down that path.

"It is difficult to say," was his common response. He did not say, "I don't know," for that would be a lie, but it seemed that whatever troubled him certainly did make it difficult for him to answer.

Finally, the night before they were to cross the border into Tarek, Myles asked Hileshand, "What do you hope to gain in all of this?"

The night was clear and moonlit, the wind soft. Hileshand removed his gaze from the patch of silver stars overhead and took his pipe from between his lips. He looked at the young man across the fire.

This was not the first time such a question had been asked. Faithfully, Hileshand had answered him, his answers usually similar in nature. Tonight, however, he chose to take a slightly different approach. "Your mother was a dear friend of mine. We talked about our lives and our thoughts about the government and a good many other things." He waited to see how the young man would respond to that.

Myles did not respond to it at all. Instead, he repeated what he always said. "You realize you are not required to help me. I can go this road on my own."

"But you do not have to go it on your own."

Myles studied him. The man's dark eyes reflected the firelight. "But what do you hope to gain in all of this? I can't give you anything."

"There is no reward, son, other than your peace of heart and hers. I would see you both safe and stable again."

"There is always a reward," Myles said gruffly. "A man does something because he has a reason for doing it. Otherwise, why do it at all?"

It was as if he had cotton in his ears. What made this difficult for him? Hileshand fiddled with his pipe and looked down into the fire, contemplating his next words. He could hear the aggression in Myles' voice, but he did not think the man was actually angry with him. It seemed more that he did not wish to be obligated to him later. But Myles did not have to worry about that. Hileshand was not going to make him work for this—he did him no favors here. There was nothing to repay. "You claim you would go this road on your own—what is your desire for reward?"

Myles frowned. "You cannot say that to me."

"Why do you wish to save her?"

"She is my mother." His tone was growing terse.

With a nod, Hileshand said calmly, "Yes, she is. You do this because you care for her. I claim friendship with you. This means that I choose to love what you love, because you love it. This means I will help you, even if I receive nothing for it. I am your friend. You do not have to pay me for my friendship. There is no reward required. It is very simple—I do this because I care for you."

A few paces away through the trees, Marcus blended

with the night shadows. He listened half-heartedly to the argument at the fire. If he were to take Myles' reactions seriously in this moment, he would wager that no one had ever lifted a hand to help him before in his life. He did not seem to know what to do with himself, now that he had a company.

Their voices eventually faded. Hileshand went to sleep and started snoring. Marcus could not ever tell with Myles whether he was asleep or lost in thought. He seemed to change position on his bedroll every time Marcus glanced at him in the darkness.

He was about to head back to the fire and wake him for the next watch when the warmth of the night air vanished in a sudden blanket of cold. The change hit Marcus so strongly that it felt like a bucket of ice had been dumped down his spine.

Usually, the perusan gave some sort of warning—a whistle in the air, the sound of bending brush—but tonight, he had heard nothing but a disgruntled argument he had heard before. He spun on his heel and reached for his sword.

A little girl stood behind him, only a handful of steps away. She stared at him with wide green eyes. Green appeared to be the color of choice among the perusan. Most had eyes the color of emeralds, yet he had also seen eyes like rubies. Her skin glowed yellow, like white gauze in full sunlight. As he looked at her, the temperature lowered even further.

No one knew much about the perusan. Some believed them to be the dead—the souls of those who had been killed in the vicinity of their sighting. Others claimed them to be beasts as much as any other creature of the woods, for they died the way other things died. It was possible to kill them, but the intense cold of their presence and their physical resiliency could make the action somewhat difficult. The head had to be severed from the body.

Some men went their entire lives without seeing one, while others saw them frequently, as if the creatures followed them through the mountains. They seemed to choose their battles and did not learn from previous encounters. Sometimes they attacked alone, and other times, they were the diversion. Marcus wondered which it would be tonight. Nothing had seemed unusual about the woods this evening, not until now.

He had never seen a perusan come as a child before. It disturbed him. He pulled his sword, pursed his lips, and whistled a shrill warning to his father and Myles.

The creature smiled.

He took one step toward the girl, who was not a girl—and suddenly realized the answer to his previous question.

Tonight, the perusan was the diversion.

chapter 9

As Marcus' whistle broke his sleep, Hileshand rolled to his feet. He withdrew his sword and stood near the fire in a crouch. He heard grunts in the woods, saw flashes of yellow light. He knew the origin of the light—they had seen the perusan several times, in the last few years especially—but all the other noises he could not place. The perusan were like ghosts that left footprints; they did make noise when they traveled, but they did not sound like half a dozen angry bears charging through the brush.

Get away from the fire. An intense urge in his abdomen. *Away from the fire!*

There was only one type of beast in these woods that had no fear of flame. Hileshand swore beneath his breath as the first roar shattered the night. Now *that* he recognized.

"Myles!" he shouted.

The man jerked out of a heavy sleep, arms raised.

"Into the woods! Away from the light."

Myles jumped to his feet, grabbing his bow and the rest

of his weapons, and Hileshand shoved him forward, directing him toward the cover of the trees. He made to follow, but the roar sounded again directly behind him, where he had been standing only moments before. He felt thunder at his back. Hileshand whirled around.

It was a goe'lah. The creature's hunched shoulders stood a good ten feet above the flames of the fire. It was covered in fur, with a face like a bear, but the hands were the hands of a man, the nails grown out like metal claws. The black eyes were horizontal and thin, as if they had been created with a single stab of a knife, one thrust on either side of the head.

Steam rose from the creature's snout. They did not fear fire because they carried it in their blood. Their touch was like a hot iron on the skin, burning a deep wound in seconds; their blood was much worse. Hileshand had once seen a brave man lose his sword arm after killing a goe'lah. He had beaten the creature to the ground and cut off its head, and its blood had sprayed across the man's limb, claiming skin, muscle, and bone before he could even cry out.

It made a bitter sort of sense that the goe'lah would travel with the perusan. Neither would be affected by the temperature of the other. The perusan were like adolescent dogs that gathered around an object and eventually tore it apart—they killed men because they could. But the goe'lah killed them because they were hungry.

There were only two ways to kill a goe'lah. The first was to kill it from a distance. The hide was fairly impenetrable, but an arrow through the eye or in the throat would often suffice. The second way involved much more courage.

Only one of them possessed a bow. Hileshand had purchased it for Myles before they left Sasha. It was a Terikbah bow, made of ustrian metal.

The goe'lah stared at him, breathing heavily. He could feel the malevolence in its gaze.

Hileshand laid a hand flat on his blade. "Abalel," he said calmly, "guide my sword."

He felt the answer in both palms. The hilt vibrated in his right. The blade began to warm the skin of his left. *Thank you.*

He pulled his hand from the metal, and the goe'lah charged him, running straight through the fire. Sparks sprayed skyward. Hileshand waited until the creature was almost upon him, then he planted his back foot and swung his sword with both hands. The blade ripped through tissue and bone, and the creature hurtled past him into the darkness, crashing face forward in the brush. It screamed but did not rise.

A second emerged from the shadows, drawn by the light of the fire. This one carried a broken tree trunk like a club. Hileshand blocked its first blow and slit the beast's stomach open as it raised the cudgel in preparation of its second.

This sword had always responded well to Abalel's touch. Light poured through the metal until he could feel the heat of it even in the hilt. The blade acted like a *kauterion*—a physician's tool that reduced blood flow. The wound on the goe'lah's abdomen did not bleed at all.

The creature grunted and brought the cudgel down in a sweeping arc. Hileshand dropped back.

Get away from the fire.

He dropped back again as the goe'lah came at him.

An arrow hissed over his head and struck the goe'lah in the right eye, jerking the head back. *Myles.* The creature roared and lost its footing. As it stumbled to the ground, Hileshand jumped over the body of the first goe'lah, whose cries had ceased, and ran into the darkness.

His eyes did not quickly adjust from the light of the fire. He had gone perhaps ten paces when something invisible struck him hard. He flew through the air and landed on his back. Gasping for breath, he heaved himself to his feet, crouched down, and waited for the goe'lah that had hit him.

Nothing happened. The trees and brush did not break before the mad rush of his bear-skinned foe.

He could hear Marcus somewhere ahead of him and to the right. Shards of yellow light flashed through the tree branches, and he knew what occupied him. He had no idea where Myles was. The arrow had come from an area to his left, but there was no sound from the trees. No call of recognition or safety.

Hileshand waited.

The shadows lightened as a perusan stepped out from behind a grouping of trees some thirty paces away. It appeared as a man, a soldier dressed in Ruthanian armor. As it came closer, it held out its hands to Hileshand, seeming to plead with him. Hileshand ignored it. The weapon of the perusan—their prying fingers—was not something that could be used over distance.

Where was the goe'lah?

The perusan did not like being ignored. Its false expression dropped into one of fury and it began to run toward him, jumping over fallen trees and pockets of undergrowth. He braced himself and met it head on. The skull had to be cut from the body. All other blows merely slowed them.

The perusan danced around before him, blocking his blows with its arms and hands. Two more joined it. Hileshand fought as he had not fought in years. He took the head off the woman on the right, evaded the reaching grip of the child in the center, and suddenly heard the goe'lah behind him. *Behind.* He had missed its movements as he had fought its companions.

Huge hands lifted him off the ground in the yellow-tainted darkness. The creature let loose an ear-ringing roar, holding Hileshand above its head and shaking him like a trophy of war. Hileshand felt himself slide in the creature's grip—his weight shifted. It gripped his cloak and trousers, not his flesh. He twisted in the air, once, then again, rolling his weight to the right side. The goe'lah's grip broke, and he landed on his knees on the creature's shoulders. Lifting his sword with both hands, he slammed it down through the layers of his cloak held aloft in the creature's grip and felt the blade rip through tough flesh.

Searing pain erupted along his thighs. He grunted, ripped his sword free, and threw himself back as the goe'lah dropped.

The earth did not catch him kindly. He landed on something that punctured his left shoulder, and for a brief moment, the pain in his thighs became manageable, over-shadowed by the pain in his arm. He had been stabbed before—multiple times, in fact; he could not remember it being this blinding.

The perusan soldier and child came toward him. Holding his breath against the pain, he staggered to his feet and fought the creatures off. He killed the child first, the soldier more slowly. In the aftermath, the forest seemed oddly quiet, the remaining activity removed from him.

Another goe'lah bellowed in anger somewhere in front of him. That had to be Myles. Hileshand glanced over his right shoulder and saw the light scattering through the trees as the perusan fled the edge of Marcus' sword. He felt a brief smile. Marcus could handle himself. He and Hileshand had been fighting perusan for ten years.

It was very likely that Myles could handle the goe'lah just as well as he had handled the dragon, but Hileshand was not willing to leave him alone. Grimacing at the way his body hurt, he forced himself into a forward jog through the shadows in the direction of the goe'lah's roar.

$\mathcal{M}$yles killed one goe'lah, the one that had rushed Hileshand at the fire, and three perusan. They had appeared as men dressed as merchants. His brother killed ten perusan and afterward seemed strangely relaxed, as if he had just returned from an outing with friends. He teased his father, who moved stiffly with much wincing. The older man was in obvious pain, but Myles would never be able to consider Hileshand's signs of pain as proof of weakness. With Hileshand, they were the highest signs of strength.

No one approached a goe'lah without a bow. Anything other than a bow was an invitation for a painful death. The blood maimed more surely than a sword and killed more readily than a plague. Enough of it, and it could eat through the skin. Yet a sword was all Hileshand had possessed this night, and he had outshone them all. He had killed his own assailants and then come to Myles, killing one more goe'lah and half a dozen perusan that Myles could not adequately attack with a bow in his hand.

As he processed this new understanding of Hileshand, Myles put on thick gloves and heaved the dead goe'lah away from the fire one at a time, dragging them into the woods. Then he sat on his bedroll and watched in silence as Marcus tended to his father's wounds. They were small, considering.

A thorn protruded from Hileshand's shoulder. The root was as wide as a sword pommel, the shaft solidly implanted in the muscle. Marcus eventually gave up trying to remove it gently, for it would not be gently removed. "You taught me to stay away from these, Father. Then the moment my back is turned…"

Hileshand grimaced as Marcus forced the shaft and it finally rotated free. Marcus held it up in the firelight. About three inches long, it was covered with hooked barbs.

A gela thorn. Myles had stepped on one as a child. It had not been a pleasant experience. The barbs bore a toxin that didn't kill but still managed to sting severely.

"I wondered what that was," was all Hileshand said.

Marcus tossed it into the woods. He bandaged the shoulder as best he could with the supplies at hand and came to the next area of issue. He looked at his father for a long moment and then demanded, "What did you attempt to do *here*? Squeeze him to death with your knees?"

Hileshand attempted a laugh. It finished as a wheeze and he scowled at himself, irritated at the inconvenience of pain. He told them briefly what had happened, without fanfare or obvious embellishment, and Myles sat there in silence, uncertain how he should respond to the tangible emotion of awe that built within him. He had not felt this before, not for a real person.

With a heavy frown, Myles watched Hileshand and

thought about all the stories his mother had told him. One of those stories, a story he had been particularly fond of as a child, contained a goe'lah. Hana had gone into great detail about how his father had killed it with the sword of Abalel—a sword that glowed with the sun's flame. Hileshand had carried such a sword this evening.

Your father touched what no one would touch, she used to say. *He was the bravest man I knew. You will be like him.*

That had been his goal. Ever since he had been old enough to understand, Myles had desired to be the man he had heard about. A good man. A brave man, who never crumbled in a fight and never failed to protect those he loved. Myles had allowed his mother's words to mold him and influence him. He had been deeply affected by the legend she had crafted for him.

Hileshand's stories of Lord Elah, his father of blood, had confused him, and now Hileshand himself confused him even more.

None of them desired to sleep again in the woods that night so they crossed the border into Tarek at dawn, arrived at an inn early in the day, and slept through the night. They stayed at the inn for a week while Hileshand recovered.

One night when Marcus was out buying supplies, Myles went to Hileshand as he sat smoking his pipe on the common porch off the front door of the inn. That was his practice. When they were in town like this, he would end the day watching passersby through a fog of pipe smoke.

Myles found him with his feet propped up on the railing, the pipe between his teeth.

Myles leaned back against the rail and folded his arms, looking down at him. They were mostly by themselves. A mother played with her two small children at the end of the porch. A maid was cleaning up some sort of accident involving a potted plant on the opposite end.

"May I ask you a question?" Myles said.

Hileshand tilted his head back and looked up at him. "Is it the same question you always ask me?"

What question is that? Myles wondered. "No," he answered. "I have never asked you this question."

Hileshand smiled. "Then yes."

"Did you serve in the Ruthanian royal military?"

For a moment, the question seemed to catch the older man off his guard. "Yes," he said eventually.

"Were you a captain?"

"For a short time, yes."

"Were you decorated for valor by King Habeine?"

"It is highly possible. Why do you wish to know?"

Hana had told Myles all about the Ruthanian military and his father's supposed involvement with it—he had been a captain, decorated for valor, which was an honor given to very few. A theory was growing in Myles' mind. He had wondered about it before, but it had begun to seem more realistic last night, when he had seen Abalel's sword in Hileshand's hand. "I would like to hear of a few of your stories."

Hileshand's feet swung off the railing. He leaned forward and said, "There have been two great stories in my life. One is the daily discovery that I can trust what Abalel says to me. He means what he says and acts on what he says. That is the first. The *second* great story is your brother." He smiled and leaned back in his chair. "He delights me. With little exception, everything he does, he does very well."

Myles had seen his love for him displayed again and again. He knew Hileshand meant what he said, though the words were somewhat difficult to accept because from a certain perspective, they were not true. "He is not the son of your blood."

"But that does not matter. It is a detail that carries no weight. He is my son because I want him to be my son, just as your mother wanted you to be hers."

Hileshand could not be aware of the picture he painted with such words. Myles studied him, debating his next question. He glanced at the mother with her two children at the end of the porch, then he returned his stare to Hileshand and said, "How well did you know my mother?"

There was something about the way Hileshand spoke of her that was unique. At the very least, the tone of voice he used in reference to her suggested that the two of them had been much more than acquaintances. *At the very least.* Myles suspected it had been something more than merely friendship, however—something strong enough to compel her to name him after this man. To tell his stories and claim them as those of his father. When Myles was a boy, she would often look at him and say, *Your father was very brave,* goshane. *I miss him. But you are here, and that makes me happy.*

Myles was watching closely, and he did not miss the flicker of depth that passed through Hileshand's eyes at that question. It was gone in a moment, but during that moment, it had been very clear. Caution crawled through Myles' stomach, a strong sense of wariness.

Hileshand sighed and lowered his pipe to his lap. After a brief hesitation, he said quietly, "If you would like that to be the first story I tell you...I am willing."

"I..." Myles did not know how to answer him. The story lay there, an open invitation that he had but to reach out and take, but he could feel the sudden tension in his abdomen, the advanced beat of his heart. Why did this affect him this way? *No,* he thought. He didn't want to know.

Finally, he said, "I do not wish to have the story. I simply...I just wanted to have an answer to my question."

Humor deepened the lines around Hileshand's eyes. "And did I answer your question?"

Myles did not know what the older man suspected here, but clearly, he suspected something.

"Yes," Myles answered.

chapter 11

They traveled deep into Tarek and arrived at the closed gates of Bledeshure the night before the King's Feast. The city was swollen to capacity. Hileshand counted a hundred tents spread out along the road, their occupants waiting for first light and the trumpet blast that would signal the opening of the gates.

"Make camp," Hileshand told Marcus and Myles. "I will come back."

An hour later he returned with the information they sought. "Galatia has not recalled her soldiers. They fear a response from Furmorea, so most of the companies sent into that land have been stationed here until the risk is abated."

Myles stared up at the imposing wall that circled the city. It was lined with Galatian archers. They stood every five paces, waiting for any offense to occur. The city had been overrun. "Do you still believe this to be a good idea?"

It was the closest Hileshand had ever seen him come to revealing fear. He wondered what the man was thinking.

The wall of this city meant something to him that it did not mean to Hileshand and Marcus. It was, perhaps, the epitome of everything that had befallen him.

Myles looked back at him, scowling.

Hileshand could see the tension on the man's face. He nodded and answered his question. "The man has not left the city." He looked back to the wall, adding quietly, "He is here."

In the morning, the trumpet sounded; the gates opened, and they entered the city with the others.

The Galatian military had occupied Bledeshure for nearly four months. The king of Tarek, an older, maturing man named Reshland, did not wish to be dragged into this war with Furmorea, his western neighbor, so he begrudgingly allowed the occupation to continue. The Galatians had taken but one city, and they offered him a substantial tribute for the use of his land, paying him from the profits they leeched from Furmorea.

In most cases, records were not kept of the sale of slaves. This was especially true when there was an influx of them, such as in a time of war. But the man who had sold Hana Rosure would likely recall details of the purchaser, perhaps even his name. That was Hileshand's plan—they needed the seller.

The man's name was Banamin Deregus, and he was a captain in the Galatian Eurspak Division. The word meant *hunter*. He was a scout for the larger company. Myles remembered his name. He remembered his face. Of course he did.

For two days, they privately made inquiries. Hileshand would take one of them or the other, never both brothers together, and as their efforts returned to them empty, Myles retreated into a vicious sort of silence. He had not shown himself to be a man of many words, and he used even fewer of them on the interior side of Bledeshure's gate.

They stayed at an inn on Wester Street across from the harbor. The Tarek River flowed as wide as a lake, and the Galatian presence did not seem to have discouraged shipping. Marcus had never seen this many merchant vessels at one time before. Any more of them, and they would be piling up atop one another. The harbormen were loud, shouting to each other late into the night and starting again long before the sun rose.

On the night of the third day, Myles and Hileshand returned to the room in silence. Catching Marcus' gaze, Hileshand shook his head and looked pointedly at Myles, who slung off his cloak and dropped it across the corner chair. He did not look up.

"See to supper, Marcus," Hileshand said quietly.

Marcus went downstairs.

The inn's main room had come alive. The temperature had elevated, and the entire space crawled with bodies— many more men than the last time Marcus had taken this staircase only two hours before. His steps slowed. What was going on? Hearing bright, tinkling laughter that clearly did not belong to anyone in this group, he stopped three steps off the floor, his hand on the rail, and scanned the crowd.

Immediately, he found what he sought.

A girl had just entered through the main doors on the other side of the room. Her eyes were the color of moulta blossoms. Stormy sky. The swell of the sea at midday. Her eyes were the first thing Marcus noticed about her. *Blue eyes in Tarek. Rare.* She was probably Furmorean. He had heard that the farmers in the north could produce light eyes like this.

He discovered he could not move. Her gaze held his as if no one else was present. Then she giggled again, turned her attention elsewhere, and finally he could breathe.

She was accompanied by guards in red and black uniforms. They were large men, fully armed. They kept the crowd at a decent distance from her as the men of the inn pressed against one another and pushed, each straining to catch the girl's attention.

She was a prostitute. Her laughter, her response to the men—Marcus immediately knew what she was and judged himself harshly. He was not a man without resource or company—he claimed to be Myles Hileshand's son. That made him altogether different than the men in this room. Why should he respond the same way they did?

Yet this girl possessed a quality that seemed almost magical. She was truly captivating.

As his thoughts stumbled all over themselves, he pushed his way to the bar and spoke with the innkeeper. The girl's laughter was highly distracting, and Marcus suddenly decided he would stay a few minutes. *Dangerous,* he thought. *Those eyes, that voice—very dangerous.* A strong sense of caution arose in his chest, but he decided a few minutes could not hurt. The room overflowed; he could not even see her now that he was off the steps.

The innkeeper, a man named Daveen, gave him a sly smile. "Not from Tarek, are you?" The man shook a glass at him as the girl's giggling filled the room again. "I can always tell the new ones. Her name is Amilia—the jewel of Bledeshure. Every man in the whole of Tarek knows who she is, and I can always tell the ones who don't." He grinned. "They look just about the same way you look right now."

Dangerous. The word returned to his thoughts. "Tell me about her." Marcus leaned against the bar, his back to the crowd.

Daveen readily obliged him. "The owner's name is Frassen Olah. He moves among kings and those who have more gold than common sense. Only the best with Olah. And that girl is his crown."

Why does he send her here then? Marcus wondered. The inn was old and did not attract wealth. He saw sailors and men who looked like they had just come from their booths at the marketplace. Most of those here were clearly not among the upper class.

He heard shouts in the crowd—men calling suggestions to her. She giggled.

Daveen shrugged. "She comes here once a week, sometimes more. I've heard she asks for my place specifically. Drives up my business, and maybe she likes the change of scenery." He shrugged a second time. "Honestly—why else would she come here? I know what I have. I know my patrons. But then, some of the men insist she isn't fond of palaces, though I could never guess why she'd prefer this sort of—"

The innkeeper looked over Marcus' shoulder. His eyes widened, and a moment later, Marcus felt a hand on his arm. The girl slid up beside him at the bar and loudly asked him what he was doing there.

The entire room groaned in disappointment.

"Him?" someone grumbled. "Why him?"

She was much more beautiful up close than she had seemed from across the room, and from across the room, she had seemed glorious. Marcus cleared his throat and said quietly in Ruthanian, "My lady…I thank you for your offer, but…" She did have the most striking eyes. He had never seen eyes this color before. Golden hair. Golden skin. He shored up his courage. "I cannot accept it. You will need to make another choice. I'm about to leave."

The words were far more difficult to say than they should have been. Marcus purposefully redirected his attention to the bottle in his hands. He wondered if it were possible to draw more attention to himself than what he currently drew. *Likely no.* He could feel the gaze of every man in the room pressing against his spine.

The girl repeated her question, this time in Furmorean, her voice low. "What are you doing here?" It no longer seemed to be an invitation.

The tension in her tone drew his head back around. She was smiling. She put her hand to his stomach, and the warmth of her touch startled him. He forgot her question. She giggled and slid her hand down his body to the inside of his thigh, and he suddenly had difficulty remembering how to breathe.

She leaned close and whispered in his ear. "Have you gone mad?"

He took the opportunity to lean close as well. "What?"

"In a moment, none of this will matter. They will assume you've run and chain you as surely as they chained you before. Why did you return here?" She pulled away.

He stared at her. The innkeeper had named her owner. The girl was a slave—from Furmorea, the same as Myles—but Marcus doubted she had been brought to the city in the same grouping as Myles. She was too comfortable in this harsh environment to have lived in it for only a few months.

Yet she thought she recognized him. She thought she knew him. Why had Myles never mentioned her? Was there a reason he had not done so? Marcus had trouble holding his focus. A beautiful girl.

He leaned away from her. He had to, if he intended to speak with any clarity. "You know me?"

"I saw you at the block," she answered simply. She took hold of his hand. "Come upstairs with me—smile, why don't you?—and I will help you leave."

Something about the tension in her voice, the clear concern, gave him pleasure. "Why? Why would you do that for me?"

He did not move from the bar, even when she tugged on him.

The false pleasure on her mouth disappeared, and with a sharp sigh, she looked at him with frustration and a peculiar sort of despair. "Deregus is here. This very night."

Deregus. Marcus looked through the room. Every face was turned toward him. Every man watched his quiet exchange with the girl. But then he saw them. A group of soldiers stood near the door. One of them, a captain, met his gaze and held it, a look of deep suspicion on his face. He signaled to the men beside him and nodded his head in Marcus' direction.

Change of plans, Marcus thought and imagined his father and brother in their room upstairs. *I hope you both are ready for this.* He squeezed the girl's fingers. She had a small hand. It was delicate. "And that," he said, "is the goal. Thank you for helping make it possible. Tell me, where will you be tomorrow? I would like to see you again."

She withdrew from him. The room instantly began to rumble and shiver like a hive of wasps, and as one, all of them leaned forward in disbelief. Marcus felt the touch of their stares grow more intense and demanding.

The soldiers dispersed through the crowd. As they did, Marcus pushed away from the bar and headed for the rear stairs. He took them two at a time but heard footsteps behind him and knew he was not going to make it back to the room. *Change of plans.*

Something struck the back of his head. Colors scalded his eyes, and the world became hazy. He thought he heard a female voice shouting in alarm and hoped it was the blue-eyed girl. It would be nice if it were Amilia, concerned for him. *No...wait. Concerned for Myles. She thinks I'm Myles.*

He didn't know anything with certainty until a bucket of hot water emptied all over him.

chapter **12**

"**Y**ou are not the farm boy we dug out of the hills."

Marcus pulled his eyes open to a blast of fiery sunlight. It appeared to be somewhere near midday, and he winced at the sting in his eyes, then grimaced at the way his skull seemed to compress in pulses. His entire body ached, and he fuzzily remembered being tied to a wooden beam, arms spread, feet chained. He could not feel his hands.

The speaker continued, "That man killed eight of my men and severely injured four more. One is never going to walk again. You have his face—but not his intelligence, nor his skill."

A sword point prodded sharply against Marcus' chest.

"Nor do you have his scar."

As his eyes adjusted to the brightness, Marcus managed to keep them open long enough to survey the man who spoke to him. It was the Galatian captain from the harbor tavern. *Banamin Deregus*. The man appeared to be somewhere around his thirty-fifth year, and his armor was deco-

rated with several bronze marks—medals for service. So he
possessed a level of courage then. And aptitude.

Four men stood with him, two on either side of the beam
holding Marcus to the ground. Two of the men smirked. One
smiled fully as Marcus made eye contact with him. A chill
spread through Marcus' body, even though sweat collected
on his face and chest. They had stripped him of everything
but his undergarment.

The sword poked his skin again.

"Let me ask you the same question I asked him," Deregus drawled. "Why would a Furmorean bear the symbol
of the Ruthanian god of night?" He smiled when Marcus
didn't answer and shrugged. "Your silence does not matter.
The moment I saw your unmarked skin, I knew what I had
found. Galatia does not practice the same rites as Ruthane,
but we honor our neighbor's allegiances; we are familiar
with their act of *parsah*, where they accept the god's blessing
by killing the chosen-born. You're not Furmorean. You're a
Ruthanian twin. Your brother was the child of favor, who
somehow missed his appointment with death."

They were on a flat roof. Distantly, Marcus heard the
shouts of the harbor guards and the calls of the merchants
trying to finish their transactions before the departure horn
sounded. So they had not brought him very far. His skin felt
like it was searing slowly over a low fire. How long had they
waited before waking him? He attempted to flex his hands
and could not tell if he was doing so.

"What were you doing in the city? Looking for him?"

One of the guards snickered.

The captain pushed the sword. It cut the skin this time, a
thin line of blood tracking down the outside of Marcus' ribs.
"Why seek the brother? You should have sought the wom-

an." His brows rose. "Finest looking creature I have seen in a long time."

He described her in salacious detail, and rough laughter passed through the entire group.

Marcus stared at him. Now that he had a face to go with the story Myles had told, that story achieved a new level of reality within him. What sort of man could destroy a woman's family and be so unconcerned with the consequences that he would later be able to make comments such as these? Marcus had not been immune to the signs of torture on Myles' face as he had told the story, but now, seeing what Myles had fought against, he truly began to understand.

Deregus smiled coldly. "The face is not all you share with your brother. I have seen that look of rage before. Is this the story? You return home and find your house burned and your family missing. Well, except for your father. I suppose you found him well enough." He laughed. "If the wolves didn't pull down his bones."

He lowered his voice and said secretively, "Our idea was to stage the Fall of Burmin-Li. The stakes through the legs were a nice touch. And the eyes were a nice touch as well." He nodded to one of his men.

The man bowed. "Thank you, Captain."

"The eyes actually gave us some trouble. Usually, they are not that difficult to remove."

They described the death of Hana's husband in detail, and by the end of the story, Marcus had never hated anyone as he hated this man. He tried to control the emotions that surged through him and did not fully succeed.

Marcus took a deep breath and rasped, "You should run. Now. Before you die."

Their laughter became a roar.

"What are you going to do, boy? No, I will tell *you* how you are going to die." As he spoke, he sheathed his sword and pulled a knife from the scabbard strapped to his calf. "I am going to carve into your chest the same mark I saw in your brother's. Then I, personally, am going to take you north and see you try to save your life in the arena. Your brother could have made a name for himself there—but you? You won't last the first two minutes. You may not even survive today."

He nodded to two of his men, and they came around and crouched at Marcus' shoulders, forcing him still, securing his arms even further. The captain sank his knee deep into Marcus' stomach, leaning all his weight against his diaphragm. Marcus couldn't breathe.

"Steady now," Deregus said, bending over his chest, knife in hand. "If you scream or shake this at all, it's going to hurt much more."

He made the first incision.

The hands at Marcus' shoulders disappeared. He heard shouts. Sounds of violent commotion. The knee came off his stomach, and he could breathe again, but the effort and the pain nearly made him wretch. His head felt like it trembled and swam about.

He briefly lost consciousness, and when he regained it, the rooftop had grown calm. A shadow fell across his face, and he looked up as his brother squatted beside him, taking a knife to the ropes around his arms. Myles acknowledged him with a glance.

"You're frightfully late," Marcus wheezed.

"'Frightfully'?" Myles looked at him with doubt. "The sun's gone to your head, brother." He cut his arms free, ripping the ropes away. "Don't move," he commanded and disappeared.

Marcus didn't think he would be able to lift his head even if he had the desire. He groaned as feeling began to return to his hands.

Myles returned with a mallet and went to work on the shackles on Marcus' feet, muttering beneath his breath. A few swings of the hammer, and he pried the metal away and tossed the locks aside. Then he pulled a towel from his knapsack and wiped Marcus' chest. Marcus winced at the roughness, and his brother, clearly amused, used gentler strokes.

Assuming the reason for Hileshand's absence, Marcus asked, "Did he get him out?"

"Yes. But Deregus fought him and required a bit of persuasion. A little bump on the head." Myles shrugged. "Actually, it was a solid hit—the man is built like a draft horse. He won't be alert for hours."

"You owe me the largest of favors."

The corner of Myles' mouth pulled in. Humor filled his eyes. "It isn't deep. You'll live."

"I'm not certain I have the desire."

Myles helped his brother sit up. Keeping a hand on Marcus' arm, Myles adjusted position and angrily kicked away the beam that had been strapped to Marcus' shoulders. Sliding an arm beneath him, he eased Marcus to his feet. Spots of light filled Marcus' vision. The world shook. His knees gave way, but Myles held on to him.

Deregus' four men lay in various throws of pain across the roof. None of them appeared to be dead or dying, and Marcus wagered that his brother had argued extensively before agreeing to this part of Hileshand's plan. As he looked at them, Marcus fought repulsion. Why allow men like this to live? Their descriptions of Hana and the death of her husband made him shudder.

Yet his father had seen much more of war and death than Marcus had; perhaps Hileshand had a better understanding of mercy as well.

Myles stopped. Without warning, he lowered Marcus to the ground and stalked over to the nearest guard. What was he doing? Alarmed, Marcus said, "Myles..."

But the warning trailed away. What could he say to him, now that he had looked into the crazed eyes of the man who had taken everything Myles loved? If his brother chose to seek vengeance here, Marcus would not be able to stop him. He could not even put together the right words.

Myles looked back. "You will need clothes," he said.

He stripped the guard.

chapter 13

In the quiet of the shipping office, Hileshand washed and bandaged Deregus' wounds. He reset the bone in the forearm and splinted it securely. Then he turned a crate upside down and sat on it, waiting for the man to return to consciousness again. After a time, he pulled out his pipe.

This building was set at the far end of the docks, and it had been deserted for quite some time. The sign above the door could no longer be read. Sitting there on the crate, Hileshand could hear the shrill crying of rivergulls and the shouts of the distant shipmen. He watched Deregus. The man was snoring.

Through war and attempts of peace, Hileshand had killed many men in his lifetime, and though he had grown older, he did not believe he had grown soft. He could easily take what he had just repaired. He could leave it broken, without aid, and never think of it again. He did not think of the others, and they had been better men than this one spread out on the ground before him. This man was not a man. He had betrothed his soul to the gods of death a long time ago.

Why, then, did he feel this quiet urge for delay in his heart? He frowned as he pulled at his pipe. He had ordered Myles to leave the others alive, but this one he had never fully decided upon, being willing to do whatever necessary to pry from his grasp the information they sought.

And Captain Banamin Deregus was not going to part with anything easily. His skull was made of stone, as evidenced by the force Hileshand had been compelled to use against him, and likely, the rest of him was just as determined. Hileshand was familiar with this type of man. Without proper motivation, Deregus would tell him nothing.

Frustrated at his unrest, Hileshand left the office and walked out into the darkness of the empty warehouse.

The room was large, the shadows expansive. Chunks of the roof had crumbled away, but the jagged openings did not allow much more than dust-filled, half-hearted shafts of light to enter. The place had been built over the river, and out here in the storage area, he imagined he could feel the current as it rushed against the old wooden piles.

Pipe in hand, Hileshand walked the wall. The dark corners of the room became familiar to him as he trudged onward and sorted his thoughts.

Marcus and Myles waited for him at the King's Southern Inn outside the city. They expected this endeavor to take a period of time, knowing the sort of man Hileshand intended to break. But he did not understand this unexpected restlessness within him. Why the delay?

His steps slowed, and he felt the floor move beneath his boots. The building shifted around him, boards and nails creaking ominously. With a frown, he glanced through the darkness and wondered if the building would hold long enough for him to complete his purpose.

He could not delay. He put aside the catch in his heart and adjusted his path.

As he approached the door to the office, he heard voices. Men speaking with one another. He swore beneath his breath and eased closer, beginning to choose his steps with care.

"...simply left him here?"

"Who could possibly care enough for Banamin Deregus to see to his wounds? Unholy, I say, the tending of any Galatian. Particularly this one. We should kill him now and be done with him."

Hileshand put a hand to his sword hilt.

"But the one who cares for him also left him bound. That does not make sense. Why see to his wounds and then bind him?" The voice grew alarmed. "What are you doing?"

"What do you think? I'm checking his purse."

Hileshand released his breath slowly, a smile moving across his lips. His purse? That he would not deny them. He put his pipe between his teeth and waited for them to leave. The eerie movements of the building began to feel less ominous. After a time, they seemed almost soothing.

"All right. Let's go."

"Stay a moment. Now, let's...let's think about this."

The tension immediately returned. "What is there to think about?"

"I ask this question in all seriousness—do you think Claven would give us a reward for killing this man?"

His companion snorted loudly. "Claven would never see *you*. Not even if you killed ten men just like this one."

"I have killed such a man before. This one would not be

difficult for me."

Hileshand returned his hand to his sword and prepared to step through the doorway.

The office filled with a mad roar. The men began to shout in panic. Apparently, Deregus was not as removed from consciousness as he had seemed. Hileshand rolled his eyes as the men who had flirted with the idea of death squealed and jumped about like frightened children. The floor creaked loudly. He felt the building tremble.

The roar choked off, dissolving into a breathy moan.

"Go! Let's go! Run!"

There were pounding footsteps and additional cries of panic. The office emptied, and the door slammed shut.

When he was certain they were indeed gone, Hileshand slipped back into the room to begin what he intended.

He stopped.

Blood covered the floor. It had sprayed across the walls, on the ceiling. Bloody footsteps tracked to the door and he saw more of them haphazardly strewn across the steps leading to the riverbank. Deregus lay on his side, gasping for breath. He had been stabbed multiple times. He was dying.

Hileshand went to his knees beside him. He put a hand on the captain's shoulder, grimaced at his wounds.

Deregus spat a curse at him.

He did not have much time. Hileshand gripped the man's arm. "The Ruthanian twin—there was a woman with his brother in Furmorea. What happened to her in the North Square? Who purchased her?"

Deregus shook his head. The words slurred on his lips. "Should have killed him."

The life faded from him.

Hileshand tried to draw him back. "Deregus!"

The man sneered at him, and that was how he died, his face twisted in that position.

Hileshand released him and leaned back. He felt gutted, as if he had been wounded as severely as the man who lay before him.

"Delay?" he said, looking skyward. "Is this the delay you intended, Abalel?"

He had hated the sight of finding Marcus today, bound, in pain, struggling to keep hold of his consciousness on the crossbeam, with Deregus drawing blood on his chest. Hileshand had known what they could likely expect in all of this. The plan, after all, had been his plan, and he knew the risks, but seeing his son in that position had disturbed him greatly. It had taken a determined focus not to kill Deregus right then, without hesitation. He had managed to restrain himself for the sole purpose of exploiting the Galatian captain for every scrap of information he possessed.

He stood to his feet and stared down at the body, feeling weary and strangely appeased at the same time. What now? It had all been for naught.

chapter **14**

That night at the inn, they discussed their options. By now, every Galatian within the city walls patrolled for Marcus and Myles, so the two of them were out of play. Deregus' men would take precautions—they would not allow themselves to be caught like that again, so Hileshand's plan would not work a second time.

Right away, an alternate plan occurred to Marcus. It was, he thought, rather perfect. He listened to the other ideas for a short while, then he leaned forward in his chair and said, "So…I think I know our next course of action."

Myles and Hileshand looked at him, waiting.

He pointed at his father. "You would return to the city."

"Of course."

"There would be some money involved." Marcus tried to keep his lips still and did not fully succeed.

His father frowned at the obvious amusement, tilting his head as he studied him.

Marcus added, "An amount entirely based on your own

whims. But probably substantial."

"All right…"

As sincerely as he could, he stated, "You would need to secure the favor of a prostitute. The jewel of Bledeshure."

Something was wrong. Bas'silia could feel it in her heart. She could see it in the girl's face as she lay there in the bed, her pale skin drained of all color. She was so still, and it was clear she was in pain. Bas'silia wiped the sweat from the girl's forehead and spoke soothing words to her.

Shelmak had come and gone this morning—hours ago. The man was a fool for hurting her like this. He had rough hands, but they were swift, which was why the master kept him on retainer. Precautions were taken to keep the girls from conceiving. But Amilia was not meant for this life. Bas'silia had known that the moment the master had brought her home from the North Square. At twelve years of age, the girl had been quick to blush and innocent-eyed—young in many ways. Those Furmorean elements of her character had long ago vanished, as could be expected in this place and as a part of this house.

But one element of who she was could not be removed from her. This was the fourth or fifth time Shelmak had been called to tend to her, the fourth or fifth time Bas'silia had taken care of her afterward. Usually, the recovery did not look like this and Amilia did not bleed this way. This was the first time Bas'silia had felt this deep sense of dread, so palpable in the air that she shuddered. Something was wrong. That old fool had done something to her. He had damaged her.

Shelmak's hands had been shaking, his forehead dotted with sweat. He had insisted nothing was amiss with him. She never should have allowed him to proceed. She should have listened to her inner warnings.

"Someday," Bas'silia whispered to Amilia, "you will not be in this place. You will have a husband who loves you and loves your babies and you will be happy."

The girl opened her eyes and looked at her. "Pleasant words."

"True words." *God of kindness, whichever of you is listening, please let them be true words.* Bas'silia ran the cool cloth over the girl's forehead again and smiled at her. "I will be happy for you when that day comes."

Amilia was not fooled. She was smart—too smart, sometimes. Nothing fooled her. "Perhaps," she said, her voice naught more than a breath, "you will come with me. Perhaps he will have a handsome brother."

Bas'silia tried to laugh. "A brother? Dear girl, I would need a father. Possibly a grandfather. You honor me where no honor is due." She leaned down and kissed the girl's forehead. "Wait for me. I will return."

Fear filled the girl's eyes. Bas'silia knew her thoughts of death and scowled at her.

"You will *not* die today, girl. Do you hear me? Close your eyes and recover in peace. You are not going to see the gates of death any time soon."

But as soon as she left the room, her tears came, and she started running down the hall, to get away before Amilia heard her. Bas'silia loved that little girl. If she died here, it would be the master's fault, for that child never should have been brought into this place.

Before stepping into the room at the opposite side of the

circular hall, Bas'silia dried her eyes with the backs of her hands. The servant opened the door for her.

On the other side, the drapes were pulled. The room was dark, as it often was. The physician wished to encourage the peace of sleep, but each day, sleep seemed to come to the master with more and more difficulty.

She walked to the edge of the bed and knelt down beside it, finding her master's hand in the dark and lifting it to her lips.

"My lord," she whispered, kissing his skin.

She knew he was awake. The pain did not allow him much rest, though he tried.

A long sigh came from the bed.

"Your face is wet," he said.

Bas'silia blinked back her tears. He would know what they meant. He would know her fears. "I don't understand why the gods do this. It's not fair."

"No, it is not," he agreed, but he meant those words in reference only to himself, to his own pain. He did not love the girl the way Bas'silia loved her. She was not certain if the master had ever loved anyone. He was not that sort of man.

She kissed his hand again. She was sorry for him. Her heart ached for his pain as it did for Amilia's, but she felt two different forms of sorrow. The girl had not chosen this life, while the master had done everything he could to preserve it, unaware of the price it would one day require of his flesh. He could not be healed. The gods had chosen not to be merciful toward him, in any way.

"Move her. I want her out of the house."

Bas'silia had suspected this response from him. "My lord, please…"

"No, Bas'silia. There is enough death here as it is." Again, he was the focus of his own words.

She reached out in the shadows and ran her fingers tenderly down his jawline. He had been handsome once. He had been dangerous and strong—thrilling in a way the others were not. Now he was none of those things. Instead, he lapsed into concerns about fairness and gave in to a heightened fear of death. He knew his time was coming. He did not wish anything in this house to prove to him his fears were real, to remind him of the future he could not stop.

She gripped his hand. "What if there was another way? What if…I could make this beneficial for you?"

He sighed again. Bas'silia felt the breath roll across her. Whenever she presented a case before him, he listened; he would not do that for the others. That did not mean he would agree to her view, but she had learned how to speak to him, and he, in turn, would listen to her.

"What do you intend?" he asked.

chapter **15**

Hileshand frequented the harbor inn every night for a week, and the girl his son described never came. Marcus had been a river of details concerning her. Specifically, he could remember colors, which had never been a point of strength for him in the past. Blue eyes. Hair the color of honey. Skin as white as sand. When Hileshand had glanced at him, brows raised in humor, Marcus had shrugged and smiled in an unrepentant manner.

You'll understand when you see her.

But he did not see her. The innkeeper became annoyed at his constant questions and eventually told him, "No one *sees* Amilia. You could no sooner win an audience with the king."

Hileshand knew what the man assumed about him and the reason he kept asking for her. He also knew that he was not the only man to pose these questions. Over the last seven nights, he had seen no less than twenty men stand exactly where he was standing now and ask the innkeeper the same questions Hileshand asked.

The hour was early yet today. Only a few patrons loitered near the walls.

Hileshand hesitated a moment, watching the man mop up a spill on the counter. Then he leaned his weight against the bar and said quietly, "Look. I believe she may have information regarding a woman who was sold as a slave in your city about five months ago. I intend to find that woman, and Amilia may be able to help me."

The man looked up abruptly. "Doesn't matter," he answered, voice firm, words pronounced succinctly. "The answer remains the same. They send a runner to alert me before she comes—she chooses the day and the hour. I know no more than you do."

The master's name was Olah. Hileshand had already attempted that route and had gained nothing from it. Olah did not see anyone who was not interested in making a substantial investment into his sordid business. Hileshand had not even been allowed inside the front door of his establishment on the city's main street, and guards had escorted him off the property when he attempted to press his case.

Heaving a frustrated sigh, Hileshand walked out of the inn to give himself time to clear his head and come up with another plan. He could not return to Marcus and Myles without anything to show for his efforts.

He had gone about fifty paces when he felt a hand on his arm. He tensed and spun around, hands raised, expecting to see a company of Galatian soldiers. He did not remember the faces of Deregus' men, but that did not necessarily mean they returned the favor.

But it was not soldiers who had interrupted his disturbed thoughts. The girl was tall, nearly as tall as he was, and she was dressed well, like the lady of a house. The gold bracelet on her wrist, however, suggested otherwise. Hileshand remembered Olah's mark from the door of his business—a rose blooming from a tower. This bracelet bore the same mark.

She looked at him for a long, harsh moment. Curious, he waited for her to address him. She had, after all, sought him out.

"My lord," she said, bowing her head to him. "I heard your words to Daveen."

The innkeeper.

Stiff-lipped, she asked, "Are these words true?"

How had she heard him speak in private? He had not seen her anywhere in the room, and he had been certain not to allow his voice to carry. He could not imagine many women frequenting a place like that—and had wondered, several times, while Amilia chose to do so. "Yes. They are true. It is very important to me that I find the young lady I seek."

Something broke in the girl's gaze. She softened considerably, and a faint but sad smile began to rise on her lips. "Indeed, she is very young, my lord. Very young. My name is Asana. My mistress sends me on errand." Her eyes narrowed as she studied him. "Perhaps you are that errand."

People flowed past them on the street. A carriage approached with a small company of heavily armed guards. Asana looked through the crowd for a moment and then turned around, motioning for Hileshand to follow her. He did so. They walked for an hour and eventually arrived at an unmarked house on Clay Street. It was heavily guarded and surrounded by a wall ten feet high.

Asana nodded to the guards, and they opened the gate.

Immediately, a woman came out of the house. Her skin was several shades darker than that most often found in Tarek, but her eyes were blue. The contrast was striking. Hileshand was not used to such an unconventional appearance. She was beautiful in a way others were not.

The woman frowned at Hileshand. Asana went to her and whispered in her ear, answering questions as the woman asked them. Eventually, she waved the girl away and approached Hileshand.

"I am Bas'silia," she said, "the keeper of this house. Is it true—what you told this girl?"

Hileshand nodded. "It is."

"You believe Amilia can help you?"

"I do." He considered the situation and decided to add, "She spoke with my son. I know she can help me."

She looked at him for a long time. "Come with me." She led him up the steps. "Amilia is very ill. I am not sure if the girl will live, but this…if she does live, perhaps this will be good for you both."

A unique picture she painted. Good for them both? Hileshand leaned forward to see her expression. The woman suddenly appeared to be in a state near tears. She was clearly distraught.

"How do you mean?" he asked gently.

She shook her head at him. "Never mind that. Listen to me now. You will get the information you require—but you must be willing to pay for it. Is this acceptable to you?"

"Aye. Completely."

"You must pay in gold, and it would be good to pay here and now. Are you able?"

"Consider it done."

She paused at the door, turning to look at him. Her vivid

blue eyes searched his own. After a moment, she whispered, "I have never heard any man ask for Amilia for a reason other than to fulfill themselves with her. You are the first."

She made as if to speak again, but then a servant opened the door for them, and she closed her mouth. Drawing herself up, she blinked away the softness about her eyes and lifted her chin.

"Where is he?" she demanded of the servant as they entered.

The man bowed. "In the walkway."

"Come with me." Bas'silia issued the words as a command, and Hileshand obeyed.

The house was richly furnished and looked comfortable. His companion escorted him through a circular hall along the outer wall, and it eventually emptied onto a covered porch overlooking the back lawn. Three men waited there, breaking off their conversation as they saw Hileshand.

"My lord Olah," Bas'silia said and curtsied before the least likely man in the party. He was as thin as his bones and stoop-shouldered, the shade of his skin sallow, similar to butter. He was not well and had not been well for quite some time.

As he observed him in his chair, Hileshand realized why he had been so difficult to reach earlier in the week. It was because of the unlikely aspect of his person. He would not have expected a man who dealt in women's flesh to be confined to a chair.

As she straightened, Bas'silia clasped her hands in front of her and announced boldly, "I have done what I told you I would do, my lord. I found a buyer."

She looked at Hileshand and said smoothly, "A *generous* buyer."

chapter 16

Hileshand paid ten gold pieces for the girl, the same amount he had paid for Myles back in Blue Mountain. He took note of that fact and wondered if Abalel intended something with the similarity. As the gold left his fingers, he felt himself making a commitment of some sort, one he did not yet fully understand. He promised something with this purchase.

Despite the sterility of this line of thinking, at the time of his purchase, Myles had not been worth ten pieces of gold. The Ansan who had accepted payment would have been content with half that much, perhaps even less. Today, Lord Olah had begun his business with Hileshand by asking for fifty pieces, apparently assuming that Hileshand had heard of the girl. Yet when Hileshand had followed the rules of trade and countered by offering him ten, the man had accepted without challenge, much to Bas'silia's surprise.

Understanding what the quick agreement meant, Hileshand released his breath in a silent sigh. The girl was as ill as Bas'silia said; her master, ill himself, wanted to be rid of her.

As soon as they reentered the house, Hileshand told Bas'silia to hire a carriage and waited while she did so. Then she took him upstairs to gather the frail, delicate little child who now belonged to him. Marcus had guessed her age to be somewhere near twenty-five. He had seen her in her element, with painted eyes and an audience. Hileshand would wager her age to be closer to eighteen. On the way down the steps, holding the girl in his arms, he asked Bas'silia, and she told him Amilia was seventeen.

He could not tell if the girl was asleep or awake. She had opened her eyes briefly as Bas'silia spoke with her in a hurried whisper, telling her of everything that had happened. Then the eyes had closed, and she had not responded again.

Now that the sale had been made, Bas'silia did not see a need to hold on to her strength. She did not hide her tears. As the carriage pulled up to the gate, she kissed the girl on the forehead.

"You see?" she whispered. "I told you."

Then she raised her head and looked Hileshand in the eyes. "Take good care of her."

He felt the severity of her charge. The girl was so light in his arms. *Ten coins. Ten pieces of gold.* He had parted with that amount before and discovered Marcus' brother. Now that he had parted with it a second time, what would he find? There was something of worth here, in this bundle in his arms. He knew it in his heart, and the conviction grew as the moments passed. This little one was important.

"I will, my lady. You have my word."

She touched him, putting a hand to his elbow, then she turned and walked back into the house with her head down.

The journey out of the city required nearly five hours. The road between the city gate and the King's Southern Inn required another three. By the time Hileshand was able to carry the girl up the steps to the inn's second floor, the sun had fully set and all light but that of the moon had faded.

A servant ran up the steps before him and knocked on the third door on the left. "Marcus. Myles," Hileshand called when no one received them. "Open the door."

The door did not open.

Hileshand nodded to the servant, and the man seized the handle and pushed the panel back. On the other side, Hileshand discovered a room as unkempt as a disorganized laundry. Clothes lay everywhere, scattered across the back of chairs and lying in piles on the floor. He'd left them alone for a week, and this was the result. He shook his head and directed the servant: "Help me with that bed there. No, the second one."

Marcus was the one who remembered all her details. Marcus could be the one to sleep on the floor.

Myles and Marcus avoided frequenting the tavern on the first floor of the inn at the same time. They discussed it and worked something out that appealed to them. Every evening after sundown, Myles would buy a jug of red wine and join his brother on the back porch, where they would pass the jug back and forth, watch the moonrise, and wax philosophical. On several evenings, others joined them, but the lighting was poor behind the inn; they knew Marcus and Myles were brothers, and no one considered it remarkable.

That night, they returned to their upstairs room and discovered it occupied. There had been an addition to their company, one that required a physician's care. Hileshand had summoned the doctor from the city, and as soon as Myles and Marcus walked into the room, they were sent out of it again.

Hileshand followed them into the hall, relaying the story quietly. "She was pregnant when you spoke with her, Marcus. There were complications afterward. She has been ill for six days now, yet there is good reason to hope. Several men recommended Aerman, including Bas'silia. He is the first physician to see her. If a physician can heal her, he will be that man."

Myles glanced at his brother. Most of their evenings had included long hours spent in discussion of this girl. Nearly every man who joined them recognized her name and praised her beauty, repeating various stories they had heard of her. One man had even been impressed enough to declare that the war against Furmorea had started because of her, which had earned him many ridiculing comments, as well as a wager or two to the contrary.

Marcus now seemed to wander back and forth between confusion and a dark sort of coloring that might have been a blush. "You mean, she is…yours?"

"I did what needed to be done." Hileshand put his hand on Marcus' shoulder. He kept it there a moment and then glanced at Myles. "Wait outside, boys. I'll come and retrieve you when it is…" He appeared to consider his words a little more closely. "I will find you when you can return."

Seeing the look on his brother's face, Myles went and purchased a second jug of wine.

Sometime later, sitting on the back porch with his boots

up, Marcus told Myles, "I think this scares me."

The summer frogs were singing at the base of the hill in the water. The river could be heard but barely from this distance, while the frogs could be heard late into the night. Myles looked toward him in the next chair, unable to see his face for the shadows. "Why would this scare you?"

"I am uncertain as to the cause yet," his brother answered. His voice grew taut. "If I…if I begin to make a fool of myself, will you stop me? Will you pull me aside and cause me to think again?"

From his brief glimpse of her face, Myles had not thought her all that remarkable. Marcus, however, did not make a habit of being loose with his compliments. He complimented as his father complimented, speaking with purpose because he meant what he said. Something about this girl intrigued him, and, clearly, it continued to intrigue him, despite the cause of her illness. The thought of terminating a pregnancy turned Myles' stomach, and the immediate response of heat within him cooled only as he remembered that she had been a slave, owned by a man who would not understand what it meant to cultivate life and watch it grow. The situation could not be considered her fault.

"If you try to make a fool of yourself," Myles finally answered, lifting the jug, "I will let you, and I will sit back and watch and take note of actions I should avoid in the future."

He felt Marcus' quick gaze in the shadows. Myles had spoken this way without thinking, teasing as he would tease one of his sisters, and he paused, the jug almost at his lips. He had become comfortable with Marcus sometime during these last seven evenings. For a brief, frantic moment, the realization alarmed him. He had not meant to lower his guard like this.

With warmth in his voice, Marcus said, "I am glad you are with me, Myles."

With me, he said, not, *With us.* He spoke for himself, applying it personally.

For the first time, Myles found himself wondering if he would want to part with Hileshand and Marcus when their search was over. He knew what he would do at the end of this venture; it was a path set deep into the earth, one that would happen no matter what other choices were made along the way. He would take his mother and return to Furmorea for his sisters, and in a safe stretch of land far from the disturbances of war, they would rebuild what had been broken. That was the path; it was going to happen.

However, he found he no longer enjoyed the prospect of doing it alone. He would miss nights like this. He would miss finding Hileshand sitting as Marcus sat now, boots propped up on the railing, observing the turn of the world around him.

Marcus spoke again. "You killed a dragon."

A corner of Myles' mouth tucked into his cheek. With a long sigh, he offered the best words he could think of: "You're not going to make a fool of yourself, Marcus."

chapter 17

Aerman, the physician, gave Hileshand a vial filled with a gray powder and essentially told him that if the girl lived through the night, which he could not predict at this juncture, she should be given a teaspoon of this medication every four hours until the vial emptied.

The container was small. It would last two days perhaps, at the most.

The gates of Bledeshure had closed for the night several hours before. Hileshand paid Aerman for his time and reimbursed him for the cost of a room, then he returned to the chair beside the girl's bed. She still had not opened her eyes except for that single time in Olah's home. Hileshand clutched the vial in his hand and simply watched her sleep for the better part of an hour, a strong sense of dread drawing his heart toward his feet.

He knew very little about caring for a woman. Now he had one in his keeping—and yet he took issue with calling this person before him a *woman*. She seemed so small to him.

How was he going to look after and comfort a little girl? This pale child had seen the underbelly of a city in its fullness; she was familiar with certain aspects of evil and sin that he had no desire to imagine or even name. Because of her history, the likelihood of her trusting him was very low. Myles had not trusted him either, not in the beginning, but they, at least, had possessed a few common foundations from which Hileshand could build. What did he share in common with someone who had been forced to live as a prostitute?

Adding to Hileshand's concern, Marcus responded to this girl in unexpected ways. Hileshand had never seen him act like this before. Obviously, the young man had noticed the female sex, but he had never *taken* notice of one in particular, not like this, with his sudden memory of detail and the awkward, almost panicked look in his eyes when Hileshand explained her presence.

This little family was a tender one already, now more than ever. Hileshand had no desire to rebuke Marcus, or even to speak to him about this, but he likely would need to have a conversation with him, simply because this was a new land for them both. A new experience. They would need to be gentle with this. Indeed, this poor girl would require a great deal of gentleness.

He leaned back in his chair and released his breath slowly. *Abalel, I don't know what I am doing.*

He was trying to locate Myles' mother. That, at least in some form, was the answer to his question; it was the reason this girl was here. Yet, as he watched Amilia sleep, he knew that Myles' mother…Hana…was not the full answer. There was something about this girl. Something important. Perhaps that was why Marcus noticed her—perhaps, in a different way, he sensed what Hileshand sensed now.

Why this one, Abalel? he asked. *Out of the entire city and hundreds of girls just like her...why this one?*

The man parted from the shadows as if he were a shadow himself. Marcus did not see him in the dark until the man was almost to the steps. He had come up from the river, instead of approaching the inn from the road.

"Evening," Marcus said as the man stepped off the stairs and onto the porch itself.

The man paused. He glanced at Marcus a moment, or seemed to do so—Marcus could not see his face beneath the hood of his cloak.

The cowl turned slowly and the man looked at Myles. This second inspection lasted a lengthy amount of time.

The shadows were thick beneath the overhang and the night stars; the man could not see their faces, yet he responded as if he did, as if he were taking note of the similarities. In the darkness, his shoulders rose and fell as he pulled in a deep breath. Marcus could hear the air entering the man's nose.

At last, the man from the river responded to the greeting. "My name is Ethan Strelleck."

He stood there, clearly waiting for their return in favor.

"Hileshand," Marcus answered.

The hooded head turned toward Myles again. "And you, sir?"

Marcus answered for him. "My brother."

"Ah." Eventually, the man pulled in another full-lunged breath, smelling the air, and said, "You should avoid the open air tonight. The breeze carries the smell of death."

He went inside. The door closed behind him.

Marcus and Myles glanced at each other.

"What do you suppose *death* smells like?" Myles asked.

Marcus heard the faint slur in his words. He motioned for the jug, and when his brother passed it, Marcus discovered it was nearly empty. He shook it once and frowned at him. "We should find out."

"Aye," Myles agreed. "We wouldn't want to be caught unawares, would we?"

They considered themselves amusing and stayed right where they were for another hour, waiting for Hileshand to come and retrieve them. By the time he did, the moon had risen above the trees, shedding silver light across the short clearing off the porch's steps. The frogs still sang down by the water. The night air was filled with the calls of nocturnal birds and the distant cries of wolves.

Myles paused, both hands on the railing, and wondered at Strelleck's words. *The breeze carries the smell of death.* The night seemed like every other night. Why make such a remark to strangers? The man stirred trouble where no trouble existed.

Hileshand and Marcus took the back staircase to the second level while Myles returned the empty jug to the innkeeper's wife on the lower level.

The moment he entered the main room, he became aware of an unnatural tension. It was like wading into cold water. As the door swung shut behind him, he slowed his steps, scanning the lamp-lit space. The light seemed bright to him after several hours in the dark.

Two tables were occupied near the front door. Strelleck occupied a third table by himself in the back corner. He still wore his cloak, but he had pulled the hood away. It hung down his back, revealing dark hair that had been cropped close to his skull and a neck and face the color of cow's milk. Myles did not believe he had ever seen anyone as unnaturally white as this fellow. It appeared he had an illness that had drained his blood of substance.

Strelleck made eye contact with Myles as he entered and did not remove his gaze. Myles could feel it strongly as he walked across the room.

The innkeeper was away buying supplies in town, and his wife busied herself now behind the bar, sending dark looks toward Strelleck's table.

She accepted the bottle from Myles' hand and returned to him a small deposit. Curious, Myles did not hurriedly remove himself.

"Quiet night," he remarked, voice low.

The woman accepted the invitation immediately and leaned forward. "He's Alusian," she whispered. "At my *husband's* inn. I would deny him a room if he didn't pay so well. That is how they get what they want and make space for themselves among men—they carry more gold than the king himself. It is very difficult to say no to them, though I would do so if I could." She shuddered.

"Alusian?" Myles shook his head. He had heard the name before, but he did not know much about those who carried it.

"Not a man," she answered simply. "*Like* a man, but they have no blood. And wherever they go, real men die. It is said they walk in prophecy. They can sense death and are present to carry men beyond the sphere of this world and into the next. That creature there—Ethan Strelleck, so he calls himself—is more spirit than he is flesh. Listen to my words, son. Someone is going to die here tonight. By dawn you will see it. I've already lost one room. They left the moment they saw

LAUREN STINTON

his entrance, preferring to risk the dangers of sleeping on the road." The innkeeper's wife met his gaze and gave him a pointed look, brows raised. "Brace yourself. It could be that little girl your father brought with him today."

Your father. Marcus had started that, and it seemed to make things easier while they traveled. Myles initially resisted the claim because it was untrue, but he had never fully corrected it. Marcus *was* his brother, and Marcus called Hileshand his father—the statement was not entirely a lie.

Myles could feel the Alusian's gaze pressing against his back.

Pausing in her work, the innkeeper's wife stared at the back table for a moment and then shifted her gaze to Myles. "He seems a good deal interested in *you*, sir." She lowered her voice even further. "Be careful. They are unpredictable."

Myles considered her words for a moment. *Unpredictable.* "He does not seem unfriendly."

A rough noise scraped up the back of her throat, and she returned to her work.

Seeing her scorn, he made his decision and asked, "What does he drink?"

The woman looked at him sharply.

Myles grabbed a clean glass off the counter. "Send back a bottle." Then he went and joined him.

chapter 18

Ethan Strelleck felt no need for purposeful conversation. He seemed surprised that Myles would seek him out, and after accepting his presence across from him at the table, he did not immediately speak again. He stared at Myles with a look Myles could not name. A few times, he pulled in deep breaths, his nostrils flaring, shoulders rising, and afterward, he would relax his lungs and breathe normally for a time before inhaling like this again.

His choice of wine was putrid. It smelled like burnt grass and tasted like tree bark and candle wax. Myles didn't know what it was, and after a single sip, he set the glass down and did not touch it again.

When he had endured as much of the silence as he could, he leaned back in his chair and folded his arms, returning the Alusian's stare steadily. "Did you mean what you said tonight?" *The smell of death.*

The man who was not a man did not require a reminder of his words. "I did," Strelleck said after a moment.

"Would you say you smell this often?"

Something flickered through the creature's eyes. He answered warily, "Yes."

"Then why mention it tonight?"

Strelleck asked a question of his own: "Why do you seek me?" He glanced around the room.

Myles was aware of how the others watched their table. Conversations had ceased. The innkeeper's wife had retreated behind the bar again and stood there staring, an unattractive frown between her brows.

He shrugged. "I am merely curious."

Without pulling his gaze from him, the Alusian again filled his lungs, a deep breath, and let it out slowly. "I am no fortune teller."

"I do not require my fortune told."

The creature studied him. Eventually, the lines about the eyes and mouth grew less noticeable, and he seemed to come to a decision. He answered Myles' question. "I do not understand you."

"What do you not understand?"

"You bear the mark of God."

There were many gods of death; Myles wondered which of them this creature served so diligently that he felt no need to specify him.

"You were intended for death and yet did not die."

The entire room watched and listened to this conversation, but the Alusian's words remained opaque in their meaning. Myles assumed that these few souls here, none of them Galatian soldiers, would be able to understand what Myles knew Strelleck meant. "Yes, I am aware of this."

"You are not fully aware of this." The black eyes narrowed. "You were chosen for death—assigned to it. The

Ruthanian gods of death were offered your flesh. They laid claim to you, but another has laid claim to you as well, and that one desires your life more than the others desire your death."

"I thought you said you would not tell my fortune."

The seriousness relaxed. A faint light of humor went through the creature's eyes. "That is not your fortune. It is the past I see when I look at you."

"So your kind does possess a prophetic gift."

"I did not give you prophecy."

With a small smile, Myles waited for him to continue.

Adjusting his position in the chair, Strelleck leaned forward. "I gave you *eshtareth*—it is vision of the past. Often, one can deduce a man's future by observing the man's past. Your kind…is quite predictable."

"And *your* kind allows false rumors to be spread about them." Myles glanced across the room at the innkeeper's wife, but as Strelleck replied, he looked back to the creature.

"I can speak your fortune." Strelleck paused. "Myles Hileshand. But I choose not to do so."

Myles figured that if this creature was of a mind to take offense, he would have done so immediately. As of yet, Strelleck had not responded with any form of hostility. If not for the white of his skin and the unusual full-lunged inhalations, Myles would not have suspected him to be any different than himself. He appeared as a man.

"So you *can* see the approach of death, even when it does not align with any action the man has taken in the past?"

"I will not tell your fortune."

"Again, I am not asking you to do so. I simply desire understanding."

The Alusian watched him for a long moment. Myles

thought, perhaps, this might be the moment when hostility finally surfaced. But with a sigh, the creature said, "Highwaymen attacked a concealed courier an hour from here. One of the children in his party runs here for protection. He will live. But his pursuers will die."

"His pursuers?"

"They desire what the boy carries with him."

Strelleck looked at the door. Wondering, Myles followed his gaze.

Light steps pounded across the front porch. Something slammed into the door, and the panel swung open. A boy of about ten skittered into the room. His face was red from exertion. Eyes wide. Lungs rasping. He looked ready to fall over.

He staggered around and shoved the door shut. His hands shook so severely that he had difficulty drawing the lock. When he had done so, he spun around and swept the room with a gaze that had been blurred with tears at some point recently; his eyes were red. Streaks of mud ran across his face. He knew fear now. The sorrow and whatever else had been put aside.

One of the children runs here for protection. Myles frowned. Why chase a child? Where was the reasoning in that? Highwaymen were not brave men; they attacked in shadows and refused to approach large companies. They were cowards—why would these men pursue this boy into a crowded environment?

"Help me," the boy gasped. He fell several steps forward, trying to hold his balance as he put distance between himself and the door. "There are men—they come." Breath sobbed out of his throat. He half-stumbled, half-ran into a chair, and a man at the front table reached out and caught him before he dropped. "I'm sorry. Sorry—"

No one in the room moved. The little boy stood there in the man's arms and tried to breathe, his entire body trembling. No one spoke to him. No one stood to defend him.

The innkeeper's wife sucked in a breath and said, "What have you done, boy, bringing evil men to this place?"

She seemed to enjoy making accusations along such lines. Myles pushed his chair back and rose to his feet. With that simple gesture, he again had the attention of every person in the room.

"You," he said, pointing at the Alusian. "How many men?"

"Six," he answered calmly. It almost seemed that he had heard the question before it was asked. "You should understand that one of them is trained as an Ethollian sorcerer, who is capable of summoning the children of the dead— creatures of spirit and stone. He is beyond your strength. You will not be able to best him."

Myles was not concerned with whether or not he could best a man trained as a sorcerer—the only concern was that the Ethollian *could* be bested. With an annoyed scowl, he demanded, "When will they get here?"

"They are close enough to have seen the boy enter. In order to possess what the boy possesses, the Ethollian is prepared to destroy everyone he finds here."

Now the room responded. As the stiff quiet erupted with alarm, Myles pointed at the innkeeper's wife. "You. Get upstairs and tell Hileshand and Marcus I need them. Go. Now."

She lifted a bottle off the counter and clutched it to her chest. "If the boy has something of value, we need to give the man what he wants! Give it to him! And spare our lives without bloodshed."

A few of the others agreed with her.

Myles looked at the boy. The child stared at him, shaking his head over and over again. He had already proved his strength. Whatever he possessed, it was of enough value to his heart that he would run for an hour over a dangerous road to keep it safe. He deserved to keep it, without strangers deciding the future for him.

"Weren't you listening?" Myles bellowed at the innkeeper's wife. The child jerked. "Six men, and *they* are going to die, not this boy. He will keep what he has. *Now do as I say.* Go."

This time, she obeyed. The bottle slipped from her hands, and she jumped over the shattered pieces as she ran for the steps.

Myles pointed at the man who had a grip on the boy's arms. He was securely in his middle years, a few seasons older than Hileshand. There were children at his table. "You. Get all these people out of here. There is a spare room off the kitchen, near the back door. Do *not* take them into the woods unless it is absolutely necessary. Go now. And be silent in your waiting."

Chairs tipped over. Bumped tables grated across the floor as the room cleared.

Myles looked at Strelleck. The Alusian had not removed himself with the others. He remained at his table, watching him, his expression continuously calm.

"Have you ever seen a sorcerer trained in the Ethollian arts?" the creature asked. "Those beyond the level of apprentice can kill with only a few words. They can speak and have a man's skin stripped from his bones. This man surpassed the level of apprentice decades ago. He can do much worse."

Myles did not have his sword. Anticipating a quiet evening, he had left it in his room. The only weapon he possessed on his person was a Galatian knife with a curved blade, hanging in a sheath on his belt. Scanning the room for additional materials, he asked, "Are you going to sit there and observe?"

The creature's brows rose. "This man is fond of killing with enchanted objects. He first enchants them, then he speaks to them, giving direction, and they obey him. You should know that that is how he killed the boy's uncle."

Myles straightened the fallen chairs and brought the room to order. "Why would I need to know that?"

"The uncle was a scout in the Terikbah military. He was the courier—still a young man, only recently retired. Decorated many times by his commanding officers. He was a warrior of some skill, yet he could not stand against the Ethollian."

Just how much had this creature seen of his past? Myles sensed strongly that with these statements, he spoke of Hileshand, also a retired soldier. Could Strelleck see more than the past and the present? Could he actually see Myles' intentions as well?

He heard footsteps upstairs and the high-pitched, fluctuating voice of the innkeeper's wife floating down through the floorboards. With a sigh, he gave the Alusian his full attention. "Answer the question. Do you intend to sit there and amuse yourself, or do you intend to give me aid?"

"I do not meddle in the affairs of men. I will give you no aid."

So be it. Myles had not expected a different response.

The creature studied him with unhindered interest. "That which keeps you," Strelleck said at last, "will one day demand a reckoning. Do you understand this? I do not believe you do."

Myles studied him in return. "A reckoning?"

"Yes. He will take your life as surely as he has preserved it. That is his way."

The locked door opened.

chapter 19

The man who entered was old, much older than anything Myles had anticipated. His back was bent, his shoulders bowed. A jagged gray beard hung down his chest, looking as if it had been trimmed by awkward chops of a dull sword blade. His clothes had been purchased many years before and lay across his bones the way banners hang empty when there is no wind. This was a great sorcerer? He had not *run* here after the boy; that much was immediately certain. Myles doubted he could even walk that distance.

"Hail, traveler," Myles said, keeping his hands at his sides, away from the knife at his belt.

The noises upstairs had ceased. There was no audible sign of Hileshand or Marcus. Myles glanced over his shoulder at the bottom of the staircase and saw it empty. They came—but where and when? Depending on what the innkeeper's wife had told him, Hileshand might not be expecting to find a sorcerer here.

"Hail," the man finally answered and came fully into

the room. He lifted a trembling hand and set it on the door, pushing it shut behind him. "Cold night, eh?"

It was warm, the strength of late summer contained in every breeze.

"I enjoy the cold," Myles answered. "Do you come far? Are you traveling on to Bledeshure in the morning?"

Rough laughter trickled through the front windows. The sorcerer had brought his men all the way up the steps.

The old man paused, looking at him with eyes as lined as tree bark. "Aye."

Myles smiled. "Well, watch out for pickpockets. They are vicious this time of year, with all the travelers in town after the King's Feast."

The man smiled at him in return. It was a slow smile, the unhurried response of a talented man who understands much more than he should. He turned his gaze to the Alusian, and Myles watched as additional awareness flickered through his expression. It would seem he was of the same mind as the innkeeper's wife—that the Alusian's presence meant someone's death.

His gnarled gaze swung back to Myles. "It will be you," he said.

"No," Myles answered slowly. "No, I don't believe that is truth."

Clicking his tongue, the old man rasped, "Give me the courier's satchel, and I will not kill you."

He said it with the same knowing smile, the same abnormal light in his eyes, and Myles knew that the promise was not built on anything resembling truth. "I will not do that."

He felt the man's gaze move over him. It spent several moments on his shoulders and arms and drifted downward to the knife at his belt. Myles again became aware that the blade was the only weapon he had readily available. It was less than the length of his forearm.

The old man shook his head. "You are promising for a fool, but a fool you remain. You will regret these words."

Myles had not doubted Ethan Strelleck's judgment concerning this man, but for the first time, he felt a faint brush of genuine doubt concerning this plan, if it could be called that. *Where are you, Hileshand?*

He shrugged. "My answer remains the same. Go your way—now, without causing unnecessary difficulty—and perhaps your road will change for you." He frowned at him. "Perhaps."

The man raised a thin hand.

Every light in the room darkened, as if the room had suddenly filled with black smoke. Myles felt nothing on his skin. He smelled nothing. But his heart began to race, and he had the distinct impression that something invisible was screaming. He could almost hear it. It was as if his ears were aware of it, but his mind could not register the sound.

Perceiving Strelleck at the table became a difficult task. Myles thought he saw the Alusian's head turn toward the back staircase.

Hileshand stepped into the room. Myles heard the precise clip of his boots on the wooden floor. Steady steps.

Hileshand's sword was not drawn. He took two steps past Myles and stopped, looking down at the old man across the way. For a moment, he said nothing. He simply stood there. The silent scream in the air slowly faded. Myles felt his head clear.

He did not fully know what Hileshand possessed, but if anyone in their party could find space and skill enough to stand against an Ethollian, it would be Hileshand—perhaps by sheer luck alone. He killed goe'lah without fear. He could coat his sword with Abalel's light.

Myles watched the emotions rage across the old man's face. He saw surprise, anger, and then blue-lipped fury.

"Leave," Hileshand said. "Or it *will* be you."

The old man glared at him. He could have melted steel with such a gaze. "You have little training. You have little power." He spat the words, froth on his lips. "What can *you* possibly hope to do?"

"Myles," Hileshand said without removing his gaze from the Ethollian. "Back door. Go help your brother."

Myles looked back and forth between them. "You are certain of this?"

"Yes. Go now."

"Yes," the old man crowed. "Run away, boy! Give me the pleasure of hunting you."

Myles frowned at him and walked away.

Ethan Strelleck stayed where he was.

chapter 20

*M*yles found a body on the back porch. The man was bleeding, lying face down in a dark pool that reflected the globe of the moon, but he was not yet dead. *Marcus' doing.* A corner of Myles' mouth tucked in. His brother killed the perusan quickly enough, despite their appearance as men, but he avoided the death of actual men as much as Hileshand did.

Six men, the Alusian had said. All six would die. His brother had not heard this prediction.

With a last glance at the door of the inn behind him, Myles pulled his fingers from the pulsing vein of the man on the porch and stood to his feet. He eased the curved Galatian blade from his belt and crept around the building.

He found Marcus standing in the shadows on the other side, waiting for him near the front porch.

"Do you attract unrest for the sake of unrest, or does it simply follow you like a perusan?" Marcus whispered with a grin. He passed him his bow and quiver. "Two on the porch.

Two on the road—and those two are talkers. When the wind slows, you can hear them cleanly across the green. One has a bow. The other claims to be a *messurah*." A man trained in the Galatian art of hand-to-hand combat. The messurah did not carry traditional weapons because they did not need them. Dangerous men, if they were allowed too close.

Simple highwaymen who were magicians and trained messurah? Myles was beginning to doubt Strelleck's words to him. These could not be highwaymen.

The inn sat at an angle from the main thoroughfare, with a garden and bushes between where they stood now and the front porch. A stone's throw beyond the porch lay the road. Myles doubled back several paces then stepped out of the covering of the building and into the solid shadows of the trees.

As he made his way forward, back bent, bow in hand, he could hear the frogs down by the river. Something hooted above his head, and briefly, the winged creature followed him, flitting from branch to branch.

Men spoke quietly by the road. One was Galatian; that had to be the messurah. The other spoke Terikbah with a Ruthanian accent.

Myles set an arrow to the string and approached silently in the dark, listening as the wind carried their conversation to him. They were quite liberal with their words—foolishly liberal, for men on a quest. They were winded from their pursuit, yet not winded enough to refrain from boasts of how many men they had killed this night and how the gods of death would be pleased at their sacrifice. Foolish talk. Myles realized they were passing a wine skin back and forth. *Foolish and inebriated.*

Once in position, his targets clearly in view, he hesitated, thinking of Hileshand and his desire to leave the lives of others untouched. Myles could understand that desire. He did not enjoy the thought of causing another's death.

But these men had come to kill something that did not belong to them. They attacked what Myles desired to protect; they intended harm to his flock.

He killed them as he had killed wolves and other predators, and he did not regret his actions.

Marcus put both hands to the railing and swung up onto the front porch. The landing thump of his boot heels was masked by a sudden commotion behind the inn. *What is that?* He paused in the shadows, listening. He heard groans and pops that somehow seemed familiar, though he could not quite place them. It sounded like wood splintering.

In the moonlit darkness, he saw the two men before him straighten. The noises behind the inn continued for a short time and then the night dropped into quiet. The birds calmed in the woods. Even the river frogs grew silent now.

"What was that?" asked the man on the right.

Marcus decided to join their conversation. "'Tis uncertain," he answered.

Both men spun toward him. Marcus raised his hands. "Now, look. We can avoid trouble. Let us consider this—"

The first man ignored his attempts at diplomacy and came at him with a dower knife, a short sword with a triple-edged blade known for its ability to cut through bone. Marcus sidestepped his awkward thrust, redirected his forward momentum, and dropped him headfirst into the railing. The porch shuddered. The highwayman crumpled to the floor.

The other man was a much more experienced swordsman. Marcus tested his skill and quickly discovered his opponent had military training. His movements bore the strong, unvarying precision taught by Ruthanian drill instructors. Though somewhat predictable, he was one of the best swordsmen Marcus had come against in the last several years.

The fight did not last long. The man gasped in surprise as Marcus took out his sword arm, driving his blade deep into his shoulder. The sword clattered out of the man's hand. He hissed and simply stood there a moment, cradling his useless arm. Then he sank to his knees and waited with cold pride, expecting the final stroke Marcus never liked to take.

"Not this time," Marcus said and cracked the hilt of his sword against the man's temple.

In the sudden quiet, he observed his handiwork lying unconscious before him and listened to the night that no longer spoke. Every sound but that of the wind in the trees had fallen away. The conversation at the road had dropped as well. The archer and the messurah had not come to the aid of their comrades, which clearly was Myles' doing.

Remembering the odd noises that had drifted from the back of the inn, Marcus, sword in hand, headed off the porch. As he stepped off the stairs, something brushed across his face and throat. *Spider webs? Across the entrance to an inn?* That did not seem right.

Pulling his hand down his face, Marcus slipped into the moving shadows of the trees and jogged around the building.

He came upon the same scene he had left earlier: the highwayman lying on the wooden slabs in the moonlight. He had lost much blood, more than Marcus had anticipated.

A scowl pulled across his features. He saw now that he

had likely killed him, which had not been his intent.

Wait.

Something was different. A moment passed before his mind registered the changes in the dark, in the midst of all the blood.

The steps were broken, splintered into halves, as if a giant weight had been dropped upon them.

His stomach leapt into the back of his throat. Half the man was missing. His torso lay there, along with his arms and head—everything above the base of his rib cage. But nothing remained below his rib cage except a dark spreading pool that reflected the moonlight.

Marcus staggered back. When his thoughts returned to him, he took a shallow breath and looked madly for the creature that had done this. He saw nothing in the moonlight. He had heard nothing other than the sound of the steps shattering beneath the creature's weight. *Where?* The wind pushed through the branches all around him, stirring shadows across the grass. Everything moved. Nothing stayed in place.

He sensed movement in the upper field of his vision, in a place where there should not have been movement, and slowly looked up toward the roof.

The creature sat to his left, on top of the porch, leaning away from the building almost as a man would, its legs bent beneath it, one taloned hand gripping the edge of the second-level roof. It easily filled the space between the first and second floors. In a way, it reminded Marcus of the dragon they'd seen in Blue Mountain, but this entity was bigger. Much bigger. The scales were as black as tar, darker than the shadows, despite the broad light of the moon. The head was flat and triangular, like that of a giant snake. A dull yellow gaze swept the darkness. The eyes glowed like lanterns. The sight of them sent a deep chill down Marcus' spine. He pulled farther into the woods.

He had heard that high-level Ethollian sorcerers were able to call forth *atham-laine,* the children of the gods of death. Creatures of the spirit world were not subject to the rules and laws of the natural world; therefore, the weapons of man could not kill them. Yet beasts such as this had little difficulty inflicting death on members of the natural world.

And, as it seemed tonight, they had particular tastes. Blood glistened on the creature's massive jaws. It had been feeding.

This, Marcus thought, *will not be easy.*

He realized suddenly those had not been spider webs.

chapter 21

The meusone were the children of Etnyse, a goddess of death that required some very particular, very invasive rituals of worship from those who had lost loved ones to disease. In certain ways, the meusone were similar to the perusan: Both shed light in darkness; both could be difficult to kill. But they varied in their choice of habitat—the meusone did not live hidden in the woods until they chose to attack. They had to be summoned. Their presence here tonight was the Ethollian's doing as well.

This was an extremely sophisticated level of effort for a group of highwaymen.

Marcus stepped behind the gnarled trunk of an oak and waited for the glowing creature to pass. His plan was not fully formed yet—he actually did not know if a plan, a *good* plan, could come together under these circumstances. Once the Ethollian was removed, that would change, for Hileshand would join them, but even then, Marcus knew from past experience that removing the sorcerer did not necessarily mean the automatic removal of his fanged companions. Sometimes that was true, yes. But it was not true all the time.

If they let them go tonight, these creatures would become the elements of legend up in the distant mountains, preying upon travelers and killing dragons and lions. It would be much more responsible to kill them here. His father would know what to do.

But Marcus had no idea how long this matter with the Ethollian would take. The windows of the inn appeared dark, as if curtains had been drawn across them. He could not remember seeing any curtains.

The meusone neared the garden, its movements fluid and graceful.

Keep walking, Marcus silently instructed. In this moment, that would be the easiest route for them all. *Do not stay here.*

For a moment, it seemed that his desire would be granted.

Then the shadows around him filled with a low-pitched hiss, loud enough that he could hear it above the wind but not loud enough for him to be able to place its exact location. It was highly disconcerting to be hissed at in the dark and not know what was doing the hissing.

Something struck his boot, just above the ankle. Tension high, his heart took a dramatic leap in his chest, and he slammed his sword down in the darkness, unable to see what had attacked him. He felt something break along the edge of his blade, and whatever it was writhed in the brush. He could hear it flopping about.

For a moment, Marcus held his position on the ground, knees bent in a crouch. He looked up at the meusone quickly, then at the strange black beast perched atop the porch roof. Neither of them looked his direction.

He let his breath out slowly. His heart ran behind his ribs like a man possessed. A snake that hunted at night? Weren't most of them day-dwellers? Its lunge had not broken his skin. He had felt pressure on his boot and that was all.

Something clamped onto his arm. Pain ricocheted through his body, a surprisingly large amount of pain. It jolted all the way up through his skull, instantly blurring his vision.

Jerking his arm to the side, he slammed the sword down a second time. Another writhing body flopped in the brush, but the jaws did not release his flesh. He had to sheathe his sword and pry the head off with his fingers, cutting himself on half a dozen exposed points that felt remarkably like teeth. A snake with multiple pairs of teeth? He threw the head as far away from him as he could.

His vision stumbled about, the pain in his skull affecting him like a screaming woman. It was immediately and thoroughly difficult for him to pay attention to anything else. Something seemed odd about this. Could snake venom have an instantaneous effect on his head? That did not seem likely.

The meusone started shrieking. It had seen him.

Abalel, Marcus thought, *this doesn't seem fair.*

Where had he put his sword? He had put his sword down—hadn't he? *Wait.* No, he had sheathed it. He had *sheathed* it, and he didn't remember.

He scrambled for the hilt in the dark, found it, and managed to pull the blade free.

But something was wrong with this as well. The sword felt heavy in his hand. He had trouble keeping it aloft. *No, no,* he thought, blowing out his breath and bracing himself for the screaming meusone. *This is not good.*

But as he watched, the meusone staggered. Finding its footing again, it spun around and ran the other way—away from Marcus. He had no idea why it would do that. He had never heard of a meusone running *away* from someone. They were not that friendly.

He could no longer focus his gaze. What was wrong with him? That had not been a snake. It could not have been a snake.

The massive shadow on the roof swung down and landed with enough force to shake the ground beneath Marcus' feet. *Not good,* he thought again.

The beast snarled at him.

Marcus backed away slowly. Perhaps it would not follow him into the woods. Certain *atham-laine* preferred open ground to enclosed areas. Though born in shadow, they were not always willing to follow their prey into shadow.

But, of course, this was not one of those times.

The creature threw back its head and screamed. The harsh metallic cry pushed a wave of nausea through Marcus' stomach. He sensed—suddenly—how ill he was. He was *very* ill.

The earth trembled as the beast charged him. Marcus turned and sprinted for his life.

Somewhere in the midst of his wild run, Marcus dropped his sword. He did not realize this until it occurred to him that the blade no longer felt heavy. He discovered his hand was empty, and with that realization came another, one that sickened him: This was likely the end of his story. Bitten by something that was not a snake. Chased through the woods by an *atham-laine.* Eventually his father would find bits and pieces of his body and mourn him.

Marcus stumbled as he ran. He did not want Hileshand to mourn him.

Trees broke and splintered behind him. The *atham-laine* roared. Every time it did that, he felt as if his pace slowed, invisible hands pulling at him. The pain in his head and arm was spreading through the rest of his body. His hands felt like they were on fire. His legs trembled.

Hot, foul breath chugged across him. His eyes began to burn. His nose and throat felt like he was trying to pour liquid coals through his face.

The beast lunged at him and raked claws across his back. He lost his footing and fell forward. The earth took an extraordinarily long amount of time to greet him. He landed hard, the air thundering out of his body.

The *atham-laine* screamed above him.

chapter **22**

As Myles turned back from the road, he saw something he had not expected to see. He paused in the shadows, putting a hand to a tree and leaning forward, and watched as a meusone walked elegantly across the green in front of the inn about fifty paces away from him.

The creature was as thin as a young sapling. Its head was level with the bottom of the second-floor windows, but the horns that grew above its ears rose several inches beyond the sills—protruding into the darkness like white spikes on the top of flagstaffs. A haze of pale silver surrounded its entire body, the smooth, scaly flesh glowing in the moonlight.

The Ruthanians worshipped these as lesser gods. They were believed to bring good fortune. The trick was to outrun them. That was all. *A small thing, is it not? Outrun the meusone, and it will make you a king.*

Myles had seen a statue of a meusone outside a temple in Bledeshure. The sculptor had not captured what was here to be captured. This was not a creature that could be blown over by the wind. It would be simple to outrun something built like a blade of grass, as the artist's work had suggested— it was a different matter altogether to outrun something that had been built to run. This creature was thin but muscled, like a city courier who had been devoted to his occupation for several years.

According to legend, a challenge against the meusone resulted in life or death, good fortune or very bad fortune. If men ran too slowly, the meusone seized them and beat them against trees or stones. Those who would be king and missed the mark paid for it with their lives. It was an expensive wager.

Myles knew no stories of killing the meusone. He didn't know if they *could* be killed, but he had no intention of running this evening.

The meusone stopped. It jerked its head around and stared down into the woods behind the inn. *Marcus*, Myles realized. Had his brother even seen it? If he hadn't yet, he certainly would in a moment.

The creature tilted its horned head back and let loose a high-pitched wail. The timbre thrust through Myles' skull like a spear. He could not think clearly until the creature paused to draw breath.

Retrieving an arrow from the quiver at his back, Myles nocked it. The creature shrieked again and began to lift its feet, running through the garden, crushing plants and knocking over posts. It had accepted a challenge that, no doubt, Marcus had not intended to give. Myles released the arrow and drew another as the first shaft punctured the back of the creature's head and brought its angry charge to a halt.

The meusone's subsequent scream drew physical pain and dropped a shield of spinning colors before Myles' eyes.

None of the stories had ever mentioned the way these things could scream. As his vision righted itself, he saw that the meusone had adjusted course. It now came down the drive toward him in a wild sprint.

He stepped out from beneath the trees to meet it.

Every shot found its mark cleanly and securely, but none of them brought the creature down. It was like sending arrows into a tree. They penetrated and remained, sticking out like pins in a cushion, but the tree did not notice. The holes in the skin didn't even bleed. *This could end very poorly*, Myles thought. As the creature neared, he slung the bow around his shoulder and pulled the Galatian blade from his belt.

The creature shrieked at him. He again saw spiraling lights, and the sound jarred him to his bones. He misjudged the closing distance and realized his error a moment before the meusone reached him.

Breathing a curse, Myles threw himself sideways toward the woods, but the creature reached out a tentacle-like arm and managed to close its hand around his throat. The ground disappeared beneath his feet in a terrific jolt. He felt an explosion in his neck and another down his spine and figured himself for lost, all because of that mind-numbing scream that had caused him to misjudge the distance.

The meusone screamed again, shaking him violently. It thrust him up into the air, aloft over its horns, then slammed him down to the earth. He could not breathe around the weight on his throat. His head rang with the creature's screams. He did not feel any pain and, because of that, knew he was about to die.

Gripping him firmly around the neck, the meusone bashed him against the ground, smashing him into the compacted soil like a maid beating a rug. Eventually, it threw him down and walked around him, leaning over to take hold of his right leg. Grunting and muttering, it began to drag him toward the woods.

At some point during the short journey across the grass, the haze parted, and Myles became aware that he could feel the meusone's cold grip on his ankle. He could also feel the ground moving across his back as the creature dragged him. He should have felt pain. The meusone was in a process of breaking him right now, and the absence of pain was a definite sign it had achieved a level of success. He *knew* his neck was broken. He had felt it break beneath the force of the meusone's hand.

But when he made the attempt, he was able to lift his head off the ground. He was able to move his arms and hands. Was it possible he had a second chance at this?

He no longer had his bow. The quiver seemed to have been crushed; he could feel something about that size mangled and broken beneath his shoulders. Shaking off the daze that threatened his vision, Myles looked for his knife and discovered he still gripped it solidly in his hand. He took a deep breath, blew it out, and flipped the weapon around, gripping the flat edges of the curved blade between his fingers.

The meusone's head floated more than fifteen feet above him. The creature jerked around and snarled at him. Arrows protruded out of its shoulders and neck, but none of the shafts drew blood—except the original one, sticking out of the back of its skull.

That was Myles' target.

Only one opportunity afforded itself to him. As the creature turned back toward the trees, Myles hurled the knife at its skull, and the blade thudded through bone and flesh. The meusone dropped him and staggered forward, slamming into a tree where it started screaming incessantly, in a weeping sort of way. Myles clambered to his feet. The world spun and danced around him, and he had to bend over, hands to his knees, fighting an intense urge to vomit.

The meusone recovered itself before he did. It pushed off the tree and rotated toward him, hissing, the knife embedded in the back of its head.

Myles prepared for impact. He would reclaim his knife and use it to dislocate the creature's head from the top of its neck. Or he would make the attempt, if such a procedure were possible.

But the impact never came. The silvery, glowing head with its white horns dissolved before his eyes. It crumbled away like crushed stone in a strong wind. The tall body wavered in the air and then thudded backward to the ground, where the flesh did not remain. The earth seemed to take hold of it, inhaling the body through the soil. Myles pulled back and watched as the entire form disappeared. Nothing remained behind.

What was this?

He felt a presence behind him and turned.

Ethan Strelleck stood only a few paces away. He lowered a long, wooden shaft from his lips. It appeared to be some sort of blowing instrument. His sword remained sheathed. What sort of weapon did the Alusian possess that allowed him to dissolve the head of a creature revered as a god?

Myles realized he'd lost his knife; it had dissolved with the head, and he scowled. He had wanted to keep that. "I thought you didn't meddle in the affairs of men," he grunted.

Strelleck took him in slowly. The creature's head tilted as he focused on Myles' throat in the moonlight. Myles felt something on the back of his neck and reached up to touch odd, circular ridges in his skin. When he lowered his hand, his fingers were bloody.

"I do not meddle," Strelleck stated darkly.

"This looks much like meddling." But then Myles gave him a brief smile. "I thank you for it."

"I do not meddle," Strelleck repeated. "But the one who marked you…he meddles all the time, and I heard his voice."

Strelleck reached into an interior pocket of his cloak and withdrew a second wooden shaft, this one small, about the size of his hand. He twisted the top of it, as if unscrewing a plug from a vial, and Myles shook his head once as the shaft began to lengthen, growing from either end. When it was about four feet long, Strelleck rotated the head again, and the shaft thickened into the haft of an ax. The end of the shaft expanded into a double-headed blade that was in-scribed with words and images. The markings continued off the steel and twisted down the wood. A beautiful weapon, elegant and solid. It did not seem to put forth light of its own, yet Myles realized he could see all of it without issue, despite the shadows.

Strelleck handed it to him. "I have been instructed to give this to you." He glanced over his shoulder at the inn. "Avoid the ante-porch for as long as you can. The ehls do not appreciate disturbances."

chapter **23**

Myles discovered the bleeding torso on the back steps. With a grimace, he eased away from the porch and into the shadows of the trees.

The boy's pursuers would die. All six of them. It did not matter if his brother attempted to spare their lives; it would seem the Alusian had spoken true words. What existed in the darkness tonight that would take the legs off a man but leave the rest of him?

His question was answered a few minutes later.

He began to hear movement in the trees. Snapping brush. Growling. The *atham-laine* wandered into the moonlight. It was as tall as the meusone but much thicker. This was not the body of a runner; this creature was muscled and sturdy, the scaled arms and shoulders like that of a wrestler. The eyes glowed yellow. The jaws were slick with blood.

Overall, it was very impressive.

"Anytime you're ready, Marcus," Myles whispered.

His brother did not appear.

The ax shuddered in his hand. Myles lifted it away from his body and stared at it as the double-headed blade began to pulse rhythmically. It had not been a trick of his eyes earlier; the blade actually did put forth light of its own. Every time it faded, it faded a little less, so the light steadily grew more pronounced. It began to resemble Hileshand's sword the night they had fought the goe'lah.

The huge head swung around. The creature saw Myles standing there in the shadows and roared. The sound struck him like floodwaters. He nearly lost his footing.

The *atham-laine* took a few prancing steps and then ran at him on all fours, covering the short distance between them in three bounds. As the creature leapt at him, Myles swung the ax with both hands in an upward motion. He felt heat surge through the wood and up his arms. The haft tore from his grip as the beast slammed into him, rolling with him through the woods.

He landed on his back. Something heavy bore down on his chest, impeding his breathing. He applied force to it and it moved, thudding into the soil next to him. An arm.

Silver light reflected off the tree branches above his head. It was a bright glow, like that of a lantern. *What is that?* The woods filled with groans and growls. Myles pushed himself to his feet.

The *atham-laine* lay on its back, a slew of noises emitting from its throat. Myles imagined it was cursing. It saw him standing there, within reach of its clawed hand, but made no move to seize him.

The ax head glowed with fierce light. Myles shielded his eyes and, at the same time, tried to look more closely.

The ax stuck out from the wide chest at an angle. Myles had barely nicked the skin; less than an inch of the blade had sunk into the scaly hide, yet the ax somehow remained in place, as if affixed there with some sort of adhesive. His blow had been a poor, hurried attempt at best—it should not have been able to immobilize the creature.

What sort of magic was this?

The beast groaned as if the life soaked out of its spine into the soil. It did not move even as he put a boot to its chest. Bracing himself with his foot against it, Myles jerked the weapon out of the skin. The creature whimpered as if he had stabbed it through the heart. It did not try to rise.

Myles hacked off the head.

Instantly, the decapitated body shriveled, dissolving into the grass as the meusone had done. He smelled burning tar. His eyes watered. The flesh disappeared, and all the grass died in the surrounding area.

But the head remained. It lay there on the ground, the malevolent eyes no longer yellow with life.

Good, Myles thought. *I could use that.*

Avoid the ante-porch, Strelleck had said, so Myles did. He made use of the rear porch instead. For several minutes, he stood outside the door and waited, the panel closed. He could hear Hileshand's voice on the other side, but it was not loud enough for him to discern the words. The tone seemed steady and unafraid, as if he carried on a conversation and nothing more.

Myles waited until he smelled the sweet odor of Hileshand's pipe wafting out onto the porch, then he pushed open the door. He carried the *atham-laine's* black head into the main dining room and tossed it on the floor. It was as large as the body of a bull, and it landed just as solidly.

He was drenched with the creature's dark blood. The ax

pulsed in his grip, the light flaring, then fading, flaring again. He ran the back of his hand across his mouth and tasted unfamiliar blood on his teeth. He did not see the Ethollian, to his surprise. He had intended to startle the old man with the *atham-laine*'s head. *So much for that plan.*

"You done in here?" he asked Hileshand. "Or should I come back?"

Hileshand stared at him, then lowered his gaze to the massive head lying on the floor.

Much of the room looked as if it had survived a fire. Portions of the walls and ceiling were scorched and blackened. Chairs were in pieces. Tables lay tipped and shattered. Myles felt as if the air should smell of smoke, but all he could smell were Hileshand's pipe and the permeating stench of the *atham-laine*'s blood all over his body. It smelled like mildew and rotting flesh.

Myles finally located the sorcerer. The old man was curled up in the corner behind the bar, his arms over his head, his entire body trembling. He did not appear to be injured, which annoyed Myles without limit. He glared at Hileshand.

"His life is not mine to take," Hileshand answered simply. Then he added a statement that did not make any sense to Myles: "I have not touched him."

He had not touched him?

The sorcerer groaned and rolled out across the floor. The breath left his body, and Myles watched the color drain from the flesh, leaving it sallow. The man died as an old man would—without strength, though tonight's events loudly testified to the strength he, at one time, had possessed.

Myles looked at Hileshand with a hundred questions on his tongue. He knew Hileshand was a warrior. He knew dozens and dozens of stories that could prove that fact without effort. But what enabled Myles Hileshand to kill a man without touching him? He had not even unsheathed his sword. His arms were folded, boots spread; it was not a position of stealth or even of strength. He simply stood there, much as Myles had left him a few hours ago.

Hileshand told him, "The universe is not balanced."

That was all he said, and Myles frowned. "What does that mean?"

"I will explain it to you in detail." But he clearly did not intend to do so tonight. He glanced at the door through which Myles had just stepped. "Where's your brother?"

Myles stared at the Ethollian's body for a long moment. The balance of the universe? Killing a man without touching him? Hileshand was not a man; he was a riddle. An enigmatic riddle.

"He comes," he answered.

Hileshand made Myles cart the *atham-laine*'s head back outside, grunting something about it disagreeing with women and children. Afterward, they cleaned up the ehls that had taken residence on the front porch—they were ugly, multi-legged creatures that spun webs like spiders. They had removed the heads of the highwaymen Marcus had left there and blanketed the inn's entrance with enough web to appear as thick as gauze. They did not appreciate fire or water. Hileshand used both.

In the meanwhile, Marcus did not appear out of the woods.

"What happened?" Hileshand asked.

Myles told him of meeting Marcus by the garden; he mentioned the meusone and Hileshand looked at him sharply.

"Meusone?"

The concern in his voice was unmistakable. Myles studied him and wondered if the same concern would appear if the roles were reversed and *Myles* was the one who had yet to return. "I saw but one of them, and it is dead at the hand of Ethan Strelleck."

"The Alusian killed it?" Hileshand's brows rose.

"Aye."

"Peculiar." Hileshand frowned toward the trees. After a moment, he instructed, "Go find the innkeeper's wife, and tell her we need a lantern." He paused. A pained expression crossed his features, and he added, "You may need to look for her under a bed."

Derek, the little boy who had run from the highwaymen, started weeping when he saw Myles. Apparently, he had remained fairly composed during the long wait, but the bricks slid out of place now, and his gallant wall of strength crumbled.

Myles did not readily show softness. His brother did—but Myles could be like a fort surrounded by armed men in an enemy land. Tonight, however, he reached out a hand to the boy, and Derek ran to him as if he were a member of his family. He wept and wept, and Myles patted his back and told him not to worry; only bad men had died here tonight.

Hileshand greatly desired that to be the truth.

The innkeeper's wife squealed when she saw the state of the dining room. She stopped squealing when Hileshand told her she and her husband would be compensated for all damages. Repairs could start in the morning. Everything would be taken care of.

One of the men—his name was Useffe—volunteered to

accompany them into the woods to search for Marcus. He was a few years older than the twins, and he wore a worn baldric that suggested he had seen a few rough encounters of his own.

"You have my respect," he said quietly, looking at Myles. "With it, you deserve my favor. I will go with you."

Hearing these words, Hileshand wondered at his courage and why the man had not volunteered his services earlier. Then he looked again at the woman with him. She clutched Useffe's arm and ignored everyone else in the room. A very beautiful girl, very young. Her face was as pale as sand, her fingers leaving marks on Useffe's arm.

Hileshand thought of the young girl asleep in Marcus' bed. His eyes were drawn upward and he let his breath out slowly. He could understand why Useffe had restrained himself. He could also understand why Useffe chose not to do so a second time.

Myles was covered with the *atham-laine's* black blood. He looked very impressive in this moment, mopping his face with a towel, the bloodstained ax leaning against the broken table beside him. As he cleared away the dark mess that covered his throat, those watching pulled back, then moved forward again, staring at him in shock.

His movements slowed. "What is it?" he asked, drawing the towel away.

Hileshand smiled, feeling a rush of pride. That was the only response he could have at this point, in his understanding of this man. "You mentioned a meusone tonight."

"Aye."

"You said the Alusian killed it."

"Aye."

"What happened to your throat, Myles?"

"Why?" he asked, putting a dirty hand to it and feeling around.

Useffe stepped closer to him. After a brief examination, he said, his tone purposefully casual and slow, "You fought a meusone? It put hands to you here?" He pointed at Myles' neck.

Myles glanced around the room at all the faces. "Yes..."

Aerman the physician slept somewhere in this building. That was good; it was possible they would need him. Hileshand took Myles by the shoulders and turned him toward the light, studying the back of his neck. "Give me the towel."

Myles obeyed in silence and stood there as Hileshand scrubbed his skin clear of black blood.

The back of Myles' neck had been punctured in several places. They were wide punctures; the meusone appeared to have had such a grip on him that it had driven its claws into his bones. But the wound had healed. If Hileshand didn't know better, he would have assumed that Myles had sustained this injury several years ago.

But he had never seen this scaring on him before. Myles had not had it last week, before Hileshand had gone alone into Bledeshure.

Morbid fascination flooded Hileshand's abdomen. "This hurt?" he asked and jabbed a finger into one of the sealed holes.

Useffe and some of the others grimaced.

Myles didn't flinch. "No," he answered.

"Myles, the meusone fight in a particular way." Hileshand paused. He glanced back at Useffe and then asked Myles bluntly, "How are you on your feet right now? This should have killed you."

"I thought it did. It grabbed me, and I thought the blow broke my neck—I thought I felt something. But it must have missed."

He thought he had *felt* something. "No, I don't think it missed." Hileshand described the marks he saw—what appeared to be old wounds.

All throughout the telling, little Derek stared up at Myles with silent but tangible awe. Hileshand could feel it radiating out of the boy's eyes like heat off a stove.

Giving in to his grin, Useffe grunted and allowed, "Wish I could have seen that fight."

chapter 24

A stone's throw from the inn, Hileshand found the decapitated bodies of the esep lizards. They were small creatures covered with red and yellow patterns along the spine. Tonight, the forked tails were twisted, arms and legs splayed, green blood splattered on the ground. One head he found. The other he did not.

The esep did not kill men if proper treatment were received promptly. Most of those traveling through this section of Tarek, where the creatures were common, carried the dried leaves of moulta plants as a precaution; the leaves could cleanse the blood of a variety of ailments, particularly the venom of the esep lizard. Relief came in a few hours— but only if the bite was treated in time.

Marcus' footprints were erratic in the soil. He had stumbled. Something had surprised him. He had run.

His route through the trees was not difficult to track. The *atham-laine* had carved out a wide path behind him, the brush flattened, trees felled. When Hileshand discovered

Marcus' sword lying in the dirt, crushed from the *atham-laine's* weight, he knew what had happened to his son and why he had not found the second lizard's head. Marcus, like Myles, did not put his back to his enemy. He did not run from him.

Half an hour later, the trail brought them to a bluff over-looking the Tarek River. Hileshand put a hand to a bent tree and leaned out over the open space, lantern aloft. He could not see the bottom, but he could hear the river tumbling through it. It was difficult to judge the distance. The moon-light fell down the rocky wall only part of the way.

The trail stopped at the edge of the ravine. Hileshand discovered fresh blood mixed into the churned soil—a small amount, not enough to signify a death. The *atham-laine* had not killed his son here. But his heart squeezed in his chest as he considered the yawning abyss before him. This drop would be dangerous enough during the day, with a clear head.

Seeing what had occurred, Myles grunted deep in his throat, frowning fiercely in the lantern light, and Hileshand had to sit down. He set the lantern beside him on the stone and covered his face with both hands.

Abalel. Not this…

The night filled with sounds of the river, croaking frogs, the distant call of an owl. Was this it, then? This could not be correct. It did not seem right or possible to him.

Where's your brother? he had asked Myles.

He comes, the man had replied. His answer had contained no hesitation. He had not questioned his confidence.

Where's your brother?

He comes.

"My God," Hileshand muttered.

THE HOUSE OF ELAH

They would find a way down to the water and scour the banks for him. They would search the currents. They would go back into Bledeshure downstream and search every step of the docks, ask every sailor. They would find him, no matter the condition of his body, whether or not he yet lived, no matter how long it took.

Useffe grabbed the lantern off the stone. Stepping close to the ravine, he wrapped his hand around the bent tree and leaned as Hileshand had leaned, staring down into the darkness.

After a few moments, with the same purposeful calm he had employed before, he said, "I say, Hileshand—there's someone down there. He waves a torch."

The sun sent broad, golden beams of light across the mountains. The day was fully upon them by the time Myles, Hileshand, and Useffe walked into the Alusian's camp. Hidden from the woods and much of the river by a network of rocks and cave-like formations, the bottom of the ravine had proven difficult to reach. They had been forced to retreat to the dock and climb half a mile across jagged slippery stones.

Ethan Strelleck had been expecting them.

"You meddle," Myles informed him. "You can no longer have an argument against this."

The creature responded as he had before. He scowled and seemed somewhat offended. "I am not the one who meddles here," he answered and did not explain himself.

Strelleck had reset the bones in Marcus' arm and cleaned and bandaged his wounds. The man was far from consciousness, but he lived, each breath clean and unrestricted. He had deep bruises across the left side of his face where he had landed against the ravine stones.

"He fell about halfway down," Strelleck told Hileshand and gestured toward an outcropping of rock above their heads. The ravine was deep enough to hold a merchant vessel set on end; Marcus had fallen more than thirty feet.

Strelleck turned back to his fire, where he stirred a wooden spoon through something housed in a black half-pot; he appeared to be making breakfast.

Hileshand observed him there for a time and then squatted down opposite him. "I cannot tell you what you have done for my heart this day. I thank you. I am indebted to you."

Only once or twice before this had Myles heard him speak with such openness, the vulnerability clearly displayed. The thought of losing Marcus had shaken him.

Myles frowned as he studied Hileshand. He stood close to him, less than an arm's length away, yet he could sense the distance. Myles did not have what his brother had. Marcus possessed Hileshand's heart. He was right to call him "Father." This man loved him.

The Alusian looked at Hileshand. "Your sons," he said at last, "bear the same mark, inscribed by the same god. One of them bears it on his heart; the other bears it in his flesh. But it is the same mark, and the same god desires them to live. So they will live, because he desires it."

The creature possessed the gift of *eshtareth*—the ability to see the past and speak it forth. Myles had no doubt that Strelleck *knew*, as few could, that Hileshand's "sons" were not his sons. Marcus, perhaps, could be labeled as such, but it seemed odd to Myles that Strelleck would use the same language for him, knowing what he knew.

As if these thoughts had been spoken verbally, the Alusian shifted position near the fire and looked up at Myles. He held his gaze for so long that Myles began to wonder what the creature was seeing. The past? The future? It would be an interesting thing to see all this creature could see.

Strelleck pulled in a full-chested deep breath, let it out. "You smell," he said. He nodded toward the river, which echoed loudly through the stone structure surrounding them. "Go bathe yourself and return."

He went back to stirring the pot.

Hileshand smiled at Myles' expression and began to walk across the cavernous room to look in again on his son, who slept on a pile of blankets near the back wall.

But then Strelleck lifted his head and called, "Hileshand."

Marcus' father looked back.

"This is not the story you believe it to be."

An odd expression on his face, Hileshand adjusted his route and returned to him slowly, with caution. "I don't understand."

"That girl you brought back with you from the city—her story is not the story you believe it to be. Do not let the surprise alarm you."

He would say nothing more, though Hileshand requested it of him.

"I thought you were opposed to speaking fortunes," Myles said, folding his arms. Allowing accusation to manifest in his voice, he continued, "You seem to change your mind on many things."

The creature looked up at him. "No," he answered smoothly, the tone rather curt. "I simply make an exception with you."

Myles left for the river as quickly as possible.

chapter 25

Amilia opened her eyes to a room filled with soft, early morning sunlight. A woman sat in the chair beside the bed. Her hair was pinned up beneath a white cap edged with ruffles, and her face bore the familiar lines of a life of hardship and disappointment. Amilia had seen many faces like this in the city. No woman among them had ever taken kindly to her, and this woman immediately offered no exception.

When she saw that Amilia was awake, the woman gave her a brittle sort of smile and said brusquely, "Hileshand is downstairs with his son. I was to fetch him when you awakened." She put hands to the arms of the chair and hoisted herself to her feet.

Amilia did not watch her go. She heard her padded steps retreat to the door and then move down the hall. The woman muttered beneath her breath, the words indiscernible.

The room grew quiet. Amilia slowly realized she could not hear the sounds of the city. For the first time in five years, she had awakened in something that, to her ears, seemed like perfect silence. She could hear birdcalls floating in through the open windows. She heard men's voices from down on the porch, but they were not the rough voices of the city, where people had to rush about and push hard to secure their fortunes. These voices were relaxed.

The fog filtered in again before Amilia's eyes, and the next time she opened them, a man was sitting beside her. He smiled at her and shifted position in the chair, as if he meant to touch her. But then, with faint hesitation, he seemed to think better of it. He leaned back in the chair instead of forward.

"My name is Myles Hileshand," he said.

She remembered him from the house on Clay Street. Bas'silia's words returned to her, whispers about a new master. This man had held her in his arms and carried her down the steps.

He was older than Lord Olah, somewhere near fifty years of age. But when she looked for the lines of hardship on his face, she did not find them. There were lines there, but they were not lines of hardship—they were the signs of simple age, and that was all. Concern built within her as she stared at his face. What sort of man was this? Relieving the stress of a man accustomed to anger and disappointment— she could do that with minimal effort. She had been doing that for years, and she was quite good at it. But how was she to please a master who did not have these lines? What would a man like this do to her if she disappointed him? She did not know.

The smile faded some. "Amilia," the master said slowly, "you do not have to be afraid here. You never have to be afraid again. I did not buy you for…the reasons you suppose. When you feel like yourself again, I will ask the question I have for you, and your answer is the only thing I require from you."

She watched him.

She knew the thoughts of men, or supposed she did, but this man she could not easily read. The concern did not abate with his unusual words; instead, it increased tenfold. Bas'silia had wished happiness for her—she had not wished a man who could not be pleased. Amilia *wanted* to please this man. Her wellbeing depended on his pleasure.

The door opened on the other side of the room. The master looked up and smiled and seemed a touch relieved.

Amilia instantly recognized the man who appeared. She would remember his face forever.

A man's name did not matter in the North Square. The day she had seen this face the first time, she had been on her way to a client who lived across the city. The coach's route had taken her through the land of the dead, where the slaves were bought and sold.

She hated the North Square. The memory of her own sale in that place remained a vivid, fiery blister in her heart—a cruel mark against her. Olah had not been ill when he had purchased her. He had shown her what the world outside of Furmorea expected from her, writing her story in his own words, with his own hands, and the first page of that book was something she could not forget. It began in the North Square.

Amilia would not remember this man's face except for the way he had treated the woman with him. He had been gentle with her, defying the horror of the moment and the threats of Deregus' men. The way he had stood there, attempting to shield the woman, had drawn Amilia to the coach's window, her hand softly to the door. Was the woman his wife? His mother? She could not tell, but in response to him, the woman had turned and put her hand to his cheek, a simple gesture that had, in turn, carved the man's face into Amilia's soul. She did not know that such gentleness could exist in a man. She had not known it could exist in the North Square.

The woman had been sold, and Amilia had watched the slave until the road turned and she could no longer see him.

This same man had appeared like a wraith at the harbor inn, ignoring Deregus and his companions, chiding her fears. She had attempted to warn him because she had to, because she could not accept the thought of him being destroyed by the evil that ran this city. He had rejected her efforts, and she had thought him a gentle but perfect fool. Now, with suddenness, she did not know how to direct her thoughts at all.

What was this? What was *he* doing here?

Her master stood from the chair. He stepped around the bed and put his hand on the younger man's shoulder. "This is Myles. I believe you remember him."

Her eyes went to those of her master. Obvious humor gleamed in his gaze as he read her expression. She dared to speak to him, the urge unwieldy and almost desperate inside her. "I-I do not understand, my lord."

"Hileshand," he corrected. "Just Hileshand."

chapter 26

The Alusian worshipped Boerak-El, the god of sorrow. The creatures, both male and female, carried a peculiar magic, for their god was one of the gods of death. *The god of sorrow—of mourning.*

Despite the ferocity of his title, however, Boerak-El had shown himself to be quite accurate with prophecy. Hileshand had never heard of an Alusian speaking a word that proved to be false. Because of that, he saw no reason to challenge the Alusian's judgment of the matter and waited to move his son until Strelleck thought it timely.

Three days later, Amilia watched as he and Myles brought Marcus into the room and transferred him from the litter to the first bed, close to the door. She was sitting up today, her color faintly returning. Two days had passed since her fever had broken.

"This is Marcus," Hileshand told her somewhat needlessly. He had given her bits and pieces of the story, almost the entirety of it now, but he was uncertain if she would recognize the man on her own. In this moment, he resembled his brother very little. The left side of his face was a host of dark colors and swollen scrapes. Upon occasion, he opened his eyes, but he did not seem to use them. Hileshand cared for him as he had once cared for Myles after his bout with the red lions in Blue Mountain.

Myles hoisted the litter and carried it out of the room. Little Amilia watched him as he stepped into the hall and then her gaze returned to Marcus. Hileshand studied her.

Ethan Strelleck had given him an odd warning three days ago. At least, a *warning* was how it had seemed at the time. The more Hileshand thought about it, the less sense it made to him.

Her story is not the story you believe it to be. Do not let the surprise alarm you. Simple words they might be, but without any sort of context, Hileshand could make nothing of them, and Strelleck had not been forthcoming.

Marcus remembered her details—the color of her eyes. For the moment, that was the only story Hileshand was aware of. That was the only one that mattered to him. He took care of his son and chose to disregard the Alusian's words.

Marcus did not fully awaken for another three days. When he did so, his speech was slow and labored, the result of effort and specific focus.

Hileshand transferred chairs and sat between the beds, Amilia on his right, Marcus on his left. He took Marcus' hand and smiled at him and forced himself to refrain from overwhelming him too quickly.

Aerman, the physician out of Bledeshure, had come twice in the last week. The man was pleased with Amilia's recovery, but he had seemed hesitant concerning Marcus, who had not quickly come back to them after the blow to his skull. Hileshand himself was not afraid for the young man, not anymore, but he did understand the reason for care and caution in his approach.

"Tell me your name," he instructed, bending closer to him.

Marcus blinked at him several times and finally answered, "Marcus...Hileshand."

Hileshand squeezed his hand. Those words were simple, too. Simple and sharp, capable of cutting the heart open. "Do you know how proud I am of you?" he whispered and then cleared his throat. "My name?"

"Myles Hileshand."

"And your brother?"

"Named after you."

"Good." Hileshand squeezed the hand again.

He glanced at Amilia across the way. Her back was to the headboard, her legs crossed beneath her, a book in her hands. She had not been reading it; she had been examining sketches of mountains and distant plains and faraway cities, many of which Hileshand had seen in his travels. He had purchased the little book from a peddler and given it to her as an offering of good will. Perhaps he could not guess a woman's thoughts, but he had discovered that a good story tended to work where guesses did not.

She did not speak much with him—in truth, she seemed somewhat nervous around him, the way a young child would be concerned in the presence of an unfamiliar uncle. But she did respond to his stories, even asking questions. She had a traveler's heart and a student's mind. By her questions, he could tell she was intelligent, though she had not received much formal training. She remembered details and did not need to be reminded of anything he had told her once.

"Do you know where you are?" he asked his son.

"This is…" Marcus widened his eyes, narrowed them, released his breath, and gave his first incorrect answer. "Blue Mountain."

"We are far beyond the days of Blue Mountain."

Marcus made a second attempt. "What is the name… that little town in Tarek?"

"We spent a few days in Basin, and no, we're beyond that as well. This is the King's Southern Inn, on the South Road. We are three hours out of Bledeshure. Do you remember? We have been here for nearly a month."

"Bledeshure?"

"Aye. Do you remember Deregus, the Galatian captain?" Hileshand put his hand on Marcus' ribs, felt the steady beat of his heart, and was pleased by it. "The man who sold your brother?"

"I…" Lines pulled together between Marcus' brows. His lips parted, and he managed, "Marcus was sold?"

Hileshand looked down at him, feeling tendrils of concern, then Marcus realized his error and corrected himself. "Myles? What happened to Myles?"

"Calm, Marcus. Your brother is fine. Do you remember where we found him? He was in Blue Mountain in the arena. He fought the dragon."

"The dragon. Right. I remember the dragon."

Of course he would remember the dragon. Hileshand smiled again, knowing what else he would surely remember. He nodded toward the little girl in the next bed. "This is Amilia. You remember Amilia, don't you? You spoke with her at the tavern near the harbor. She thought you were Myles."

Marcus moved his head slowly. He stared at the girl for a long time. When he turned back to Hileshand, there was a look in his eyes that Hileshand did not believe he had ever seen before. He could not name it, not fully, and its unexpected abnormality here in this situation reopened the alarm inside him.

"I don't know who that is," Marcus said.

Hileshand reached around and placed his other hand on top of the one he already grasped. "It is all right, son. Get your rest. You will recover completely."

"Are you...are you certain it is all right? Am I supposed to know who that is?"

"I am sure it will return to you. You suffered a long fall— a hard hit. You've been in bed for a few days."

Again, that atypical look swarmed through Marcus' eyes. "What happened?" he asked.

"What do you remember?"

"I...I remember Blue Mountain. I remember perusan—and goe'lah—in the woods. Is there more than that to remember?" He frowned as he pieced together what Hileshand had just told him. "We have been here a month? In Bledeshure?"

"Aye."

Marcus relaxed against the mattress, closing his eyes. "Why does my stomach hurt?"

"The evil but necessary effects of rhusa bark. For the knock on your head and the claw marks on your back."

Marcus did not ask about the claw marks, as Hileshand had suspected he would. Instead, blurry humor crinkled his eyes, and he said, "Please tell me I did not throw up as much as Myles did."

The rhusa bark had not sat well with either of them.

Amilia pulled her bottom lip between her teeth and turned her head, something much like a first smile spreading slowly across her face. Marcus, of course, did not see it, and Hileshand had to work to keep his own lips still.

He was uncertain how he should answer the invalid's worry, so he finally patted his son's hand in silence. Understanding the gesture, Marcus groaned and made a weak attempt to pull the blanket over his head.

Hileshand captured his hand and made him lie still.

chapter **27**

"**H**ave you ever seen a dragon?"

Young Derek had not departed from Myles' side for more than a handful of minutes in the last six days. Word had been sent to his father in Helsman, the city of the king beyond Bledeshure, and until he came to fetch him, Derek slept on a pallet on the floor of their room. Hileshand insisted upon it, and Derek was much more than pleased to comply. The boy was polite around Marcus and Amilia, but he had made a clear choice with his affections. He ate what Myles ate. He went where Myles went. He made certain his pallet was within an arm's length of Myles' at all times through the night. More than once, Myles had awakened to hear him scooting it closer.

Myles did not mind the persistent company. A persistent child was different than a persistent man. In a way, the boy reminded him of his sisters, and he did not realize the ache in his heart until Derek revealed it to him. It was more than just nostalgia for familiar times and places he had known in the past. He could not quite decipher what it was that the boy stirred up within him.

The question about the dragon came following an afternoon spent repairing the river dock. It had been damaged by a passing merchanter headed into the city to trade. Myles and Derek had assisted Hessek, the innkeeper, with felling trees to serve as piles. Derek had cut his hand on the double-handed saw and seemed quite pleased at the prospect of a new scar.

Myles and Derek sat now on the hillside that sloped down into the river, watching the ships pass. They did not pass often, but when they did, Derek would point at them and make up stories about what they carried and why. He seemed knowledgeable about such things, and when asked, he said his father had taught him about merchants and vessels and all things related to shipping.

"Yes," Myles said at last. "I have seen a dragon."

"Where?"

"In Furmorea. It was killing the sheep, carrying them off in the night. A farmer expects such things every once in a while, but this creature came often and was in the process of slaughtering the entire herd."

"What did you *do*?" The last word was emphasized strongly, the sounds drawn out into multiple syllables.

"We camped in the woods and watched for it. A few nights later, it returned, and we trapped it and killed it."

"You killed a dragon?"

Myles smiled slightly. "In that instance, I *helped* kill a dragon. I did not actually kill it myself."

"Have you heard the story of the man who killed a dragon with his bare hands?"

The smile ebbed. "What?" Myles looked over at him in

surprise. "Who tells a story like that?"

The boy threw his hands in the air and replied with fervor, "My uncle! He said there was a man in Edimane who fought a dragon with his bare hands and cut him up into pieces. And the sielkis came, and the man fought those, too, and there was a great battle and blood everywhere, and it was amazing! He saw the fight."

Then the rush of Derek's words paused. His hands lowered a little, and he shrugged. "But I think your stories are better. Fighting the evil meusone? Killing the *atham-laine* that tried to kill your brother? These stories are much better. My uncle would have liked these fights more than the fights in Blue Mountain."

One man had come out of Blue Mountain, and the story had traveled with him. Just one man, and here the story was, being handed back to him. Myles did not know how to respond to this.

Someone called for the boy from the top of the hill behind them. Derek twisted around, and when he beheld the man standing there, he leapt to his feet and ran up the slope.

This, apparently, was the father, come to retrieve his son. The man's name was Lord Persus Claven, a nobleman—and a close friend of the king, Derek had proudly informed them. He advised the king on matters of finance. When the innkeeper realized whose son this was, he first had paled. Then he had rubbed his hands together in glee, foolishly expecting a substantial reward for Myles' efforts. For a brief moment, Myles had considered hitting him for such a response, for the innkeeper behaved like this in front of the boy. Derek was smart; he would know he had been reduced to his weight in gold, by a man who had not even been present the night of the attack.

An armed escort accompanied Claven. Some thirty men waited at the top of the hill, fully armed. With a cautious frown, Myles rose to his feet and walked up the slope, his journey much slower than the boy's had been.

Derek ran into his father's arms and at the same time, loosed a torrent of wild words, trying to speak within the span of only a few moments everything that had transpired. Myles heard something about the uncle, the highwaymen, the king's message kept safe, the Alusian named Strelleck. Lord Claven laughed and smiled and held on to him. He did not immediately request the document the boy had valiantly saved at great risk, and for that, Myles felt a faint, begrudging respect. The man did not treat his son the way the innkeeper had treated him. He seemed to genuinely care for the boy.

Derek broke free of his grasp to point at Myles.

"*This* is the man I wrote you about. *This* is the one who fought the meusone and killed the *atham-laine*." He spun back to his father and declared, "They sold the head to a peddler for fifty pieces of gold! You should have seen the head! It was as big as a bed! He chopped it off with a magical ax."

Myles grinned, in spite of himself. "You exaggerate, Derek."

"No, I do not exaggerate. I saw it. I stood beside it—it was as big as me. And he killed it with an ax, though it would have eaten him. It almost ate his brother, but he can run very quickly—even after an esep has bitten him in the dark!"

Myles felt the stares of the guards and scowled at the curious mix of awe and respect that came with them. They took the boy's tale seriously, despite the happy, frantic manner in which it was told.

THE HOUSE OF ELAH

Derek's father patted his son's head and sent him away with a few of his men. The boy went willingly enough, calling over his shoulder, "Myles! Myles, tell him about the dragon. He would like the story about the dragon, too." They took him into the inn through the back door.

Myles faced the father. "My lord," he said, greeting him officially now that they were alone, the tide of happy words abated.

"My son tells me that you came to his defense when no one else would. That you protected him when the others wanted to give the enemy what he possessed. Is this true?"

"Your son is very noble. He has great strength. He ran for an hour to get here, through the darkness, even though trained men pursued him. He won his life, in my eyes."

Claven studied him. "Are you aware of the message he protected from these men?"

"I am aware of its existence. That is all."

Claven's gaze continued its detailed study for several moments. He took in the scars on Myles' forehead and jawline, the bruises on his throat. Myles thought they had begun to fade over the last few days, but unfortunately, they were still present enough to draw attention like a peddler shouting of his wares in a corner booth.

Claven stepped around him and, without reservation, examined the sealed holes in the back of Myles' neck. Myles grimaced as he called one of his men to him, who also examined Myles.

A few moments later, Claven reappeared in Myles' line of sight, a slight smile on his lips. "He seems quite enamored with you. From these marks you bear, it would seem his story was not as exaggerated as I expected it to be. You truly did fight a meusone. You also slaughtered this *atham-laine* creature?"

Myles allowed a small smile as well. "Derek is a good boy." The words sounded trite, but he could not think of anything else to say. He did not wish to appear as if he gushed. Derek possessed a delight that was tangible, and Myles had not expected his company to be such a relief. And, oddly, such a discomfort.

He again found himself thinking of Hileshand and the hours the man had invested at the bedside of his son.

Claven glanced back at the inn—and the faces that quickly pulled away from the windows as he did so. He nodded toward the woods and asked, "Will you walk with me?"

The man chose a meandering path toward the trees. A slow path. Each step required the normal time of three. "Your name is Myles Hileshand." It was not a question, and Claven did not wait for an answer. "And you are a man who fights meusone and kills dragons."

"In truth, my lord, it has been but one dragon."

Claven smiled. "Derek," he said, "is the only child of his mother and very dear to my heart. You saved more than his life, Hileshand. You did me a..." The words tarried on his tongue. He released his breath slowly and said, "You did me a great service with his salvation. That boy means more to me than anything I have achieved in my lifetime. As I am certain you know, I will give you anything you desire as reward." He laughed in the back of his throat, a short laugh that sounded rather bitter. "I will have the king give you land and a title, if that is what you want."

"I do not wish a reward, my lord."

Claven glanced at him. "You do not understand. You have put me in a unique position. I am willing to give you anything you want."

"I will not accept reward. Your son won his life. I did

what any man—" Myles realized what he was saying. There had been other men present, men who had not responded as he had responded. Perhaps not every man would have done what he did, yet he had done what was needed. It had been a simple decision to act, and one could not be rewarded for simplicity. "You owe me nothing. The cost was not high."

"On the contrary, the cost was dreadfully high to you." Claven's tone became slightly less friendly. "I have had many dealings with Furmorea, and consequently, I have run head first into the great Furmorean pride many a time. Have no fear—I do not mean to offend you with my offer, nor do I mean to monetize your services toward my son. I mean to express my gratitude. If you do not allow me to honor you, in some way, I shall be offended." The smile returned, yet the cool steel in his voice did not withdraw entirely. "And it would not bode well for you to offend me."

That fact did not need to be stated. Myles could have put that together on his own.

No one had ever asked him what this man asked him now. It was not merely pride that made the answer difficult for him. *Anything you want.* It was a very broad statement, one that required a line of thinking that Myles had never before employed. When given the option of reward, how was one to answer? What was suitable, in this case?

His gaze on the ground, he finally said, "My bow was broken. I will need to replace it."

Claven stopped walking. He turned to face him with unwarranted amusement gleaming across his face. "You ask me to replace a bow?"

Myles stood there awkwardly.

Claven saw the awkwardness, and his smile became full fledged. "So it is not pride with you. A curious thing. Yes, I will fulfill your request and replace your bow—and I will do much more than that as well."

chapter 28

That night, Amilia descended the steps of the inn for the first time.

Lord Claven, Derek's father, was staying the night before departing for Helsman in the morning, and a large dinner had been prepared in his honor. In the past, Amilia had endured the company of many important men, and she had no desire to be surrounded by gaiety and frivolous people intent on capturing the lord's attention. But Hileshand had issued the invitation to her, and it was in her to please him.

Hileshand had purchased clothing for her. She had no idea how or where he had done so; a small satchel had simply materialized on the chair beside the bed one day. She had approached the bag with caution, but Hileshand proved to possess a better eye for details than she would have given him credit for. The dresses were simple and rather plain—the clothing of commoners, of village folk who had nothing to prove. She liked them right away, and everything he had purchased fit her loosely, concealing her form. She knew he had done that on purpose, and she smiled.

The dining room had been painted ivory and decorated with barrels of flowers and glittering streamers of colorful fabrics. It was a poor man's feast, and that helped set her at ease. She did not keep the company of kings tonight. With the exception of Claven, she kept the company of simple travelers, simple people.

To her relief, she did not recognize Claven's face. He was not one of Olah's associates.

Hileshand sat on her left and Myles on her right. She noticed a few stares—there were several men present—but none of them contained that familiar flicker of recognition.

Lord Claven was the entertainment for the rest of the room, and he had chosen Myles to be the source of his own entertainment. The more he drank, the more pronounced his decision became.

"He asks me to replace his bow." Claven waved his goblet in the air and announced to the rest of the table, "His *bow*. Does he ask for gold? No. Does he ask for position or station or a rank greater than anything his fathers have seen? No." The man smiled sloppily. "He asks me to replace his bow."

Hileshand grinned. Amilia thought that even if her eyes were covered and all the lights put out in the room, she would still be able to sense his pride. He had paid gold for Myles in Blue Mountain, just as he had paid gold for her in Bledeshure, and in a little more than two months, Myles had become just as much his son as Marcus, who had been raised by him. Hileshand's affection for the man was like a lamp set in a dark room; in his sight, Myles could do no wrong.

It made a level of sense for Myles to be accepted this way; he was the brother of Hileshand's son. Amilia was much more a slave than Myles had ever been. A slave and a stranger to Hileshand, without any previous ties to his heart, without any roads already set in place. Every time he smiled at her, she wondered at his thoughts and intentions. So she would seek to please him. Always she would do this.

Myles shifted in his chair, obviously uncomfortable, and Claven rejoiced in the action. "I have never before beheld a man who finds praise such a discomfort. Hileshand, you realize, do you not, that if you instill greatness in a man, you should also instill within him the ability to receive praise? For such a thing is necessary when the man does what his father has asked of him and becomes great. Others will take note of him."

Derek sat beside his father. Every time Myles was mentioned or addressed, the boy's eyes lit up, the smile widened, and it seemed as if he might begin floating out of his chair. Myles had treated him with the same gentleness Amilia had witnessed from him in the North Square.

The woman had been his mother.

"The great man," Claven continued, waving the goblet again, "will find himself in the presence of kings."

"King Reshland!" Derek cried, citing the aging king of Tarek whom Claven served. "He needs an audience with the king. Father, you should tell his majesty about the meusone, and the king will want to meet him."

Myles did not seem to like that idea either. He again shifted position in the chair, glancing at Hileshand with a scowl. When the front door opened across the room, he turned his scowl that direction, and his movements paused.

A moment later, a smile broke across his face. It was sudden and forthright. He turned back to Claven. "You think an audience with the king would be appropriate?"

Amilia stared at him. He unexpectedly appeared relaxed.

Derek grinned, thinking he had won, and Claven matched his son's smile. "Yes, I do, man. That is what I have been saying. Come with me to Helsman."

"Come with you to Helsman? To meet the king?" Myles repeated. He leaned back and draped his arm along the back of Amilia's chair, drawing his hand forward until it rested on her shoulder. His fingers were warm.

He had never touched her before this, not a single time. At his touch now, she could not move.

Myles turned to her and smiled, and Amilia's eyes began to burn with fire. The tears seemed to begin in the bottoms of her feet. She did not understand this sudden urge to weep with gusto, letting go of something she could not name.

Myles raised his eyes to Hileshand and with his look directed the older man's attention toward someone standing at the front door.

Amilia followed his gaze, and the air caught in her throat, just below her jawline.

Myles felt the girl stiffen beneath his touch. *She does know him.* The man at the door very clearly knew her. He had halted where he had entered. His hand still rested on the latch, the door standing open into the late evening and a sky shrouded with heavy clouds.

The man appeared to be somewhere near his thirty-fifth year and wore a jeweled sword at his hip. Multiple strands of gold hung around his neck, and his fingers glittered with gemstones. The quality of his clothes was purposeful and apparent—elegant and rich, not at all restrained.

He was a man of means, who, Myles guessed, had been thrust into wealth suddenly. He could not reason that a man born into wealth would have a mind to parade it like this.

The man's guards probably bunked in the stables alongside most of Claven's men. Dressed in garish finery like this, he could not have come alone, risking the threat of bandits and highwaymen.

Myles knew very little of the life of a slave girl living in Bledeshure, but he suspected that this tension beneath his hand now was abnormal for Amilia. Marcus had informed him of a great many things about her—details Myles did not believe he had shared with his father. Amilia was practiced. She was not new to this profession, and she possessed a level of talent in her work. Her response to this newcomer said much about the newcomer. Myles watched him and, with silent statement, dropped his hand down Amilia's arm, taking a firm hold of her. *Do not venture here*, he commanded.

Amilia began to laugh. As if a door had opened into early morning, her voice filled with light and tiny, flickering bubbles, like new Ruthanian wine. Myles froze there, his hand wrapped around her, and eventually suffered the thought that Marcus had not mentioned Amilia's laughter—and he should have. How could he have mentioned so many other things about her and yet failed to mention this?

Myles was aware this laughter was false, a contrived thing meant to somehow divert the man at the door. But he had never heard anything like it.

"Have you ever seen the city of Helsman, Myles?" she asked, turning toward him. In a single moment, she had gone from a little girl who seemed lost at this table to a woman of means who could influence and direct with grace.

Her gaze connected with his, and it was like being hit in the head with a fence post. He lost all ability to think or reason and answered her question with a fierce scowl, helpless and unable to do anything else. What she presented to the room right now—this could not be real, but how could something entirely false manage to dislocate his head from the rest of his body? He would not have been able to find his tongue even under threat.

She continued with barely a pause. "The city is lovely, a vivid image of golden spires and streets made of marble. King Reshland loves beautiful things, and his city reflects his tastes like a mirror of gold."

Myles could think of nothing to say. Every intelligent thought avoided his mind.

The girl looked at Claven, who stared at her, something he had not done before this. Her gaze now averted, Myles was able to close his mouth, and he realized every man in the room stared at her in a very similar fashion.

"Have you lived in Helsman long, my lord?" Amilia asked.

Claven's face lit up at her attention. He answered her, but Myles did not listen.

The man at the door seemed to recover himself. He shook his head once and shut the panel behind him. Hessek the innkeeper appeared at his side, and the two of them carried on a short conversation before Hessek led him toward the back steps to the second floor.

At the base of the steps, however, the man paused. He looked at Amilia again. His narrowed-eyed gaze moved slowly across Myles' hand clasped around her arm, and abruptly, he adjusted course, walking toward the table.

Amilia acted as if she did not see him, the fullness of her attention devoted to Claven. Myles watched his approach openly and considered the repercussions of removing him with force. He did not appear to be a man of strength. The sword at his hip was far too ornate for someone who actu-

ally intended to use a sword, and his shoulders bore a peculiar slope that suggested he had never lifted anything of true
weight in his life.

Claven looked up as the man greeted him by name. For
an instant, displeasure washed across Claven's features—dis-
like, abhorrence, a dozen other things—then he blinked rapidly, and every sign of rancor vanished. He stood to his feet
and wobbled a bit from the wine. Discreetly, he took hold of
the back of his chair. "My lord Hadenfeld. This is an unexpected pleasure. What do you do here?"

chapter 29

Amilia sat on the end of her bed, her hands folded neatly in her lap, her gaze on the carpet, her back straight. She possessed an air of regality, despite the darkness that swirled over her head like storm clouds. Something clearly bothered her, but Hileshand doubted she would tell him on her own. She had yet to volunteer anything to him. He knew nothing of her past, other than the obvious.

On any other night, Hileshand would have taken his pipe and retired by himself to the porch for an hour. Myles would eventually join him, and the girl would be asleep by the time they returned. Myles was not pleasant company this evening, however. He had stepped from the room a few minutes ago without warning, and Hileshand could not guess where he had gone or what bothered him.

The inn was quiet now, after many hours of playtime and festivities. Claven and his son had retired, as had the distinguished Lord Hadenfeld. Neither man seemed like the type to frequent the front porch of a country inn, so Hileshand, after a long moment's observation, decided on a route to relieve Amilia's stress.

"Come with me," he told her.

Her head jerked around. She looked at him with the eyes of a doe that had been startled in a field. He wondered at her thoughts of him in this moment and scowled at the likelihood.

He grabbed his pipe on the way out the door.

The night was dark and quiet. Last night had been clear. This night was damp and sultry with low clouds and no wind. Hileshand directed Amilia to the chair on the right. He took the chair on the left, lit his pipe, propped his boots on the rail, and released his breath in a pleased sigh.

He let the owls speak for him for about half an hour.

Finally, the child beside him said, "I answered your question."

He glanced at her in the darkness. Hana Rosure—her married name was Gaela—had been sold to a wealthy Paxan finance manager named Tressar, who came to trade in Bledeshure at this time every year. Amilia did not say how she knew his name, and Hileshand did not ask. He had no desire to confirm the uneasy assumption within him. The girl was certain of this purchase; apparently, the Paxan manager had had an avenue in which to tell her of it. Only one avenue came to Hileshand's mind.

His master, Amilia had told him, *a man named Lawvek, has several children, and he required another nurse. The son has many illnesses and cannot walk. Hana was not purchased for unmentionable reasons. Myles does not need to be concerned for her.*

That was how the Furmoreans spoke of prostitution. Judged strongly by their high morals and often rigid standards, it was deemed an "unmentionable" activity.

Amilia was Furmorean. She spoke Terikbah as Myles did—her words sounded like his, and Hileshand, as he had several times in the last few days, wondered what she thought of herself. She had been torn from her family just as Myles had been torn from his, but a more difficult path had been laid out for her. Olah had assigned to her a lifestyle considered shameful by her people. They would not even mention it by name, though the men of Furmorea were no different than the men of any other nation. The "unmentionable" business of harlotry had as secure a home in Furmorea as it did in Tarek, for example; it was merely concealed in Furmorea.

If Amilia were ever to return home, likely as not, she would be forced to take the same path that had been forced upon her here, but in Furmorea, her situation would be worse. She would be mocked and considered an object of shame. She would have little future and little hope for good happenings in her life.

Hileshand set the pipe between his teeth and considered her statement. Yes, she had answered his question. He knew who owned Hana Rosure. He knew the city the man lived in, even the name of the street. Amilia's information had been very thorough. The Paxan manager had told her many things.

"You did answer my question. And I thank you for it."

"What will you do now?"

Did she not know? It seemed to him that they had discussed this before. He let his breath out in a sigh, enjoying the quiet. At one point in his life, he had put much effort into crowds of people and the goings-on of the wealthy, but the fascination had long since drained away from him. There were other things more important than gold and what the wealthy liked to say about themselves.

"Marcus improves. When he is able, we will begin a slow journey north. It will be very slow, I imagine." He thought he could feel her gaze in the shadows. Hileshand pulled the pipe from his mouth and smiled at her. "The fall approaches, with cooler temperatures and snow in the highlands—I have no desire to press you to your limits."

His attempt at teasing received no reply. A frown crept between his brows, and he wished to see her face because he did not know what she was thinking.

"Are you all right, Amilia?" he finally asked.

He could hear her voice clogged with tears. "You…you mean to take me with you?"

A moment passed before he understood what she meant. "Of course I mean to take you with me. Did I fail to make that clear to you?" He had thought his intentions very clear.

A noise much like a small sob escaped her throat. "I thought—Lord Hadenfeld does much business with Lord Olah. His coming here tonight…he would be willing to buy me for much gold. More gold than you paid. A fortune. He sought very hard to obtain me and Lord Olah always refused him." Her voice broke. "It would be a beneficial transaction for you, my lord. Lord Hadenfeld is a wealthy man. He would give you anything you desired."

"I am not going to sell you, *goshane*." The word was a Furmorean endearment, something parents would use with their young children. Hileshand had learned it many years ago, and it had struck him as something to remember, something he could use in the future, should he ever find an avenue in which to do so. This avenue worked nicely. "Hadenfeld could offer me the king's purse, but I would not part with you."

"I answered your question," she said. "I did what you wanted."

Hileshand's understanding of her thoughts slowly increased. She expected what she had known—to be "finished" when her services were completed. He frowned. "Yes," he answered, "you did. But that does not mean I now wish to be rid of you. I am not going to put you to use and then discard you."

There were things to be said here, important truths for her to understand. He paused to gather his thoughts. When he was ready, he said, "Marcus is my son. He is of my flesh and carries my bones in his body."

He had, of course, shared with her the story of the twins' past. Without it, it was not easy to explain why one son spoke Furmorean with an accent and the other did not. Hileshand smiled to himself.

"Myles," he continued, his heart warming, for this topic was dear to him, "is also my son. He is also of my flesh and carries my bones in his body. One son was given to me in Gereskow. The other son was given to me in Blue Mountain. But both are mine. I claim them as mine. There is no difference between them and children who would be born to me in wedlock. They are both my sons.

"Marcus understands this. Myles does not yet—he has not had the time with me that Marcus has. But one day, I hope he will be able to see what I see. I know the treasure I have been given, and I intend to steward it well."

He allowed for a moment of quiet, and he could tell that she was listening to him. It was as if she pulled the words out of him. He could feel the invisible tug in the darkness, and he was happy to comply.

"I paid the same price for you that I paid for Myles." He did not speak of gold now. "Of course you are coming with us. You may part with me, if you have the intention of doing so—but I will not willingly part with you. That was my decision when I traded gold for your life, and I do not regret my actions. When I told you you were safe now, I meant it. You will never be a slave again."

Stretched out on the green, his hands behind his head, Myles stared up at the stars he could not see through the clouds. The ground dampened everything it touched; the back of his tunic and trousers clung to his skin. The air smelled like wet earth.

He listened to Hileshand's sincere voice rise and fall in the midst of a conversation Myles was not meant to hear. He had come out here to think, not to have his unasked questions answered, in a way. Did Hileshand know he was out here, hidden in the dark with his thoughts? Or was this just uncanny luck? Myles knew that Hileshand possessed such luck—the man called the universe *unbalanced*.

At one point in the festivities tonight, an inebriated Claven had leaned down and given his dearly loved son a kiss on the top of the head. Myles was twenty-one years old, a man by any country's standards, but he could not explain why that action bothered him so. Was he truly this desperate for what Hileshand spoke of now? He did not desire a kiss on the head any more than he desired the "reward" Claven insisted upon giving him.

Yet somehow, his heart ached tonight in a way it had not ached in a long time, the severity piercing. And the ache had not started until Claven's unexpected act of affection.

Myles is also my son. He is also of my flesh and carries my bones in his body. Myles and Marcus. *Both are mine. I claim them as mine.*

Hileshand positioned him with Marcus. He did not do what Myles had feared these last several days—he did not hold him separate from the son he loved. *Both are mine.*

This was so confusing. Myles sat up in the darkness in hopes that the elevated position would help his thoughts come to order.

Marcus laughed with his father. He told stories with him and was at ease and at rest in his presence. He made the whole situation seem simple. Myles knew nothing about doing that—about being a son under these circumstances. He knew how to finish his work. He knew how to think ahead, adjust what required adjusting, and plan for the future so he could finish his work more smoothly. Rand, his mother's husband, had never said anything like what Hileshand had just finished saying.

Marcus seemed to have no trouble walking this road, but Myles had no idea how to do what Hileshand wanted. He knew nothing about responding to a man who offered him these things, about living with him in close proximity, every day.

But those words were excellent words. *Both are mine. I claim them as mine.* Myles put fingers to the bridge of his nose, closed his eyes, and tried to understand. Hileshand's words were excellent words. Myles *would* accept them—if he simply could put his hand to them and know how to make them work.

Hileshand had mentioned time. How much time was required here? How long would this take?

Myles did not return to the room until dawn. Awakening to the sound of the door, Hileshand rolled over and glanced at the window, seeing the pale gray light intruding through the crack between the curtains.

The young man sat on his pallet. He did not lie down; he simply sat there, head lowered. After several moments, he reached up and ran his hand over his face.

"Myles?" Hileshand said, keeping his voice low.

The man lifted his head.

Hileshand waited for him to speak. But he did not. Myles looked at him for a long moment, then stretched out on his pallet.

Odd, Hileshand thought. Where had he been all this time?

chapter **30**

Amilia did not see much of Myles for two days. On the afternoon of the third day, Hileshand had Marcus up and walking outside in the cool air, the aftermath of rain. The clouds were still heavy overhead, but they were quiet now. The storm had passed. Sitting in the window seat, she watched Hileshand and his son slowly walk the drive.

The door opened and Myles stepped into the room. He stopped when he saw that she was alone, surprise flickering across his features, but he made his decision and came all the way in, shutting the door behind him.

He approached her, and she attempted to quiet what did not wish to be quieted within her, whenever he was near. She did not know why her stomach, her lungs, and her heart responded this way. Did he frighten her? She did not believe so. Most men did not, and this sensation did not feel as true fear would feel. It had not been fear in the North Square; that she knew with certainty. So it likely was not fear now.

For a long moment, both of them watched Marcus and

Hileshand on the ground. The men spoke with one another. Every so often, the wind would carry up to the window a few of their words.

Wetting her lips, she whispered in Furmorean, "I do not know what to make of him."

His breath rolled across her shoulder, and he answered, "Marcus is the best of men. The very best. You will never have a concern with him. He will see to that."

She glanced at him. Did he purposefully misunderstand her? "Hileshand," she said. "I mean Hileshand."

"Oh."

Again they watched in silence. The clouds began to clear away in the west, displaying the first orange lights of sunset.

"Do you think…?" At first, that was all he said. Then he took a deep breath and began again. "You have known Hileshand for less than two weeks. Do you believe he speaks the truth to you?"

It was a peculiar question, especially from someone who would know the answer much better than she. Indeed, the answer had become so obvious to her that she had stopped asking the question. "Yes," she said. "I know he speaks the truth."

Myles frowned. "How do you know that?"

Another peculiar question. Had he never considered all these things before, never put together an accurate picture of her circumstances in his head? Was he truly this naïve? She looked up at him, a bitter sort of amusement pulling at her lips. "I know when a man lies, my lord."

He did not seem to appreciate that answer. The frown altered. He began to look uncomfortable. "I, least of all, am your lord, Amilia. You should not say that."

Watching his expression with care, she tested him and

said, "You are the son of the man who purchased me. I believe that makes you what I call you."

He did not have to answer verbally to communicate what he thought of that.

She remembered Hileshand's words on the porch three days ago. She had heard the affection in his voice when he had spoken of this man. She had heard the longing, even. Never had she experienced a man who spoke so honestly and freely; in that moment, Hileshand had seemed like a river without boundaries. Nothing held him back. Nothing restrained him from doing what was on his heart to do, and his heart was to care for this man. Why did Myles find this difficult? He was being offered what she had always wanted: safety and peace.

No one had ever done for her what Hileshand had done for her.

"He believes you are his son. He calls you that." She prodded, "Is your heart loyal to someone else? Does Hileshand…act in a way against your wishes?" She doubted that. Hileshand had told her about the House of Elah in Gereskow. Marcus had been awake for that story and had supplemented his own additions to the narrative. Their blood father had wished them dead; both sons had been tossed away, in different manners—Myles especially.

"There is no one else."

She watched the emotions appear and disappear across his face.

He repeated, "No, there is no one else." After a period of silence, he continued, "I heard what he said to you."

She looked at him. "When?" she asked. Hileshand had said many things to her.

He frowned and turned to look out the window. "That

night on the porch. Three days ago."

He had heard *that* conversation? Curious, and somewhat cautious, she asked, "Where were you?"

The frown intensified. "On the green. I heard the door open and figured it for Hileshand. He often frequents the front porch in the evenings. I did not know he had brought you with him until you spoke."

Her words had been spoken in fear and honesty. After hearing them, Myles would now know how she thought; he would know her for what she was—a slave of the basest sort.

She would wish that he did not know these things, that he had not heard her words, yet in the end, she struggled to think it mattered. In his thoughts and attitudes, he was as Furmorean as she; certain things neither of them could overlook. Those things were unmentionable things. A disgrace before the gods.

Last year, a Furmorean had ridiculed her in the presence of several of the rich and influential men of Bledeshure. The encounter had happened at a party thrown in honor of the visiting governor, and her fellow countryman, a merchant of some renown, had filled his head with wine and attacked her as a child would attack an older sibling who had embarrassed him before his young friends. He had said ridiculous things. The others had mocked him and laughed, and she had laughed as well. In truth, she could not remember a single name or description he had given her that night, but the *intent* behind the words she had never been able to clear out of her heart. How could she? He was right. Her father, if he had lived, would not have accepted her back into his house. In all likelihood, Myles questioned Hileshand's wisdom and why he gave her such grace. *She* wondered that.

Amilia sighed deeply, and Myles heard it. He looked down at her.

He said gently, almost apologetically, "I did not intend to eavesdrop."

He did not mock her.

She pictured him again in the North Square with his mother and sighed a second time, for a different reason. She wanted him to touch her again and did not understand how one man's touch could mean something entirely different than that of another. She had not *wanted* to be touched before. Part of her trembled in fear at this desire she could not explain, and part of her wanted to laugh because it was as if she had come upon a candle burning in the middle of a dark forest. Something stirred here. The land was not dead.

"If you ask me, Myles, I will tell you anything you want to know." She spoke truth. She intended it as a promise.

A knock sounded on the door.

Myles went to answer it.

Ten men stood there, all of them armed, all of them with their hands full. Two of them carried a huge chest between them—as large as a seaman's trunk. Another bore multiple packages almost as long as Amilia was tall. Every object was wrapped in tan fabric that was held in place by white ribbon.

These men had come by ship. They could not have come by way of the South Road, for Amilia had been watching. She would have seen them come up the drive.

"Myles Hileshand?" asked the first soldier.

Myles hesitated, so Amilia chose to answer in his stead. "Yes," she said, stepping forward. "This is Myles Hileshand."

She ignored his swift look.

The man bowed. "My lord. I have been instructed to inform you that what we bring you today is not payment for services rendered." A corner of the man's mouth turned up and his eyes crinkled. Apparently, the situation had been explained to him. "It is the gratitude of a father who loves his son. The son chose many of these objects himself and desires you to know that you will like them."

Lord Claven had left with little Derek two days before.

When Myles did not respond to his announcement, the man asked, "Where would you like us to leave these, my lord?"

Myles blinked and seemed to regain his senses. "In here," he answered stiffly.

They brought in the chest and set it against the wall. They then began to cover the first bed with article after article; the items piled up on top of one another. Three or four of the soldiers removed purses from their belts and left them on the blanket as well. Amilia had heard of this Terikbah tradition; if a man wished to show his esteem for another's act of courage or service, he would leave that man what he carried in gold. It was meant to be a sign of significant honor.

Myles seemed thoroughly overwhelmed. He stood there, his back slightly bent, shoulders elevated.

When their arms were empty, the soldiers filed out of the room, leaving the first man behind.

"We understand you are soon journeying into Paxa. My master leaves a ship for you at the lower dock. Until two days ago, it bore the name *Warman*, but yesterday, it was re-christened. It now travels by the name of *Atham-Laine Folmerkah*."

In Furmorean, the words meant "One Who Slays the Monster." The corner of the soldier's mouth twitched again, and Amilia grinned. She could imagine Derek jumping up and down with glee. That change in title had been his doing, surely.

"The captain has been instructed to serve you for as long as you need him. There is one other matter as well."

Elated by all of this, Amilia looked up into Myles' dark expression. There were so many gifts! And they were all wrapped in secrets, hidden away. Perhaps he would let her open one.

The soldier stepped into the hall and motioned to someone. A young man followed him into the room. Unruly red hair sprouted from his scalp in all directions. He had pale skin and hundreds of freckles, and he was strapped with half a dozen different leather bags, some long and thin, some bulky and wide. He bowed before them, and the bags shifted in their places all around him.

"This," the soldier said, "is Antonie Brunner. He is a scribe. Master Derek hopes that you will allow him to accompany you in order to secure a written account of your further adventures—adventures Derek deeply regrets missing." The man paused. "Is this acceptable, Lord Hileshand? His lordship requires an immediate answer."

At the mention of Derek's name, Myles' expression seemed to soften. He released his breath in a sigh and said at last, "Fine. Tell Derek that's fine."

The soldier bowed. "Very good, sir. May the gods grant you peace and continue to steady your hand."

Before he left, Claven's soldier removed his purse from his belt and dropped it on the bed with the others. A sign of great honor.

May the gods grant you peace and continue to steady your hand.

Amilia smiled. There was no question of that.

part two

God of Sorrow

chapter 31

The attack occurred at dawn, just as the sun was appearing above the eastern horizon, spreading a broad, golden reflection across the Paxan Sea. The ship gave a single tremendous shudder. That was the first and only warning.

Hileshand grabbed the rail with both hands. His gaze snapped to Josson, first mate, who stood beside him. The man had his hands around the rail as well, and his face went as white as the froth breaking along the ship's prow.

"What was that?" Hileshand demanded, hoping he was mistaken.

He was not a sailor; he knew only the stories of sailors, all of which began as this one seemed to begin—just after dawn, as the light touched the water, there would be a single, unexpected shudder from beneath the ship, a violent caress meant to ascertain the vessel's weight and composition. The niessith did not attack a vessel without first judging the strength of that vessel.

Hileshand's stomach turned over as he thought of his

children asleep below deck.

They had exited the Tarek River six days ago. The Paxan coast filled the eastern horizon, looping along in a jagged line of muted color, with rocky peaks and plateaus rising into the sky. The tallest points were cloaked in heavy blankets of snow.

The closest projection of land, a band of stone jutting out of the angry, sun-swept waves, was more than five miles away, and this far north, the waters were cold. Much too cold to chance a long-distance swim—in truth, *any* period of time in the water. It would suck the life out of a man's bones.

But perhaps this unexpected jostle was not what Hileshand feared it was. Niessith attacks were rare. There had been only two in the last one hundred years—the probability was not high.

Perhaps this bump was caused by something else—something large but friendly and clumsy, coming up too close to the surface. This was their fourth week aboard this ship, and they had experienced no trouble. There was no reason for trouble to start now, here, a mere twelve hours from their next port.

The first mate did not allow for the possibility of peace.

"All hands," Josson wheezed. Then he blinked and filled his lungs and shouted, "All hands on deck!"

Jarred out of a fitful sleep, Marcus Hileshand rolled out of his hammock and landed on his stockinged feet, the wooden floorboards frigid beneath his toes. He knocked over his boots in the dark and waited there a moment, his consciousness slowly clearing. *Boots. I need those.* He crouched down, feeling around for them. He found them and pulled them on.

"Myles!" he whispered loudly. "Myles! Antonie!"

The snoring did not falter.

"Myles!" He kicked the appropriate hammock.

Myles grunted. Marcus heard him stir, imagined what he had seen before when he had put a boot to the bottom of his brother's form like this.

"What?" his twin grumbled.

"Get up. I think we hit something."

There was quiet. Then Myles said again, "What?" Same dark tone.

The quiet broke as a fury of shouts sounded on the main deck. Marcus tilted his head and listened, the inside of his chest tightening as he recognized the sounds of panic. The crew did not respond now to a storm's violence or to a minor mishap—these were screams of fear.

"We hit something," he repeated, though he doubted now the truth of that statement. A collision surely would not fill men with this level of panic. "Get yourself up. Hurry!"

Myles groaned and swung free of the hammock. He hit the floor and tripped over his boots, too.

Marcus made his way to the wall and reached for his cloak. His sword hung beneath it. Even below deck, with a covered stove on the other side of the small room, he could feel the cold bitterness of the sea. The wind was forceful out here and ridiculously unpleasant, as if blowing off ice.

"Antonie," Marcus called again.

The scribe suddenly filled the space right beside him. "Here," he answered.

Marcus jerked away from him, glaring toward the face he could not see. What was he doing, standing so close in the dark? "Did you feel that?" he asked, pulling the cloak over his arms.

"I did." Antonie's voice lowered and, rather sarcastically, he said, "You know what lives in these waters, Marcus? You know what can strike a ship like that?"

Marcus paused.

Antonie did not normally speak this way. The words themselves were somewhat alarming, but Marcus was more greatly concerned because Antonie was the one who had said them. The man kept to himself as much as possible. As far as Marcus could remember, he had never willingly volunteered information to the rest of them. Hileshand had tried to draw him out of his cave of seclusion, and with very little exception, Hileshand had failed in his quest.

"What lives in these waters?" Marcus repeated and scowled at the sounds of movement. He could hear rustling. Antonie was doing something in the dark.

The man grunted once. When he spoke again, the words sounded stiff—he spoke through a clenched jaw. "Something that does not like the smell or texture of blood. It preys upon men, but whole men. It will not take the injured. Stay, Marcus—and forgive me in advance for my effort."

Marcus didn't know what he was talking about until the man rammed something sharp through Marcus' bicep. Marcus responded without thought and struck out blindly, managing to catch the corner of Antonie's chin with his fist. He heard the man hit the ground, flat on his back.

"What do you imagine you're doing?" Marcus hollered, feeling heat dribble down his arm, draining into the sleeve of his cloak.

"Saving your life!" Antonie hollered back. "Myles—"

Across the small room, a sleepy Myles grumbled, "Stay away from me."

"No! I tell you, this is the way—"

Something slammed into the bottom of the ship. Wood snapped. Beams. Panels shattered. The roar of rushing water. Marcus lost his footing as the ship rotated, careening sideways. He grabbed the nearest hammock as his arms brushed it in the dark. He hung on with both hands.

The water broke into the cabin. Currents of cold swept across his legs, and he struggled as he tried to pull himself in the door's direction. But he wasn't certain where the door was anymore. The floor was tilted.

"Myles!"

"Over here!"

Something bellowed outside the ship. A massive cry.

Marcus heard the stove break on the other side of the room, the iron bending, screaming as it twisted. Metal slammed against metal. The room filled with piercing, high-pitched hisses, like the warnings of a thousand snakes. The sound seemed to drag across his spine, through his skull. What was that? His brother cursed.

The cold hardened into a physical form that wrapped around Marcus' legs and coursed upward. It happened so quickly that he had lost control before he knew what was going on. He had no idea where his sword was. He slammed his fist down on the cold, scaly link around him. The flesh thinned out beneath his hand to reveal a network of bones and sinew. The creature was sensitive. Something came near his head and hissed viciously in the wet darkness.

Then the creature touched his arm, the one Antonie had bloodied. Even through his cloak, with water rushing over him, the reptilian arm found his wound. The weight disappeared from his chest, backed off his legs.

The hissing near his head pulled away. Then all of it pulled away. The banging stopped near the stove. The room dropped into something that seemed like silence, now that the piercing hisses were gone. Marcus' heart raced.

The ship shook violently. He held on to the hammock as his body banged against the floor, which now stood up next to him like a wall. Back and forth. A terrific shaking. Then the ship plunged. His stomach rolled into his throat.

The fall seemed to last several seconds. Marcus clung to the hammock and held his breath. Antonie was screaming.

The hammock ripped off the ceiling as the ship's downward spiral slammed to a halt. Marcus hit the wooden panels below him. Salt water coursed over his head, filling his mouth.

"Marcus!" Antonie's voice again. Marcus could hear the man slogging toward him through the water. "Where are you?"

Marcus flung the broken hammock aside. He did not know where the ceiling was. He did not know if he was standing on it, or on the wall, or on the floor...He didn't know where the door was. The roar of rushing water filled the room. "Here," he said. His waterlogged cloak pulled him backward. He unclipped it and let it fall away.

Antonie found him, grabbed his arm. "The ship is sinking. We have to go."

Marcus pulled away from him. "Myles!" he shouted.

He heard the continual rush of water. He heard screams in the distance, on other decks.

That was all he heard. This time, his brother did not answer.

Fear laced itself through Marcus' ribs, tightened around his stomach. His brother did not answer him.

Antonie's grip became like a band of iron. He steered Marcus in the darkness, pushing him forward. "Marcus."

His name was spoken apologetically but firmly. "The room is empty. We have to go. Over here. Here's the door. That's it. Good…"

The hall was mostly dark on the other side. Marcus saw a square of sunlight falling across the steps at the distant end. The ship was sitting in the water right side up. He could hear the entire structure groaning as it filled with the sea. The water was high enough to cover the bottom steps of the staircase.

"What," he rasped, "was that?" The water pulled at his boots.

"It's called a niessith," Antonie answered.

Marcus' thoughts came together with a snap, and he jerked his arm free and started running for the captain's cabin. The first door by the steps. Amilia's room.

The door wouldn't open. He threw his weight against it. It shifted but barely. Antonie helped him, and the panel finally moved.

"Amilia!" Marcus shouted.

She did not answer either.

The room appeared to have been ransacked. The dresser was overturned, trunks scattered. Water stood two feet deep. But what he noticed more than anything else was the hole in the wall. It was the size and shape of a wagon wheel. He could see sunlight on the other side, though the captain's cabin was several rooms away from the exterior of the ship.

Antonie was breathing hard. "The niessith have spikes on their palms," he said, lifting his own hands to show him where. "They drive them repeatedly into a ship, puncturing multiple openings like this, then thread their tentacles in. They are…very large entities. Bigger than the ship. They stand as a man does, their feet on the sand."

"Amilia," Marcus said again. He staggered inside the room and dropped into the icy water, hands out, searching. He cut his palm on a shard of wood. His fingers went numb. He did not find her. She was gone, just like Myles.

On his hands and knees in the water, Marcus stopped. He felt as if a piece of him had been cut away from his body. The mere thought of this, the horror of it, made it difficult for him to breathe. He could not move.

Antonie returned his firm, directing grip to Marcus' arm. "We have to go," he said sharply and heaved him up out of the water.

chapter **32**

They had set out from Tarek with four passengers and forty-three crewmembers, including Captain Isule. Now there weren't enough of them to fill a single longboat. Marcus counted twelve miserable, shivering men, all of whom sat there in silence and watched as the *Atham-Laine Folmer-kah*, Persus Claven's ship, sank beneath the waves. The top of the mast disappeared, and Marcus looked away, letting his breath out slowly.

His father sat beside him. The man said nothing, his hands in his lap. He was very still and did not seem to notice the cold as the rest of them did.

Several long, silent moments passed.

Then a man shouted at them from the wreckage that floated on the sea's surface. He waved an arm and shouted again. The captain gave the order, and his remaining crew set to work, putting the oars in motion. They had already pulled three survivors out of the water; this fellow would make thirteen in the longboat.

Without a word, Hileshand made his way to an empty seat and began to work alongside the others. Marcus could not. His arm ached where Antonie had stabbed him—with one of his quill pens, he realized, pulling up his sleeve and examining the wound. The hole was small, but it hurt and it still bled, red water dripping off his hand. He was shaking. He felt as if he could not control his body, or his mind.

He could remember the sound of Myles' curse in the dark. That must have been when the niessith grabbed him. His brother had realized what was happening and given his customary curse. The niessith would have taken Marcus, too, if not for Antonie, the redheaded man who had never expressed a will or an opinion before this day.

Marcus raised his head and looked at him. Antonie sat on the bench facing him. "Thank you," he whispered.

Antonie studied his expression a moment. Then he nodded slowly.

Save for the one waving man, the sea was quiet. Nothing stirred along the surface. *Myles. Amilia.* Marcus ached as he had not ached before. This could not be true—this emptiness of the sea. But the silence proclaimed the loss.

The loss.

Marcus shuddered, staring at the shimmering surface. What happened beneath the waves—right now, in this moment? Had they died yet? Or were they still struggling somewhere? Marcus grew ill and forced his thoughts in a different direction. He could not think that way.

Captain Isule searched out Hileshand and called to him, "Destination, my lord?"

The question was asked with stiff words. The captain mourned. Marcus knew him to be an honest man, one who cared for those who trusted him to keep them safe. There were tears in his eyes, though drawn by the cold or the sorrow Marcus could not tell.

Hileshand had been expecting the query. "Survivors first," he answered.

Myles and Amilia. Was there any hope? Marcus looked out over the water.

Hileshand continued, "Then take us three miles south."

Marcus glanced at him, wondering. Port Soren was to the north. The longboat would add hours to the journey, yet they would be there before midnight. What was south? He had studied the map again last night and could not remember there being anything of interest along this stretch of coastline. Port Soren, meanwhile, was a major stopping point along the Northern Trade Line.

Isule did not question the order. "Aye, my lord. Right away."

With a mile remaining before the completion of Hileshand's strange request, Marcus focused on the hilt of his father's sword and realized it was covered with green blood. As his thoughts slowly returned to him, he saw that the same blood also covered his father's arms and was splayed across his tunic.

The hue was unnatural. It seemed almost metallic in the early morning sunlight, glowing vibrantly, like the underside of a fresh leaf.

"What happened?" he asked, nodding toward the sword.

Hileshand grimaced, a deep line drawing between his brows. "The head came up over the side of the ship." His gaze flicked to Marcus', held for a moment. "It looked like something you would see in the darkest of dreams. A god of death, like the images they worship in Ruthane. It was hideous. I've…I've never seen anything like that. Covered in horns. The mouth did not have any teeth."

Because it did not like the taste of blood. It swallowed people whole. Marcus glanced at Antonie and wondered how the scribe had known that, where he had learned it was necessary to spill blood before an attack of this nature. Perhaps he had simply read about it—he was a scribe. No doubt he had read many things and knew many things because of it.

The captain was listening to their conversation. He nodded toward a few men at the oars. "Your father saved four of my men as they were dragged off the ship. He wounded the creature badly. It lost an eye and a good portion of its skull. I would wager everything I yet possess on the probability that your father killed it. Likely, it will drag itself ashore and die on the beach in a few days."

He paused. He looked down at his hands. "More men drowned today than lived to fill the belly of the niessith. A noble act, that of drowning. Your father did well."

Hileshand looked north, back across the sea to the area where the attack had occurred. "Not good enough," he murmured, then redirected his attention to the approaching coastline.

chapter 33

The old man reached his sitting rock and did as its name suggested. He sat. As the weight eased off his bones, he sighed, first in pain and then in pleasure. He surveyed the rolling landscape before him and thought what he always thought when he looked at it like this: *You have made a beautiful place.* He had lived in these mountains for fifty years, but that would always be his first thought.

"Beth!" he called down the slope. "Beth, what are you doing?"

The sheepdog responded with a swift bark and charged up the hill with much more stamina than he. He transferred his walking stick to his other hand and reached down to give the dog the obligatory scratch behind the ears.

"What now, Beth?" he asked her as she rubbed against his knee. "What do you think we will find today, eh?"

He smiled to himself. What other man on this earth was as blessed as he?

Three hundred miles and two mountain ranges separated him from the sea, where he had spent his young years with his grandfather. He had learned to fish there, which he still enjoyed doing. His grandfather had taught him other useful skills as well, such as reading and cabinet making; his grandfather had been a very wise man, who could speak several languages and was proficient in more than one occupation. *Should the winds change,* he had said.

Well, the winds had changed for him. They had changed for his grandson, too, but the transition had not been a painful one. The grandson, now much older than the grandfather had ever been, smiled again. He put his hand on his knee as the sheepdog took off across the hill in hard pursuit of a rabbit.

His little house sat at the bottom of the next mountain, near the waterfall. It was not far from here, perhaps an hour's walk. At one time in his life, the stroll between his garden and his sitting rock had taken him only fifteen minutes, but those days were long past. He carried the stick now. He glanced at it and struck the end against the rocky soil.

He had his little house, his little flock, and a life of peace. He missed the sea, but Issen-El had provided for him in that way, too.

"Come along, Beth," he called, putting his weight to his walking stick and climbing slowly to his feet. He had two hours of steep climbing before he reached his destination. He had gotten a late start today; the sun would be setting shortly after his arrival, so tonight, for the first time in five years, he would sleep in the cave. He had restocked the cabinets last month. He would have everything he needed.

He and Beth crossed the snowline. The temperature lowered slowly. By the time he reached the cave near the top of the mountain, his breath was leaving him in steamy clouds.

The old man paused at the entrance, leaning on his walking stick, and stared out across the land. *You have made a beautiful place.* The same thought as before. It would always be the same thought. He was very grateful.

With a sigh, he turned and faced the darkness of the cave mouth. He was especially grateful for this. For his little bit of the sea.

The lantern lived in the first cabinet on the left. He brought it out and set it on the rock table, taking a moment to run his fingers across the designs he had carved into the sides of the stone. He had spent hours on this project. No one would ever see it but Beth, but he was content with that. He loved the way it felt beneath his fingers. He loved that he had made this. He had never worked with stone before or after this, and he thought the table had turned out very well.

After fumbling with the match kit, he opened the lantern's little glass door and managed to light the wick. A warm yellow glow spread through the front room. He shook out the match and tossed it aside.

Issen-El, the god of the sea, had built this cave for him. He had fashioned it out of the mountain with his own hands and given him the location in a dream. Every week for thirty years, the old man had made the trek up the mountain to see what Issen-El had brought to him. The sea god had been faithful with his choice of treasures.

One time, it had been a small chest filled with gold pieces. The old man had finished his house with that. He had also used it to help build a house for the new doctor down in the town, as well as a few other buildings, and the chest was still over halfway full. He would never be in need, because of that one, single gift from the god of the sea.

Another time, it had been a seashell—a beautiful gift

that he kept on his mantel. The last time, one week ago, it had been a huge fish, which he had spread with butter and spices and cooked over the fire, and he had enjoyed it very much. Though he lived three hundred miles from the sea, the distance did not matter. He still had the sea because Issen-El was generous.

In the next room, near the cave's back wall, was a rectangular frame in the stone. It was the size of a trapdoor, but it was uncovered—without a door—so he supposed it was more of a "trap." When he knelt down beside it and craned his head, he could hear the rolling sounds of the sea, even though to his eyes, the trapdoor was a solid fixture. It enclosed stone and that was all. When he touched the center of it, he felt stone. Yet somehow, Issen-El could send him gifts through it. The stone was no different than the sea to Issen-El.

Beth came bounding up next to the old man, barking loudly. Her cries echoed against the stones.

"Stop that," he told her, frowning down at her.

She didn't listen to him. It wasn't like her not to listen to him. Her hackles rising, she crept to the entrance of the next chamber, where the trapdoor was, and took position before it, growling into the darkness on the other side.

Perhaps Issen-El had brought him another fish and it was flopping about. Beth had barked at the fish, too.

The old man lifted the lantern by its handle and made his way into the next room. Holding the lantern high, he paused. In the wobbling light, he saw something he had not seen in thirty years. Every time Issen-El brought him a gift, it was a good gift. But this was unexpected.

A young man lay on the floor, his back to the wall, a girl sheltered in his arms. They were soaking wet and neither of them moved as the light fell across their faces. Were they alive? The old man shushed his dog again, and this time, Beth obeyed. She growled. He set his hand on her. She fell silent.

In the quiet, he could hear ragged breathing. Yes, they were still alive. He shuffled closer and saw both of them were shivering, even in their sleep. It was not good to be wet through to the skin here on top of the mountain, with the wind and snow.

A gift from the sea.

"Issen-El," he said quietly, "why do you bring me these?"

chapter 34

First, the old man went to the second cabinet on the left and found his blankets. They were special blankets, a gift from Issen-El several years ago. He had discovered right away that whenever he thanked Issen-El for them, they grew warm, as if flames glowed in their fibers. He carried them into the back room, thanking Issen-El all the while, and by the time he reached his new gifts from the sea, the blankets had already begun to ease the pain in his hands. Heat would do that. He had held these blankets like this, wrapped around his hands, many times before. He kept one of them down at the house—the other two he kept here.

It wouldn't do to undress them, he thought, staring down at their faces. He could not bring himself to touch the girl that way, should she wake up in the midst of it and fear him, and he could not imagine the boy being all that pleased with it either. They would need to get out of these wet clothes eventually, but for now, the blankets would do.

He tucked them in soundly. Then he went about building a fire. For that, he opened the third cabinet on the left. It was a very deep cabinet, very tall. He had filled it three months ago, and he was glad now he had done so. The firewood it yet contained would be more than sufficient for one night.

"What do you think of this, Beth?" he asked her. He returned to the first cabinet for the match kit.

The dog wagged her tail at him and watched over the sleepers as he built the fire beside them. He did not know where the smoke went here in the back room, but it never made his eyes water. He tilted his head back and looked up at the stones of the ceiling and thought again that Issen-El always knew what he was doing.

The girl awoke first. That took him by surprise for, by this time, he was frying strips of dried beef in a skillet over the fire and he knew very well how boys liked to eat. He had made certain that the skillet was full.

She stared at him, peering out from beneath the blanket, her head resting near the crook of the boy's arm.

"Finlan," he said.

She just stared at him.

"That's my name." He tapped his chest.

Blonde hair and blue eyes. Many years had passed since he had seen coloring this fair. He held his breath, trying to remember the right words in a language he had not spoken in decades. *Ah, yes. There it is.* He could remember his grandfather teaching him these things. Whenever they had studied languages, he had not allowed young Finlan to speak anything other than the correct words in the language they were studying. *Someday you will need this,* he'd said.

"My name is Finlan," he said in Furmorean. "Do you

speak Furmorean?"

Her eyes widened slightly. She nodded against the boy's arm.

He smiled at her. "Good. I am making you supper here, and I have clothes for you. They'll hardly fit you and they're not for a girl. They're for a man—but they're dry. You should get out of that dress before you catch ill. We'll dry it by the fire."

She didn't move, and he supposed he could not blame her for that. She likely had no idea where she was. She would have questions for him—eventually. Many questions. He nodded toward his dog.

"This is Beth. She herds my sheep for me. We are friends."

At the mention of her name, Beth rose to her feet and approached the girl slowly, bending down to put her nose near the girl's forehead. Delight skittered through the girl's eyes, and she pulled the blanket up over her face.

The boy roused at her movements. He opened his eyes, blinking in the light.

Finlan saw the blankets move as the boy tightened his grip around the girl. Trying to set him at ease, Finlan smiled at him, too. "Finlan," he said again. "I am Finlan. Hungry? You'll need to change your clothes first."

The boy sat up slowly, pulling the girl up with him. He was bigger than Finlan had thought him to be. He was used to work, and judging by the scars running across his forehead and jaw, he had seen a few scuffles other than the one that had brought him here.

The girl reached a hand out from beneath the blanket. Beth padded closer and sniffed her fingers.

"Where are we?" the boy asked.

"Two days out of Galwin," Finlan answered, adding, "In Paxa."

"No, I mean…" The dark eyes again swept the room. "What is this?"

A reasonable question, considering where Finlan had found them. His gifts of the sea, handpicked by Issen-El. The corner of Finlan's mouth twitched. "A cave," he answered simply. "A cave on top of a mountain. I found you here, lying as you were lying just a moment ago. Sopping wet."

The boy looked at him for a long moment. "Who brought us here?"

"Issen-El brought you here. This is his cave. He made it for me, and he built me a door that brings me gifts from the sea." With the spoon, Finlan pointed to the trapdoor, fixed into the stone less than a foot away from where the boy's head had lain. "You were in the sea?" He did not need to ask the question, but he wanted to put the boy at ease.

A frown had crawled its way across the boy's face. He nodded slowly.

Finlan shrugged. "There you go. Issen-El brings me many things from the sea—but he has never brought me people before. There are clothes for you in the other room. Dry clothes. I will feed you when you are done changing. I imagine you're hungry."

The boy, like the girl, was not one who moved quickly. "I don't understand."

"What do you not understand?"

"Our ship was attacked by something in the water. It was large enough to stand on the bottom of the sea, and it lifted the boat off the waves."

Finlan grimaced. "A niessith."

"Excuse me?"

"What you describe—it is called a niessith. It attacks ships so it can eat the men aboard."

The boy looked at the girl. Both of them became very still, and Finlan guessed they had not been traveling alone, that they had had companions with them, and they were now dead.

"I do not understand how we are here," the boy said at last.

"I told you—Issen-El brought you. He brings me gifts from the sea. Not that *you* two are a gift, of course. Not in the same way." He smiled briefly. "I don't intend to keep you like a shell on my mantel."

The girl's gaze jerked to his. His jest seemed to have alarmed her.

"I'm teasing, my dear. I will help you reach wherever you wish to go. If you are feeling up to it, we can head down the mountain in the morning and see about buying you supplies in town. There would even be men to guide you, if you wished."

The boy glanced away, thoughts turning behind his eyes. He looked back. "How far are we from the coast?"

"About three hundred miles."

The girl paled.

The boy didn't move at all for a long time. When he finally did, it was to lean forward and exclaim, "Three hundred *miles*?"

"Yes. That is why I am so grateful to Issen-El for this place." Finlan leaned back and waved his hand about in an encompassing motion. "He brings me the sea. I was raised on the Paxan shoreline, just south of Port Soren—I am the end of a long line of fishermen. I miss the sea. I miss the water and the sounds of the swells and the salty scents of the breeze. But Issen-El made this cave for me, and he gives me gifts from the sea, even though it be at a great distance."

The girl made a decision for them both. She looked Finlan in the eyes and said, "My name is Amilia. This is my brother Myles."

Finlan smiled. "Very pleased. I am very pleased to meet you both."

chapter 35

Two hours later, old Finlan made up his bed and fell asleep on the other side of the fire. He soon filled the cave with the fierce growls of his snores. He could have silenced even Hileshand, who, until tonight, had been the loudest sleeper Amilia had ever witnessed.

She found she could not sleep. Every time she closed her eyes, she saw the niessith's face again. She felt its grip on her, squeezing the breath out of her. She again felt the same fear. She knew she was safe now—but that understanding did not help her heart to calm.

Myles feared nothing. Yet the moment she touched his shoulder, he sat up, looking down at her in the firelight. He had not been asleep either.

"I'm sorry," she whispered, glancing at the dog that lay at Finlan's feet.

Beth raised her head, ears pricked forward.

"This is just so odd. All of it. And I keep thinking about this morning..."

He motioned for her to come closer, and she did, pulling her blanket near his blanket. He leaned back against the stone wall, and she cuddled under his arm, shivering though she was no longer cold. It felt as if everything she feared had come to life today. She didn't know how she would ever be able to sleep again. She had been asleep when the niessith attacked.

After a very long time, Myles said, "I think Marcus may still be alive."

She looked up at him. Until this moment, she had not given much thought to Marcus and Hileshand. She couldn't. Her heart wrenched inside of her just at this one mention. "Why do you think that?" she whispered in reply.

He dropped his hand down her arm, gripping her near her elbow. "Something Ethan Strelleck said. I didn't understand it at the time. Still don't. But he talked about one of the gods of death wanting both of us alive."

"You trust the Alusian's words that much to…?" *To risk it?* she almost said. Almost, but the words jammed on her tongue. *To risk the hope of your brother's life?*

She felt his hesitation.

"Well," Myles said, "look at us. We're alive, and we shouldn't be. Someone obviously intends something. This Issen-El…I don't know who that is."

Neither did she. She had no understanding of the gods of Paxa. She sat up from under his arm and turned to face him. Her heart pounded. "What about…what about Hileshand? Did the Alusian say anything about Hileshand?"

Myles looked at her in silence. That told her as much as his words ever could. He reached out and caught her first tear, wiping it away with his thumb. "It is difficult to say," he finally answered.

"I need Hileshand," she whispered. She didn't want to cry, but now she was thinking thoughts she had not allowed herself to think, and now she was crying. "I need him to love me."

He brushed his thumb across the tears again.

"He told me I was worth something, when I didn't know why anybody would ever say that. He didn't just tell me he loved me. Every day, he did something different, just to prove to me how..." Her voice broke as the back of her throat filled with fire. "How much he meant what he said and that I was safe with him. I *need* him, Myles. I need that confidence." She tried very hard not to sob. "I need him to keep telling me how much he loves me. To remind me."

Amilia wasn't certain what happened after that. Her heart felt as if it were in jagged pieces. She was weeping. Her entire body ached with fear and sorrow, and suddenly, Myles leaned forward and kissed her. A small kiss. Not more than a touch. It was a brother's kiss, meant to comfort her. Marcus had kissed her this way as well.

She leaned away from him, staring at him in surprise. *A brother's kiss,* she thought again. *Nothing more. He can't handle your tears any more than Marcus could. He's just trying to make you feel better.*

But the ache in her chest dulled the voice of her wisdom. She couldn't function with this heartache, with the fear and the torment eating her alive. This had to stop.

She moved forward and put her mouth to his. She kissed him to alleviate the pain, to make room in her chest so she could breathe again.

Myles did not pull away from her.

She had wanted to kiss him like this for so long. He was the only man whose touch she had considered, desired even.

The only one, she thought, her fingers on his jaw.

But as the ache grew less severe, she began to think clearly. Wisdom, the little she had, returned to her, and she stiffened, her lips to his lips, feeling his breath. This was not what she wanted, not like this.

Slowly, she eased back. He watched her, his eyes dark. She could not tell what he was thinking.

Then he spoke. "Feel better?"

The words were gently asked, but still they jarred her. He knew the reason for her kiss, what the kiss was and what it was not.

"I'm sorry," she whispered. "I am so sorry. Sorry…"

What sort of creature was she? Every day for a month now, Hileshand had allowed her to live in a level of freedom, of shamelessness, that she had never expected to experience. But now Hileshand was dead, and what did she do straight away? She proved what she was. She revealed what she had known and used Myles to abate her pain.

"Hey, hey," Myles whispered. "Why do you cry this time?" Both of his thumbs were on her cheeks, his fingers on her ears, along the back of her neck. She saw the warmth of his smile in the firelight. "Don't be sorry."

He put his hands around her waist and lifted her into his lap, pulling her head to his shoulder and not allowing her to move it away when she tried. She wet the front of his borrowed tunic. She cried until she had no tears left for anything. She cried for Hileshand and Marcus. She cried for herself. She cried for Myles and the way he tried to comfort her, even when he shouldn't.

He just held her and kept running his hand over her hair.

An hour later, Myles became certain that she had fallen

asleep on his chest. The hiccupping sobs had dissipated, the touch of her breath growing slow and even against his throat. He thought about setting her down beside him but decided against it. He did not wish to disturb her, not when she so clearly needed to sleep.

Over the last month, this little girl had become as dear to him as the sisters who had grown up with him in Furmorea. He would do anything for them—he would do anything for her. He had comforted each of them in this way, in his arms—he would comfort her in this way as well.

But that kiss had not been a kiss for a brother. And his response to that kiss had not been a response for a sister.

Marcus' girl.

He looked down at the top of her head in the firelight. "What are you doing to me, little one?" he whispered to her, words of breath, not his full voice. She did not hear them, and she did not stir.

Marcus was the one who spent the most time with her. Marcus was the one she sought out first. Marcus had heard her cry much more often than Myles had, and subsequently, Marcus had comforted her much more often. No doubt, he had understood her thoughts as well, much better than Myles—why she did what she chose to do. Marcus had obviously cared for her.

Myles leaned his head back against the cold stone wall behind him and closed his eyes. He could understand all her tears, her desperation. He missed Hileshand. He missed his brother. The not knowing felt like a knife to his throat, something he could not handle or deal with, something that would kill him, unless he removed it as quickly as possible.

But there was no way for him to remove this. Not yet. Perhaps he never would be able to. There was the possibility of that. They may never know exactly what had happened today.

But for now, Amilia slept in his arms. She trusted him, and she slept here, with him, in his protection. This god of death that Ethan Strelleck had mentioned—he apparently did not wish for Myles to be alone. He had left him a companion.

Marcus' girl.

For a few hours at least, Myles could allow himself to imagine she was not Marcus' girl. He drew his hand down her hair again and felt her sigh.

chapter 36

As he always did, Finlan awoke just after dawn. He rubbed the sleep out of his eyes and turned toward what remained of the fire, fully expecting to find his companions as he had found them yesterday: sleeping like rocks.

But only Amilia lay there, facing the fire, her body wrapped up like a bundle in the blankets. Myles was not present. Neither was Beth, Finlan realized.

The old man walked into the cave's front room and found the third cabinet on the left, his wood cabinet, open and three-quarters filled. His ax was missing from its hook on the wall. Myles had exchanged Finlan's extra trousers for his own, which had dried last night by the fire, but he had left both shirts behind, draped across the table.

Finlan frowned as he picked up the boy's tunic. He hoped Myles wasn't too cold. It could be chilly up here on the mountain. The sun had barely risen.

He heard his dog barking, and he went to the cave mouth, peering down the slope.

Myles was coming up out of the trees, a final load of cut firewood set on his left shoulder. Beth was trying to herd him as she did the sheep. She barked madly and ran in circles around him, nipping at his boots. He grinned at her and made goading remarks.

Taking up his walking stick that leaned against the wall, Finlan stepped into the morning light and eased his weight down on the large stone to the right of the cave entrance. He held the walking stick in both hands and watched as his dog fell in love with a stranger.

Myles had a peculiar scar on his chest. It was shaped like a half-moon, the lines finely drawn, as if made on purpose.

Perhaps it had been. Finlan had lived a quiet life, away from the traffic of cities and different countries. He had visited Port Soren, the king's capital, only once and barely remembered it. He knew very little about Furmorea and her ways. Finlan studied the scar as the boy approached, then turned his gaze upward, to the boy's eyes, so he would not appear rude.

"Thank you," he said, "and good morning. How long have you been awake?"

"Awhile," the boy answered.

He carried the wood into the cave, and Finlan shakily stood to follow him, asking, "Did you sleep at all?" Issen-El had brought this boy and his sister to him—Finlan wanted to take care of them.

"I'll sleep better tonight," Myles answered and swung the wood off his shoulder with a single, smooth motion that made Finlan grin. He remembered what it had been like to be this age. Of course, he had been a Paxan fisherman, not a Furmorean farmer. There would be some obvious differences.

"I have something I would like to ask you," Myles said as he loaded the cabinet.

"Please do."

Instead of speaking his question there and then, Myles emptied his hands and walked over to the last cabinet on the left. It was a small one, built for small things. The door was open, which Finlan had not noticed until now. Myles picked up one of the small things—a short cylinder made of ash wood. It was about the size of his hand.

"The cabinet was open when I got up this morning," he said simply. "I saw this." He held up the piece of wood. "You have several of these."

Finlan nodded. "Aye. They are gifts from Issen-El."

Myles' brows rose. "All of them?"

The cabinet was nearly full. Finlan would need to make a second cabinet if Issen-El continued to bless him with little pieces of ash wood. He nodded. "Aye. In truth, I don't know why he likes them—but he does. There are few gifts he has repeated so many times through the years."

"These appear in the back room, just as we appeared?"

Finlan nodded again. "I can show you many other things he has given me from the sea as well. Why are you interested in these?"

Myles glanced at him, then turned the small piece of wood until he held it vertically in his left hand. "Because," he said, "I have seen one of these before. It was given to *me* as a gift, and I lost it when the niessith attacked. These are... unique."

He twisted the end of it with the fingers of his right hand. Without sound, the shaft began to lengthen. It grew until it was as long as Myles was tall, then the movement seemed to slow. Myles twisted the end a second time. Beneath his fingers, that end became a spearhead.

"Huh," Myles said, examining his handiwork more closely. "That is not what mine did."

Finlan did not know how to react to this. "It is a spear?" he said, reaching up to scratch the top of his head. Issen-El had given him gifts in secret. What glorious gifts these were! Full of surprises. He had thought them simple things, when they were not simple things.

Myles pointed at the small cabinet. "Do you know what you have here? Enough weapons for a small army. Why would your god give you weapons like this? Does your town come under attack? Are there creatures of the woods to way-lay you?"

"No, we are very peaceful."

"Then why would your god give you these things? You could always sell them, I suppose."

Finlan shook his head abruptly. "No. No, I do not sell what Issen-El gives me. I share them sometimes. On occasion, I have had good cause to give them away. But why would I sell something that he has given me as a gift? It must be that there is some other purpose for these little sticks. Perhaps he intends something other than war."

Myles held up the spear, ran his fingers lightly across the razored edges. "I believe a spear has but one purpose, Finlan. Issen-El would not give you a spear and anticipate something other than violence."

After completing his examination of the spearhead, Myles turned his attention to the haft and brushed his palm along the wood. Then he paused. He adjusted his grip and looked at the end of the shaft more closely. "There is writing here."

Beth barked from the doorway. Finlan shushed her with a waving hand at his hip. He approached the shaft himself, and Myles turned it so he, too, could see the words that had been etched there with a swirling, talented hand. They were beautifully written words, elegant and flowing—and, Finlan thought, completely difficult to read upside down.

He was delighted with all of this! He could not ease the smile on his lips. To think he had had this for so many years and never knew it was anything more than a stick of ash wood! This had been in his cabinet, just sitting there. What could the other sticks do? Myles had made it sound like they might be able to do all manner of things.

"It's a name—*Constance Perebole*," Myles read aloud. Raising his head, he frowned at Finlan. "Who is Constance Perebole? Does that happen to be someone you know?"

All words of depth and wisdom took wing and flew out of Finlan's head. Constance Perebole? Now, there was a name he had not heard in a long, long time.

Myles was staring at his face. "You know her, don't you?"

Finlan did not know what to make of this. He blinked several times and raised his gaze to meet Myles'. The young man had fire in his eyes, the passion of excitement. "It is a man," Finlan told him. "Not a woman. A man. And do I know him personally? No. I have only heard of him."

"Well, who is he?"

Finlan's brows rose. "A prophet. A prophet of Abalel. He lives near the sea and teaches a school in the woods."

He leaned forward and touched the wooden shaft with his fingers. It *felt* like real wood, but how had it grown like this? Issen-El was truly the most powerful of gods! He could create metal from wood, and he could send gifts through stone—he could save *two* people from a niessith and send them through stone, too. Who had ever heard of such strength? "If this belongs to him, shouldn't we take it to him?"

"You desire to take the spear to Perebole?"

"It has his name on it. Doesn't that mean it belongs to him?" Finlan gestured toward the cabinet and cried, "Open another! We shall check. We will see if there are more names."

They opened all of them. The entire cabinet's worth. By the time they were finished, Amilia had joined them and the sun had risen to a point directly above the mountain, spreading broad light like a curtain over the cave mouth.

With only one exception, every weapon bore the same name in the same script: *Constance Perebole.*

The exception was carved into the metal shaft of an ustrian bow, just below the grip.

Myles Elah Rosure Hileshand.

Four names. Finlan scratched his head again and wondered aloud, "What sort of man has *four* names? 'Tis your first name, boy, but the rest of it—sounds like a king. Four names." He laughed in the back of his throat. "'Tis no know I would possibly know."

Amilia put her hand on her brother's arm as he stood there staring at the bow in obvious surprise. He turned to her, and beneath his steady gaze, her look become as shy as the sun on a cloudy day. She almost pulled her hand away.

The old man observed this reaction, and a frown moved between his brows. This *was* her brother, was it not? She had introduced him that way. But he had seen looks like this before—and they were not given to brothers.

The girl swallowed, the muscles moving in her throat. She whispered, "Issen-El wanted to be sure you knew it was for you. So he used every name."

chapter 37

For three days, Marcus, Hileshand, and the rest of their party trudged east through a forest so thick that the trees grew up like blades of grass in a field. The ground was uneven in the darkness, distressed by layer upon layer of different root systems and decaying trunks and branches. Marcus doubted this soil had felt the warmth of sunlight in twenty years. A gnarled, twisted canopy hung above their heads. He had never seen a forest as overgrown as this one.

Their group consisted of thirteen men—every man who had been in the longboat. Captain Isule had refused to leave them. On the beach, he and Hileshand had almost come to blows about it, and Marcus had been somewhat surprised when the captain was the one who had arisen victorious.

Lord Claven gave me specific orders—sir. You saved the lives of ten of my men, myself included. I would bear a curse stronger than any grave if I defied my conscience, and Claven's orders, by leaving your side now.

No one understood loyalty more than Marcus' father,

and, being something of an intelligent man, Isule had formed his request with care and ultimately been successful in its delivery. *I will not leave your side, my lord. I owe you a great debt.* Every one of his men had agreed.

Hileshand did not tell them where they were going. But slowly, Marcus began to suspect their destination. His suspicions became fact when, on the afternoon of the fourth day, the trees unexpectedly parted, and the group came upon a gate and a red stone wall.

Marcus had never been in these woods before; he would have remembered the strangeness of them. But he had seen a gate like this some nine years ago, and the red wall stood out in his memory like a beacon. The first red wall had been in Galatia near the Supple River—a great distance from this location. Yet this wall had been built with the same stone.

This far north, the days were cool, the nights as amiable and neighborly as a winter's storm. Antonie had not been prepared for a wild march through the woods, and despite the current temperature, he was soaked with sweat. He imagined steam rising from his body. His legs had started bothering him the first day, and they had not adjusted to the expenditure of energy. Hileshand had driven them at a fanatical pace over miles and miles of vicious, unfriendly ground.

The destination, apparently, was a gate in the middle of the woods, set in a wall made of dark red stone that Antonie had not seen until they had come upon it. For the past six miles or so, he had been aware of eyes in the trees—something followed them. They were being watched. The feeling grew tenfold now that Hileshand's gate stood, closed and forbidding, before them.

The trees had been cut back from the wall, denied the touch of it. Antonie saw sunlight for the first time since they had landed on the beach, and he thought it lovely.

"Where are we?" the captain asked.

Antonie noted with some disgust that the man was not as winded as he should have been. He was twice Antonie's age, but that didn't seem to matter. Was Antonie truly this out of place with these men?

Hileshand glanced at the captain but otherwise ignored the question, something that had become his habit of late. Antonie had heard no more than a handful of words from him since the niessith had taken his children.

With that thought, Antonie looked over at Marcus. At least one had been spared. At least he had been able to save this one. The guilt swelled again in his gut, and Antonie released his breath in a huff, running the back of his hand across the sweat on his forehead. He should have been able to save them both. He had not realized the taking would happen so quickly. The beast was large and moving through water and wood—it should not have happened so quickly.

On the other side of the gate, soldiers appeared. They wore silver armor over purple and black garments—polished armor that reflected the sunlight like molten gold. None of the pieces had been touched by struggle. They were perfect, as if completed yesterday. These were not men who saw many battles.

They opened the gate.

One of the men bore the insignia of a Paxan captain over the left breast of his armor. Antonie wondered why there would be a military presence at Abalel's School. The man was about Hileshand's age and looked him in the eye, held his gaze. Then he nodded. "You have been expected.

Welcome to Ausham."

At that name, audible concern washed through the sailors.

Antonie was stunned. The weariness in his bones vanished. This was Ausham? The School of the Prophets? The gate was old, covered with ivy that stopped abruptly where the metal touched the wall; the red stones were clean of all living things. Through the iron bars, he could see nothing but trees and more trees—ancient, wrinkled trees, when he had heard this place contained an entire city.

He had also heard that the gate of Ausham was impossible to find. He could understand why people would say that, considering the "road" they had just traveled. How had Hileshand found it?

Immediately, the answer swept through Antonie's head, and he felt silly that he had even allowed the question to come to him. *Because Hileshand has been here before.* Realization filled him, an understanding so potent that he turned and looked at Hileshand in amazement. Hileshand had been here before.

Antonie wondered at his blindness. *That* was how Hileshand had bested the Ethollian sorcerer who had stood against him in Tarek. *Because he has training as a wizard.* Antonie had heard of followers of Abalel who had an ability to hear the god's voice. He had seen few Ruthanians as committed to Abalel as Hileshand was, a point that had made Antonie wonder.

What was the story here? Had Hileshand heard the god's voice as a child and been brought to Ausham by his parents? Had he heard it later in life, as a youth? Why had he not completed his studies? According to Antonie's reading, some men spent their entire lives behind these walls, while others went on to become priests or monks, speaking to Abalel and hearing his voice in the quiet of a monastery.

No wonder Hileshand had strode through the woods with such purpose, knowing exactly where he was going. This was a road he had taken many times before.

In addition to this surprising—nay, *startling*—discovery of Hileshand, Antonie marveled that the guards at the gate had been expecting them.

But perhaps that should not surprise him. This was, after all, the School of the Prophets. Those who heard Abalel's voice.

chapter 38

Antonie was not afraid until he stepped through the gate. On the outside of the wall, near the trees, he had felt nothing but fascination. *The gate of Ausham.* He had not expected fear, and he was not prepared for it.

Stepping through the gate was like walking through a vat of fire—fire he could not feel on his skin, yet it somehow made its presence known *beneath* his skin, which was far more alarming. He could feel something unknown and foreign sliding through his veins, drawing probing fingers along his muscles and ribs. In a matter of moments, severe panic had stripped his lungs of breath, and he stopped, just inside the gate. He did not mean to stop, but his boots became rooted to the ground and they would not move forward. *I have to leave. I have to get out of here.*

Several of Isule's men suffered the same reaction. Four or five of them stopped just over the threshold, appearing frozen all the way through their bones.

This is not a good place, Antonie thought rapidly. *I have to go. I can't stay here.*

Hileshand, unaware, with Isule beside him, followed the Paxan captain away from the gate. Antonie could not follow and could not understand why he could not follow. *What is this? I have to leave. Right now.*

Marcus came up beside him. Antonie stared at him, and Marcus, with a brief look of compassion, said, "It passes. Eventually." He shifted position and looked back at the rest of Isule's crew. Lines drew between his brows.

Antonie's heart pounded. "But what is it? And why does it come?"

Marcus returned his gaze to him. "You're a scribe. I assumed you were well read."

Antonie was well read. He was very well read. Lord Claven had insisted on that, and when Derek requested a scribe to accompany Myles, Lord Claven had done nothing less than offer the best he had. Antonie had been working for the king and his libraries when Claven had found him and pulled him away to work for him instead. "I…I don't know what this is."

"This is the place where Abalel dwells."

"I still don't understand."

"His touch affects men in different ways. Some step through the gate and feel nothing. Some step through and experience fear." His brows rose, and Marcus glanced down at the clear rigidity in Antonie's frame. "That is, as you can see, a common response. Others come through the gate and suddenly know what holds the answers to their questions."

"What questions?"

Marcus hesitated. He shrugged. "The important ones, I suppose."

Antonie's heart pounded severely, and he wondered if

he would die on his feet. Did Abalel mean to kill him? *Why are you doing this?* "What happened with you—when you came through the gate?"

"Marcus." Hileshand had stopped. Leaving Isule and the Paxan, he came back to retrieve his son. "I need you with me."

"Antonie and the others have…"

"They'll be fine," he answered shortly, without looking at any of them. "There is someone I want you to see. Come with me."

This time, the words conveyed a barely concealed order.

Marcus studied his father, the frown returning between his brows.

Antonie grimaced at the thought of being left here, at this infernal gate, and when it happened a moment later, he liked it even less than he'd thought he would.

The Paxan captain had said they were expected, and the statement was true. The abbot of Ausham, Jonathan Manda, appeared to be a generation older than Hileshand. A beard the color of cotton hung to the center of his chest, and the color was striking, for his skin bore the dark, weathered lines of a man who spent considerable time in the sun. Marcus wondered about that until he noticed the garden off to the side of the abbot's house. Most of the plants bore the browning leaves of autumn and other signs of the season's end. The trees had been cut back there, allowing for open sun. Jonathan liked to work the soil.

This was the first house they had come to—or, perhaps more aptly put, it was the first house Marcus had seen. They had walked for a quarter mile beyond the gate, and though he had heard voices several times drifting out of the woods, and had even seen other walkers, until now he had not seen anything that suggested people actually lived here. The School of the Prophets in Galatia was in the middle of a port city—there were buildings and fences and lampposts, not trees.

The sloped roof was covered with fallen leaves; they clung to it like crumbs in oil. The walls were nearly invisible beneath the dark reddish-green leaves of amber ivy. It was certainly the home of a gardener, someone who enjoyed the outdoors and growing things.

The old man had opened his door before they had knocked. His face was already glowing, and the light spread even further as he searched out Hileshand and saw him standing on his doorstep. "Myles," he exclaimed warmly.

The years seemed to bleed off his face as he smiled. The change was startling and left Marcus wondering how old the man actually was. Perhaps he was closer to Hileshand's age after all.

The two men embraced.

Jonathan patted Hileshand's back and said over his shoulder, "I have been waiting for this visit for years."

His voice squealed like the hinges of a door. It was not a pleasant voice; it was like the voice of a little boy, one who had not grown past four or five.

Hileshand pulled away from him, and the slight smile Marcus had seen on his lips, just briefly, ebbed into a thin line. Hileshand had not smiled in days. He rarely spoke. He had lost his pipe—the signature of his peace. In a short time, everything had changed about him. In a way, he felt foreign to Marcus. A stranger.

Jonathan had an uncanny ability to hear Abalel's voice. Hileshand had told many stories of this man, all of them impressive, all of them unique. The welcoming embrace now over, the abbot reached out an age-spotted hand and laid it on Hileshand's shoulder. Marcus thought he could almost feel the gesture. A touch of compassion. Of shared sorrow.

"I know the trouble that befell you on the ship," the old man whispered. "I am sorry for your loss."

His father nearly broke in that moment. Marcus, the pain squeezing his throat shut, looked away from the sudden emotions that filled Hileshand's eyes. He had been a slate of anger, an unmovable stone. Marcus now understood the reason they had come here, the reason his father had driven them so hard to get to this place. He had come in search of hope. One final chance at hope. And now, with the abbot's words, he did not find it. *I am sorry for your loss.*

Captain Isule, along with the three members of his crew who remained unaffected by their passage through the gate, stood there as true companions would stand. They turned their heads but did not falter as Hileshand struggled to contain what he had been containing for days.

His father drew a deep breath, let it out slowly. The sound trembled severely.

Then he did something Marcus had not anticipated.

He stepped behind Marcus and clamped his hands down on Marcus' shoulders. His grip was surprisingly strong. He shoved him forward a step.

"This," he told the abbot, "is my son Marcus."

Jonathan's smile reappeared slowly. "It has been thirty-five years, Myles. I am pleased that you have not forgotten the words spoken to you."

Stiff-lipped, Hileshand said, "You told me I could not return without him."

Marcus glanced at Hileshand over his shoulder. His father ignored the look.

He knew Hileshand had left Ausham under strained circumstances, but the exact details had never been shared with him. All Marcus knew was that a prophecy had been spoken—he did not know by whom—and it had been a difficult prophecy, one that had divided the council. Jonathan Manda had sided with Hileshand, while several other members of the council had sided with the former abbot, a man named Constance Perebole. Eventually Hileshand had been asked to leave.

His father spoke again, the words dangerously slow. "You told me that the next time you saw me, you would see my son."

The abbot stared at Marcus until a strange mixture of cold and heat began to twist through Marcus' stomach. *You told me I could not return without him.* He supposed he was about to find out what those words meant. But he could not fit this into his mind in any way that made sense. *Thirty-five years ago.* What had Jonathan Manda seen of him fourteen years before his birth? How had he been able to predict the steps of the journey that would lead them to this day, here, standing on his front stoop? The heat slowly disappeared from Marcus' stomach, and only the cold remained.

The old man shuffled forward and put a hand to Marcus' chest, pushing his fingertips into his tunic. He adjusted his touch and finally settled his right palm flat against the skin above Marcus' heart, as if he could, through his hand, feel something that lived on the other side of his ribs.

He had a peculiar touch. Marcus could feel it *inside* of him, shifting things within him. He began to see images in his head—things he knew had not happened yet, but they were inside him as if they already had, like memories. He saw an Alusian who was not Ethan Strelleck and a mountain that appeared to be on fire. He saw the rough, detail-less outlines of four little children he immediately knew were his own, and he stood there and marveled. There were other images as well, many others, but they were shadowed and he could make out none of them.

Hileshand's grip tightened on Marcus' shoulders.

At last, Jonathan shook his head and pulled his hand away. "This is your son," he said, stating the obvious. He looked at Hileshand with a disapproving frown. "But he is not the son I have seen. Is this how you desire to treat me after so long an absence? I see that bitterness has made you grow cold toward those you once cared for. You mean to mock me with your actions here—you have another son."

Before Marcus could process what all of that could possibly mean, his father's hands slid from his shoulders down his arms, and, gripping him around the elbows, Hileshand bent over and began to weep. His head came to rest on Marcus' back. Marcus felt every sob, every jagged intake of breath.

The ache in his chest became more than he could bear.

But then, as quickly as the tears had come, Hileshand was done with them. The weeping stopped. The hot, bruising grip on Marcus' elbows disappeared, and all at once, his father stepped in front of him and threw his arms around his neck, jerked him close, squeezed the breath out of him.

Marcus was searching for something to say, for some words of comfort, if they were possible here, when Hileshand started laughing. It was deep laughter, from the bottom of his belly. Hysterical laughter. Marcus had never heard his father laugh like this.

The grief had proven too much for Hileshand. His mental faculties had slipped into self-preservation.

Hileshand sucked in his breath and pulled away. He drew a rough hand across the wetness on his face and grinned at his son. "Your brother's alive. That bastard Ethan Strelleck was right."

He spun to face Jonathan, his friend. Hands lifted, he said, "Forgive me. I did not intend mockery. I simply had to know if there was hope." He laughed once, deep in his throat. "And I find there is." He gestured toward Marcus. "This is but one of my sons. I have a second."

chapter 39

They reached the town of Galwin on the evening of the second day.

This was Finlan's town. Amilia had not walked through the streets of a town this small for many years, since before her father's death. It was peaceful, just as Finlan had described, and she found she liked it. She liked the quiet, the way the walkways were nearly empty.

She also liked the way Finlan knew almost every person they saw. He waved and called out people's names. They waved back and wanted to know how he was. A few of them smiled in a pitying sort of way and asked what Issen-El had brought him recently. Finlan smiled back and said, "A great many things."

Myles saw to the horses while Finlan and Amilia stepped into the Inn of the Third River to reserve a room.

Just inside the door, the old man paused. He scanned the room quietly and reached back to clamp his hand around her arm.

"I think we should spend the night on the road again," he whispered and returned them both outside onto the covered porch.

"Why?" she asked, glancing back at the door.

He shook his head and scowled. "Did you not see the Alusian?"

Myles was still in the stables, rubbing down the gelding. Finlan told him what he had seen, and Amilia, who had been looking forward to a bed tonight, folded her arms and huffed in protest.

"An Alusian," Myles repeated, coming alert. He looked out through the doorway across the inn's small courtyard.

The inn was an older building. At one time, it had been painted red, but the color had faded to a dull brown. The paint had cracked in many places, peeling back to reveal the gray wood below. In a way, its appearance spoke of the entire town, as well as Finlan himself—it was old yet comfortable. Perhaps it was in need of repair, but no one minded.

"Finlan, you said we needed a guide to this school. You said it was difficult to find."

The old man frowned. "Aye, that I did."

"A *guide*, Finlan. The Alusian would be a perfect choice."

"Have you lost your senses, boy? Don't you know what an Alusian is? Don't you know what her presence means here tonight?" His brows screwed together, and he said in a whisper, "'Tis a small town. I know everyone who lives here. And tomorrow, one of these dear families will have suffered a loss. Someone will mourn what happens tonight forever."

"You blame her for this? Would not the death have occurred whether she was here or not?"

Finlan reddened. "What is your intent with this, Myles?

I don't understand why you think this a good idea. I know you are not a fool. I know you are not daft—so what is your intent?"

Myles smiled darkly. "Conversation," he answered.

Amilia and Finlan stood there and watched him walk out of the stables, headed for the inn.

Finlan shook his head. "Are you certain the two of you share blood?"

"I think he knows many more things than he says," Amilia answered. She met Finlan's gaze, smiled at him briefly, and then ran across the court to fall into step beside the man who was not her brother.

"I'm coming," she told him, remembering all the stories she had heard about Ethan Strelleck. Alarming stories, to be sure. But in the midst of everything that had happened, he had saved two lives that were very dear to her. So she did not think he could be *completely* frightening.

She felt Myles' gaze and the warmth of his approval, and at that moment, she didn't care if the Alusian killed them. These steps she took now were worth it.

"Good," Myles answered. "I am glad."

The Alusian was uncommonly beautiful. Amilia knew the price of beauty like this, what a face of this grandeur would sell for in Tarek. She could not help her thoughts as she and Myles approached the creature's table; they resulted from years of training, which could be undone only with time.

The creature had white skin, eyes that appeared like black stones beneath her brows, and dark hair that hung in a braid over her shoulder. She wore a cloak, even though she sat near the fire—alone at a table in the back corner.

There was a glass of something dark near her right hand and a book in her left. She had been reading, which Amilia thought curious.

However, as the two of them stepped into the room, the head came up, and the book lowered.

They stopped in front of her table.

Amilia slowly grew aware of how quiet the rest of the room had become. People had been trading hushed whispers when she and Myles had entered; now they did not. She felt their stares.

The creature pulled in several large, full-lunged breaths.

"Evening," Myles said quietly.

The Alusian stared at him. The dark eyes turned to Amilia, who tried very hard not to reveal the tension that spilled forth in her stomach. Myles wanted to do this—she was going to stand here with him, and she was not going to be fearful.

After completing a long study, the Alusian returned her gaze to Myles. The clear eyes narrowed. "I am Bithania Elemara Amary."

An elegant name. Somehow, it perfectly matched the image she presented. The skin. The eyes. Every element in place. The smooth sort of darkness that, no doubt, drew the eyes of every man in the room.

"Who are you?" the creature asked.

"I am Myles Hileshand."

Again, Amilia tried not to react. With apparent ease, he stated something he had never stated before. *Myles Hileshand.* Why did he claim that name now, after resisting it all this time? She smiled without meaning to, and the creature glanced at her again.

"And you?"

Her mouth suddenly felt dry. "Amilia Hileshand."

The dark brows rose as the creature studied her. "I will not speak your fortune."

Bithania looked directly at her as she said these words, and Amilia knew she meant them for her alone; she did not mean them for Myles—his fortune she would speak. Amilia began to smile a second time, and the Alusian frowned at her.

"You do not understand," she said. "There is a reason I will not speak your fortune."

Amilia's smile faded.

"We do not require our fortunes told," Myles answered. "I have a request. Will you say yes to it?"

The silence in the room became as loud as a shout. Amilia began to feel it pressing against her, almost as if it had hands. Her heart jumped forward in its paces, and she did what she could to hold to her peace. What was Myles' understanding of this creature that sat before them now? He did not even *make* his request; he desired an answer to a request he had not spoken. Could he do that?

Yes, apparently he could.

The creature stood from the table, book in hand. "Yes. I will accompany you as your guide. But you should know that this journey carries a high price—for you."

The dark gaze moved back to Amilia.

Amilia found herself trembling.

"And it carries a higher price for her. It is a price neither of you will wish to pay when the time comes."

A severe sort of chill raced up Amilia's spine. She began to think that perhaps, this had been a bad idea after all.

But Myles was not concerned. In fact, he smiled. Amilia heard the mild amusement in his voice as he said, "Say what you will, but I have yet to meet an Alusian who does not tell me my fortune. Your terms do not alarm me. We leave at first light. Does this suit you?"

The creature measured him with a heavy stare. Her gaze flickered through the rest of the room, at the faces that watched with wide eyes, and then she returned to her seat. "It does."

"Good."

Myles took Amilia's hand and walked her out of the room.

chapter 40

"A high price, Myles. What do you think she meant?"

The hour was late now. Finlan lay on the other bed, snoring like one of the *atham-laine*, his back to them. Amilia would always be impressed with the noises this old man could make.

Myles sat on the edge of her bed. She was sitting next to him, her feet tucked up underneath her, the blanket gathered around her legs.

A moment passed in which Finlan's minor roars were the only sound.

When Myles did speak, he did not answer her question. Not exactly. "You told me once that you would answer any question I asked of you."

Amilia looked at him. "Yes," she said slowly, "I did. But...but why do you say this now?"

He moved on the bed, turning to face her. His gaze intent, he asked, "Are you in love with my brother?"

Everything in her body grew very, very still. He asked that now? *Now* he asked that? That was what he desired to know? She wet her lips and whispered, "No," wondering what he was doing.

Her answer caused no reaction in his eyes. She could not tell his thoughts, except that they were strong; there was a firm intent behind what he was doing now.

He asked another question. "Is he in love with you?"

Her voice quieted even more. "No."

He stared at her for a long moment. She began to feel his gaze inside of her, as if it pushed on her heart.

"You are certain of this?"

There had been many conversations. Many long talks. Because of them, Marcus was well aware that she loved another. "I am certain. Why, Myles? Why do you ask me these things?"

With incredible slowness, he said, "I know the high price the Alusian meant."

She waited for him to continue. He did not. He simply sat there on the bed, his gaze moving over her face with a strength and a sincerity she had seen from him only in certain moments. They had been brief looks in the past, nothing more than flickers that quickly disappeared. But this time, they lasted until, slowly, she began to realize what she was seeing. As a result, she could not breathe.

"Do you know what Ethan Strelleck told me, Amilia?" he asked in a conversational way. He already knew the answer to his question.

He loved her. The one he shouldn't love—he loved *her*.

Ethan Strelleck? She could not think of anything else except what she knew now, what Myles showed her now. How could he love her? How could all her hope possibly be telling her the truth right now? But Myles would not do this weakly or without putting long thought into it. Everything he did, he did on purpose, with the fullness of his strength.

Then he spoke again, and the glowing hope within her froze.

Myles said in a whisper, "He told me I was going to die." He blinked and looked away. "I haven't told anyone that. No one heard him say this to me. Hileshand doesn't know. Marcus…" He shook his head, and his gaze returned to her. "Only you. That is the price, little one. A price that neither of us will want to pay."

The backs of her eyes felt like they were on fire. "I don't…I don't understand. Did he not tell you that you were to live? Hileshand said—"

Myles nodded. "Yes, but he *also* said, outside of Hileshand's hearing, that the one who preserved me would eventually take what he preserved. Life for a time. Only a season. That is what he meant."

He put his fingers to the side of her face, brushed hair behind her ear, touched her chin. "A high price."

Her stomach, her lungs, and her heart responded the way they always responded when he touched her. She could not move. Breathing remained difficult. She thought of all the things they had never spoken of but he could likely imagine—the darkness of her history. Unmentionable things. Then she did, of course, consider again the one element he would not be able to imagine, the thing he could not expect. She wondered at all the fears that kept her silent, when she needed to tell him the truth. *Myles.*

Drawing in her breath, she made her decision. The fear could wait. She knew what she wanted.

"I have paid high prices before," she whispered.

He frowned and shook his head. "This is one you will not pay."

"But..." She swallowed. "I would pay it anyway. I *will* pay it anyway. Do you understand? It doesn't matter what you say. It doesn't matter what you decide to do now." Her voice broke. "I still would be lost."

Sliding a hand around the back of her head, he pulled her to him. The last kiss had removed her pain and calmed her fears. This kiss did the same, but it was entirely different. He had her heart with this kiss. It was a first kiss. For Myles.

He eased away from her and released his breath in an uneven sigh. "I will not have you walk this road."

"I am going to walk this road, Myles. It is out of your hands."

"I will not do this to you."

"Myles...Why do you not understand me? Do what you will—your choice tonight does not matter. My heart will be broken either way."

All she saw in his eyes now was resignation and resolve. Another sigh escaped him, this one much longer, and steadier, than the first. He was considering.

This is one price you will not pay. Horrific words.

The burning in her eyes became full-fledged tears. She touched his face. "You don't understand," she repeated, her voice trembling. "The price will be paid whether you wish it to be or not."

She leaned close and used her mouth to demonstrate her heart, and gradually, Ethan Strelleck seemed less and less important.

She slid her hands beneath Myles' tunic. The ends of her fingers formed a slow, purposeful acquaintance with the lines of his chest. The sound of his breathing changed with every movement of her hands across his skin.

She would have done anything Myles asked in that moment. She intended to. Finlan slept like the dead, his snores proclaiming his distance from the living. Essentially, the two of them were alone.

But Myles caught her hands and leaned forward, putting his forehead to hers.

After a time, he whispered, "Not now, Amilia." The Furmorean words were thickly spoken. He pulled a finger down her cheek and held to what the land of her birth had taught him, traditions she had forgotten. All at once, she remembered them and cursed them in her head.

But then he spoke again. "I will not do to you what others have done. I will give you what you are worth."

He kissed her as she had kissed him. He did not hurry and he said many things without words. She could barely breathe by the time he returned to his pallet on the floor before the fire.

After hours and hours of thinking and anticipating and hoping as she had never hoped before, she fell asleep to the sound of Finlan's jagged snores, a smile on her lips.

chapter 41

At dawn the next morning, the Alusian was waiting for them in the main room downstairs, sitting at a table,
her book in her hands. When she saw them, she breathed
one of those full-chested sighs and stood to her feet, sliding
the book into her bag.

Finlan thought this a terrible idea. He shuddered as the
creature's dark, alluring gaze swept over him, and he wondered which of the families had suffered loss this night.

The creature looked at Amilia until the girl shifted un-
comfortably. Then her gaze went to Myles. "We should leave
now."

Finlan knew it—she had killed someone.

They saddled the horses and rode out of town by way of
the westward road.

For five days, Bithania compelled them forward at a
pace Finlan had not intended. At times, her prodding was
subtle—a word placed here or there. A fierce frown. At other

times, she was much more forceful and, in Finlan's opinion, drastically unpleasant. He knew Myles noticed her behavior, but the boy did not comment on it. He seemed content to give her her head, as he would a horse, allowing her whatever pace she desired.

Not healthy, Finlan thought. *Not a healthy practice.*

They were going to visit Abalel and his School of the Prophets. They would present Constance Perebole with a brilliant gift—a knapsack full of pieces of ash wood. Then, if Abalel chose to be gracious, Myles planned to ask for information regarding his brother and father. The boy had a good deal of honor in his soul; Finlan suspected he would have made this journey even without the enticement of prophecy, if Finlan had only asked him. But still, Myles suffered hope. He wished for good news.

Finlan knew the brother and father were dead. As a boy, he had seen the niessith destroy a ship, and several *years* had passed before he had been able to enter the sea again without fear. The niessith were evil. Issen-El had saved Myles and his sister, bringing them up from the waters, but the father and brother were not here. Finlan thought that answer enough. Myles, of course, would not accept it. He wished to know what Abalel would say.

In the late evening of the sixth day, they reached Gar'rodd at the base of the foothills. Finlan knew this town was much larger than his home of Galwin, but he had not made this journey in several years, and he was unprepared for how quickly the town had grown. It was a small city now, with multiple temples and trading districts and a flourishing harbor. He sat on the back of his horse and looked around in a stupor.

They reserved a room at the First House, an inn near the harbor. The window had a very pretty view of the river.

Finlan pushed the pane open and pulled in a deep breath, smelling the familiar stench of the Redaman River, as well as bread baking in the little shop across the street. Good smells, both of them. His old bones ached. He looked forward to a bed.

The Alusian had reserved her own room. To Finlan's relief, she did not intend to bed near them. The sleeping arrangements were fine out on the road, in open spaces, but he did not enjoy the thought of her sleeping near him when walls were involved.

For a few minutes, she left them alone. Then she appeared in their doorway, unbidden.

"Myles," she said.

All three of them stopped what they were doing and stared at her.

"Myles," she said again, "walk the street with me."

She did not intend it as a suggestion.

Myles slowly sat down on the edge of the bed and pulled off one of his boots. He dropped it on the floor with a thud and looked up at the creature in the doorway. "No," he said calmly.

Finlan and Amilia looked at each other. The old man frowned, gripping the windowsill beside him with one white-knuckled hand. Had the boy lost his senses? He told her no?

"First light," Myles said. "I will walk with you then. But not tonight."

Without frown or word, Bithania nodded and returned to her own room. Finlan shivered and wondered if any of them would be alive come morning.

True to his word, Myles pulled on his cloak the next

morning and stepped out into the hallway just as the first touches of gray were extending beyond the eastern peaks.

He found Bithania on the porch.

She did not greet him. She simply walked down the steps and headed east, toward the haze of gray light over the now-distant mountains. He fell into step beside her. In the early morning shadows, her race was not distinguishable from any other. Those they passed on the street did not stare.

For half an hour she did not speak to him. She walked only.

He waited. It would appear that something was on her mind.

"I will not speak the girl's fortune," she said at last.

Myles glanced at her, immediately wary of those words. "You said you would not. You have already made this clear." When she said nothing more, he prodded, "Why do you feel it necessary to state this again?"

"To speak her fortune, I would have to speak yours."

Her steps slowed. She stopped on the wooden walkway, the river to her right, the rest of the city to her left, and faced him. A corner of her mouth rose. Myles sensed it was as much of a smile as she could give.

"The males of my kind," she said, "will not interfere with the affairs of man. If given the choice, they will not do so. I know you understand this. I, however, am female, and the situation is different for us. We interfere all the time. I am going to tell you things that you will not enjoy knowing. I do not speak your fortune here. I will not do that. But I will speak your current journey."

Myles folded his arms and, again, waited for her words. *An interesting turn of events,* he thought. Until now, a child who was just learning his letters could have transcribed the words Bithania had spoken during their journey—they were that few. This was, by far, the most she had said in his hearing.

"The woods of the lower country, near the sea," she said, nodding her head in a northwesterly direction, "are inhabited by the miron. They often resemble men. They live in the trees. In a few days, they begin their mating rituals. I had hoped we could be beyond the lake by this time, but the old man cannot travel as quickly as I would wish. Because of him, your journey is going to be much more difficult."

"Why?" Myles asked.

"Because the girl is pregnant."

The words did not quickly fall into order in Myles' head. He almost asked her, *What girl?* But there was only one girl she could mean. He leaned forward slightly. "Pregnant," he repeated.

Bithania studied him. "The girl," she said with undue clarity, "had relations with a man, and now she is pregnant. The later she is in her stages, the more the miron will seek her. I will not tell you why. I do not wish your anger. She nears her fifth month. When she enters the woods, they will find out, and they will know she is with child."

Myles attempted to set aside the emotions that rose within him as she said these things. It was difficult for him to do. The memory of Amilia's kiss seven days ago was not something he could easily shove away. He had not touched her since then, but thoughts of doing so were becoming more and more difficult to manage. *You don't understand,* she had told him. *The price will be paid whether you wish it to be or not.* The words haunted him.

How could she be pregnant? Why had she not told him? Hileshand had said the pregnancy was terminated.

Was it possible the Alusian lied to him in this?

Myles watched the dark eyes returning his stare steadily. He remembered Ethan Strelleck and could not conceive of a reason for either of these creatures to stoop to falsehood. Yes. He believed her. He wished he didn't.

Pulling in a deep breath, he forced a level of calm through his tone. "This is a thriving city. Children are born here. The city walls are low, with trees on both sides. Surely, if your words were accurate and true danger existed here, I would have heard this story. The city would not prosper within the shadow of a woods filled with things that seek pregnant women."

"The miron are dangerous only during their mating season. And this is their mating season."

Time was sliding by them. The sky had lightened enough to make the pallor of her skin and the darkness of her hair and eyes visible and gleaming to those who passed nearby on the walkway. She was no longer unobserved. People avoided her the way polished men of the court would avoid a carcass dragged in from the field.

He noticed stares directed toward himself as well, some curious, most fearful. "Then give me *eshtareth*. Tell me the past. Help me to understand this." Nothing was going to touch Amilia. Nothing was going to harm her. Nothing at all.

Bithania stared at him. She drew in a full-lunged breath, released it. She reached out her hand and set it on his chest.

He could hear gasps somewhere nearby. People watched this. Myles heard the word *companion* whispered several times.

"You," the Alusian said slowly, "cannot save her."

She was wrong. He was going to save her.

Bithania appeared to have heard his thoughts. "No," she

said, stepping closer to him. She was tall for a woman. She could look him in the eyes. "You cannot save her. If you try, you will discover your limitations and come to understand I speak the truth. This is out of your hands."

He didn't care what she told him. In this instance, she was wrong. "Then we will take another road."

Her fist tightened on his tunic. "You made a request of me. You wish to reach the gate of Ausham. The god of Ausham desires a certain road be taken." Her free hand jerked up. She pointed northwest angrily, toward the miron-infested woods. "*That* is the road. I told you my services required a price, and I told you that the price was high, that the girl would feel it the most severely. You should have considered my words."

$\mathcal{F}$inlan was waiting for Myles. He saw the boy's expression and knew the Alusian was everything he had feared her to be.

"What's wrong?" Finlan asked in a quiet voice.

Amilia was yet asleep, the blankets pulled up near her head. The road would be long for them today. The woods beyond the harbor were unsafe, and it was wise not to spend the night in them. Yet the next town was about ten hours away, so a very long day awaited them. *Best let the girl sleep while she can.*

Myles came next to him and leaned against the windowsill. He folded his arms and demanded, "What do you know about the road to Ausham? Is there only one road that can be taken?"

Oh, so that was what it was. Finlan shrugged. "I cannot tell you that, Myles. I already told you all I know about Perebole's school." His brows rose. "Several times, in fact."

The boy's expression grew more severe. "Every man who

would wish to reach Ausham *must* take the northern road from here?"

"I don't know," Finlan repeated. He hesitated. "Ausham is not like Galwin, Myles. It is not like Gar'rodd either, or any other city of men. The road to the city is difficult to find." That was why they needed a guide. Myles should know all these things.

"What do you know of the miron? They are creatures that look like men and live in the trees."

"Was *that* what the Alusian told you?"

Myles closely examined Finlan's response. "Yes. And she…" The anger of his expression began to ease as he looked toward his sister, asleep and quiet in the bed. He blew his breath out. "You know what the miron are?"

"I have heard of them. They are unique to northern Paxa, and I also know they have unique rituals—things they do with fire. The northern woods are considered unsafe. In addition, I know that many avoid the road we desire to take because of thieves."

"What road do they take instead?"

Finlan offered a half-shrug and nodded toward the river out the window. "I believe most prefer the river." He watched the boy and tried to determine what frustrated him this way. "Did the Alusian tell you something would befall us on the northern road?"

The boy grunted. "She said the miron would attack my…" He stopped speaking. After a moment, he said, "She said Amilia was in danger." The anger returned. "And she *refused* to believe I could keep her safe."

"Of course you can't keep her safe, boy."

Myles glanced at him sharply.

Finlan shrugged. "You can put up a good fight, but in

the end, only Issen-El can keep anyone safe."

Myles rolled his eyes and pushed off the windowsill. Then, quickly, he realized the visibility of his thoughts and grimaced. "I'm sorry. My anger is not against you."

Finlan knew that. "If you want to take another road, we can take another road."

"If we make that decision, I am not certain Bithania would continue with us. Would we be able to find another guide in Dorsare?"

Finlan smiled grimly. "If Issen-El wishes it, we could find the king in Dorsare."

The possibility of parting company with the Alusian gave him a peace of mind that he had not experienced since before he had first seen her, back in Galwin. He nodded to himself. *A good decision.* That creature was dangerous.

Myles went and sat on the edge of Amilia's bed. He put his hand on her shoulder. "*Aufane,*" he whispered, using a Furmorean word Finlan had never heard before. "Time to rise."

The girl stirred. The blankets moved. She saw Myles there and a glow of perfect contentment slid through her sleep-filled expression. "Myles..."

Her brother ran his hand over her hair. Again he used the word Finlan did not know. "*Aufane,* we need to go."

The girl stared at him. Then a smile parted her lips and she reached for the hand that brushed her hair, drawing it to her mouth and kissing the back of it.

Myles knocked on the Alusian's door. She did not answer.

"Bithania," he called.

He tried the handle. The door was unlocked. He pushed

it back slowly.

The room was empty. Her pack was gone. A piece of paper had been left on the bed.

Slowly, with another wary look through the room, he walked over and lifted the page off the blanket.

Myles, she had written in a sharp-edged, tight script, *I understand the decision you made, and despite your thoughts concerning me, I appreciate that you made it at all. Your kind is not fond of making difficult decisions, nor are they eager to argue with me. I have never had a man oppose me as you oppose me. Thank you.*

Myles smiled.

What you seek awaits you at Ausham. The easiest road is the northern road; traveling by river is much more difficult. I give you a word of caution: Once you are out of the harbor, do not enter the water between here and Dorsare. Do not touch it at all.

Her closure gave him pause. He read the words three times before the pace of his heart realigned itself with something resembling calm.

Amilia's child is male, and his name has been decided. It is your name. But you should know that the girl did not do this. He was named by another. The one who preserves you considers him yours. This story is not the story you expect it to be, Myles. Do not let the surprise alarm you.

She had signed her full name: *Bithania Elemara Amary.*

For a long moment, Myles simply stood there, letter in hand. He looked through the room again, then folded the page and slid it into the interior pocket of his cloak, beside the ash stick that belonged to him, the one with all four names. He set his hand on top of both items.

This is not the story you expect it to be.

He had heard those words before. Not about him, but about Amilia. Ethan Strelleck had looked at Hileshand and said the same words Bithania had written here. Myles was no closer to understanding them now than he had been the first time he'd heard them.

To speak her fortune, I would have to speak yours.

He scowled fiercely. Why the interest? Why did both Bithania and Strelleck—in addition to this other entity, the nameless god of death who *preserved* him—wish to be so involved in the processes of his life and heart? *Why?* What did they imagine they would receive in all of this?

Bithania and Strelleck claimed they would not speak his fortune, but that was, in essence, the only thing they did. The child was his child. Amilia's fortune was his fortune. Were not these prophecies? Didn't these statements suggest a certain future?

The room remained quiet. The direction of his thoughts formed nothing tangible. The answer did not appear before him.

chapter 43

Amilia was quiet after Myles informed her of the change in plans. He watched her as she laced up her boots and gathered her things, the motions stiff and oddly sterile.

Finlan glanced at him behind her back.

Myles shrugged. He did not know what this peculiar silence was.

She did not speak her mind until after Finlan left to see about booking passage on one of the vessels waiting in the harbor. The moment the door closed after him, everything became wet and weepy and something of a disaster.

She tried to speak and could not do it. Myles held her against his chest as he leaned on the windowsill and waited for her to calm.

Eventually she managed to say, "Not a ship, Myles. I couldn't be on a ship."

He frowned. "Amilia..."

"Do not ask this of me. I could be on the road for a year. I wouldn't mind a longer route. I wouldn't mind the rain or the snow—just do not take me on a ship, Myles. I could not be on a ship again."

He ran his hand over her hair, kissed the top of her head. "*Aufane*," he whispered, "my love, this is a river. It is not the sea. We are yet miles from any saltwater port. You will never see the niessith again."

She trembled severely.

"Six days. That is all. Our journey by boat would consist of six days."

She shook her head. He could hear every quiver in her lungs, every throb of fear down her spine. "No, Myles. I...I cannot do this. I don't care what Bithania told you about the northern road."

He had not told her everything. She had heard a warning of creatures in the woods; that was all. As a result, she thought this a small concern for him, that he was just trying to make the journey easier for her. She had no comprehension of the strength that stormed within him now.

She was so small. He could hold her so well here, covered in his arms like this. Slowly, a new thought came to him. He did not hold just one person against him now—he held two. *Her fortune, your fortune. Her child, your son.*

He was not about to allow that creature of death to dictate any course in his life, especially not this one. But her words were like the key to a door he was trying to keep closed. They were words of power and magic. Somewhere within him, he suspected that everything Bithania had told him, everything Strelleck had told him, the positive words and the negative words—all of it was true.

What are you doing to me, little one? he asked Amilia silently, staring down at the top of her head.

This was his if he wanted it to be. He could have this,

until the god of death was successful in his final purging.

As he thought about that, as he held her like this, he felt the bonds within him give way just a little bit more. The door unlocked. *Curse it all*, he thought.

"Amilia," he said.

She did not respond, but the tears were sniffed back and she tried to hold still.

"Is there something you would like to tell me?"

Slowly, her head leaned back, and even more slowly, she looked up at him, concern in her blue eyes, vibrant with her tears.

He waited.

She wet her lips and whispered, "Yes. But not now. Not yet."

A smile pulled across his lips. He could accept that answer. Words came to him, something he could say and mean, but he refrained. *Not now. Not yet.* If he spoke those words at all, it would be when she trusted him fully. In the meantime, he would show her she could.

Finlan walked in at a mildly awkward moment.

The old man stopped on the threshold, his hand appearing stuck to the door handle as he stared at them. Confusion washed across his features and then, more quickly than it should have, the light of realization. He had suspected. Myles grinned, and Finlan pointed one gnarled old finger at him.

"That," he said, "is not your sister." He paused and added, "I trust."

"It's an interesting story," Myles answered.

Amilia leaned against him and released her breath in a sigh, her head coming to rest on his cloak and a folded piece of paper in the pocket.

Myles was incredibly aware of her every small movement, her every breath.

Nothing could happen to her. He would never put her in danger or in any situation in which he could not save her.

He would soothe her fears. They would take the ship.

chapter 44

Two days after their arrival in Ausham, Marcus and Hileshand left for the coast. Antonie and Isule accompanied them, as well as several of the captain's men.

One full day before the trees parted and the long, white stretch of sand became visible, they began to smell the niessith's decaying body. The stench grew much worse as they neared the beach. They held cloths to their faces, covering their noses, but the relief was slight.

Marcus stepped out of the trees and beheld the repugnant sight he had been preparing himself to see for several days. It was worse than he had imagined, and standing there on the sand with the others, he wondered if he would ever be able to get this scene out of his head.

The beach was strewn with signs of massacre and death. There were pieces of the ship and items from her cargo, bodies and pieces of men—ripped apart and dragged by creatures of the woods and, likely, creatures of the sea as well. Marcus had heard of water-dwelling animals that could come out of the waves to take flesh off the sand. It had happened before.

The niessith lay on the sand almost like a man, half in the water, half exposed. The green head was tilted back against the sand, mouth agape, arms out to the sides. The horde of tentacles spread out from the body like a carpet in all directions. The end of one curling, vicious appendage lay near Marcus' boots. He squatted down for a closer look. The rotting flesh was covered with small suckers, like mouths—the reason for all the hissing. And the reason he had been unable to pry the cold loops off his body.

A small piece of wood stuck up out of the sand near the niessith's tentacle, barely noticeable amid the wreckage that covered the beach. It was about the width of his finger, and the end of it was flat, as if it had been cut off with a knife. Something about it looked familiar to him. Shifting his footing in the sand, he reached over and pulled it free. It left the sand easily.

He knew what this was. Cold washed down Marcus' body as he realized he held the ax Ethan Strelleck had given to Myles in Tarek, the night Myles had fought the *atham-laine*. High tide must have washed the six-inch piece of wood ashore. It truly did resemble nothing more than a stick, but Marcus had seen Myles with it countless times. They had discussed it at length, both of them examining it.

How would this day have been different if this weapon had been used against the niessith instead of a sword? The double-headed blade contained magic. Myles had brought the *atham-laine* down with barely a hit.

Thinking of Myles and Amilia, Marcus scowled and stood to his feet.

Isule stared at the niessith's body. Sprawled on the sand

like this, the creature was as tall as the trees standing behind them. It was huge, even in decay.

Isule reached over and patted Hileshand on the back. "Well done," he said simply, the words subdued. "Well done."

They were not the only ones interested in this ghastly scene. Three ships were anchored to the south. Several men of the different crews were poking around the dead. Marcus gripped the Alusian weapon in his hand and wondered how anyone could show such disrespect to the dead. He had known the men who lay here—during their voyage, some of them had become his friends. No one among the scavengers was interested in burying them properly. There was no sorrow here. There was only greed.

Marcus noticed that some items belonging to Hileshand were now in the possession of others. Marcus looked at him, more than willing to see them returned to him, but his father shook his head.

"It's too late, Marcus," he said quietly.

Marcus looked away. His eyes burned.

Hileshand told everyone they saw the same thing: "We are looking for two people." He described them, gesturing toward Marcus, detailing the scars on his twin's face. He described Amilia: blonde hair, blue eyes—and more lovely than others, the most beautiful girl they had seen in their lives. Surely, these things would make her memorable.

No one had seen them.

That was the answer in Port Soren as well. They spent three days on the docks and another three days in the city itself. No one recognized Marcus. No one remembered Amilia.

"Destination, my lord?" Isule asked finally.

Hileshand ran his hands over his face, was quiet as he thought. Marcus could sense the weight on his father's shoulders. He felt the same weight himself. Both of them were fully convinced of Myles' life, and for Amilia, Marcus had hope as well. If Myles unexpectedly lived, then *surely* the sister did as well. *Surely.* Abalel could not be predicted, but Marcus knew from experience that the god of the sun made decisions that were beneficial for those who revered him.

But how to recover them?

"If he assumes we are dead," Marcus said at last, "he will head east to Red Sands." That was the city of Tressar, the Paxan steward, who had purchased Hana Rosure in Bledeshure.

"We will go with you to Red Sands," Isule stated.

The city was home to the Paxan governor and many of his ambassadors. It was ten days inland, and Hileshand had told them it could be a difficult road. He looked toward the harbor, and Marcus became aware that his father did not wish to leave the coast. Having escaped the niessith, Myles and Amilia would have come ashore somewhere near here. Port Soren would have been the logical city to receive them.

"We will hear what Abalel will say," Hileshand said at last. "We will return to Ausham and seek his counsel...then we will journey to Red Sands."

Four days later, the Paxan captain opened the gate of Ausham for them, just as he had before. Again, he said, "We have been expecting you."

He looked grim. "The council has convened. They wait for you outside the Council Chamber."

chapter 45

The Council of Prophets met within the walls of Ausham's austere Council Chamber. Two days a week, the students would gather there to hear their elders argue about prophecies and what they thought Abalel was saying. At the end of each session, students had the opportunity to stand before the council and ask questions and present their own ideas concerning what the council had discussed.

One day during Hileshand's thirteenth summer, he had stood up in the Council Chamber and boldly declared that the prophecy they were discussing was about him. He did not claim this about one of the smaller, more insignificant prophecies that Abalel had given the council—he said it about a prophecy that had been spoken six hundred years beforehand. It was a foundation stone of Ausham—a prophecy that, during the time of Hileshand's studies, had been discussed more than any other. The boy stood up and announced that Abalel had told him *he* would be the one who held the Ruthanian throne in his hand. *He* would be the one to direct the steps of that nation.

The abbot of the time, Constance Perebole, had possessed little grace for the boy. Hileshand's actions that day were only one of several reasons he had eventually been expelled.

Jonathan Manda had been a much younger man back then, and he had found Perebole's harsh attitude toward the boy difficult to stomach. Jonathan had spent time with young Hileshand; he knew the boy was gifted and, therefore, when Hileshand claimed the prophecy, it made Jonathan wonder. Hileshand was many of the things Perebole believed him to be—arrogant, used to his own way, willing to take risks. This was not the first time young Myles had stood up before the council. But Hileshand was not the sort to pretend and make false assumptions. Jonathan knew the difference between Hileshand trying for attention and Hileshand stating what he believed to be fact. He could tell that Hileshand fully believed what he had proclaimed to the council.

After Hileshand had been thoroughly ridiculed by his peers, as well as the council themselves, Jonathan had pulled the boy aside and asked him why he believed Abalel had said this to him.

Calmly, Hileshand told him, *Abalel said the man's name is Hileshand. That is my name. My father is dead, and I am the only one left.*

It was simple logic that could not be put aside. Jonathan's heart burned within him, and he knew the boy had heard Abalel's voice accurately—he had merely come to the wrong conclusion.

The man in the prophecy, the one who could direct a throne—his name would be Hileshand. *Hileshand's son.*

Even after Jonathan's explanation, Marcus did not know

the entirety of the prophecy that had dropped his father in such trouble with the council—but it didn't matter. He had no doubt that his father was a powerful man, in every way possible. Perhaps that power had cost him with the council in the past, yet Jonathan Manda, now the abbot, knew the truth about him.

Marcus smiled to himself as they approached the lawn of the Council Chamber.

Giant fir trees surrounded the green like a troop of heavily armed guards and kept it hidden from the main road. Marcus didn't see anyone until the path looped around the corner and the massive trees parted. His steps slowed.

About six hundred men waited here—every student and every member of the council. Many of them turned and looked at Marcus and his father as they approached. He felt the concern immediately, as if the breeze propelled it. The tension was thick.

Then he saw the reason for it.

An Alusian stood with the abbot in the middle of the clearing.

Hileshand saw the Alusian and felt a wave of surprise roll through him. A man could go years without seeing a male. That same man could go *lifetimes* without seeing a female. Hileshand had only heard of them. They were scattered and few, much more reclusive than their male counterparts. With only a glance at her, he could guess the reason for that—she was fantastically beautiful, her face and form nearly breathtaking. She stared at him hard, and he scowled, annoyed at the way her look affected him. He did not like the immediate draw he felt toward her. It was not safe.

The males were difficult. Ethan Strelleck—he had been difficult.

The females were worse.

Jonathan's face was pale. Hileshand's concern increased tenfold.

At the gate, the captain had said they had been waiting—for them. What was this? Something felt amiss here.

Jonathan whispered, "The Alusian has called for a quest." He nodded to servants who ran to fulfill orders they had been given before Hileshand and Marcus' arrival.

A quest.

Hileshand had little understanding of Boerak-El, the Alusian god of death. He did know, however, that the god was like a spring storm at sea; he was dangerous and unpredictable, familiar with pain, and the Alusian took after him. He was the god of mourning, his people the conveyors of the dead.

Abalel was not unfriendly toward Boerak-El, though the relationship between them had never been explained to Hileshand's satisfaction. Here in Ausham, it was considered foundational knowledge, a truth that remained true even though it could not be unwrapped and deciphered. Hileshand had no idea why the god of the sun—and, therefore, the bringer of life—would choose to associate with the Alusian god of sorrow and death. Yet upon occasion, Abalel chose to do so.

Namely, when an Alusian female called for a quest.

This was not done very often. Hileshand could think of three times a gathering such as this had been called in the last fifteen hundred years. Five centuries had passed since the most recent event, and in that particular case, the man the female had chosen had died on the journey. She had killed him, or so the story went.

He folded his arms and stood there with his son, waiting to see how this would go. He felt pity for the one to be chosen from this group. He himself was not alarmed, however. Neither he nor his son was part of Ausham. The female could not choose either of them. It had to be someone from the school.

The creature pointed at his son and uttered one word, only one, but the finality of it caught him unawares. Her voice was like a knife through Hileshand's heart.

"Him."

Marcus looked at his father, confused.

Jonathan groaned and hung his head. He was taking this seriously, and at his friend's response, Hileshand's bafflement vanished and his anger found firm ground.

He glared at the creature. "My son has no part of Ausham."

"He is here."

A simple and infuriating answer. She was not following the road that had been laid for her to follow. Hileshand repeated, "You cannot choose a man who has no part of Ausham."

"He has a greater part in Ausham than you know," she answered, adding, "Myles Hileshand."

She knew his name.

"You are *not* taking my son."

He heard movement in the crowd, the concerned intakes of breath. He didn't care about protocol. He didn't care about offense. Boerak-El was not going to draw near his son. This was one soul the Alusian god of sorrow and death was not going to influence or touch.

She stared at him, her look intense. She pulled in a deep

breath, one that seemed to fill her entire body, let it out.

Without warning, she reached over and put her hand on Marcus' shoulder.

Marcus jerked once, shoulders elevating. A grimace passed over his face and he bent forward with a groan.

"Marcus!"

Hileshand watched with a deep sort of horror as his son did not respond to him. Marcus did not rise. Instead, he dropped lower, putting a hand to the ground, braced himself against whatever her touch had thrust inside him. His shoulders shook.

The anger stormed through Hileshand's senses again. He pulled his sword.

In his peripheral vision, he saw men running toward him. He heard shouts of caution.

He made no move to attack her. Not yet. He stood there, sword drawn, and spoke quietly as half the clearing came at him. "If you hurt my son, I will find a way to kill you, and in that quest—*my* quest—I will be successful."

He did not touch her. Jonathan waved the men away, shouted at them, and they came within a few paces and stopped. They could see that Hileshand had halted and foolishly assumed he did not intend to kill the creature.

Oh, he intended to kill her. But not yet.

"If you have done something to my son that cannot be undone, you will wish you were dead. Repeatedly."

She stepped closer to him. Looking him in the eyes, she said haughtily, "There is only one sword I fear among man and it is not yours." There was heat in her voice, obvious anger.

Then something flickered through her eyes. A line drew between her brows. The anger ebbed, and she hesitated.

Drawing another full-lunged breath, she set her hand on Marcus again, and the young man gasped, bent closer to the ground. "It is his sword. The sword of Marcus Hileshand."

"Touch him again, and I will remove your arm from your body."

Her mouth twisted in a hideous smile, and she pulled her hand away.

"What have you done?" Hileshand demanded.

"I have done nothing. If you possessed any level of wisdom, you would see this."

He stared at her. The words did not fit with his rage, so he tossed them aside as mockery because, clearly, she *had* done something. She had caused Boerak-El to touch his son. Marcus did not stand. He appeared to be having trouble breathing.

Jonathan leaned forward, head tilted. He made as if to speak, but the Alusian ignored him.

Looking at Hileshand, she repeated, "My touch does nothing. It is what he hears. Boerak-El speaks to him. If this road does not please you, speak with the one who has chosen your sons. Do not speak with me. In the meantime, you will not follow us, or more than Marcus will die."

She took his son.

Before they left, Marcus had put his hand on Hileshand's arm and said quietly, "Look. It will be all right. She's done nothing to me. Don't worry." He had said these words with a calm countenance, his body now still, his grip firm, his back straight. He seemed out of sorts—but not impaired.

Hileshand did not know if he could do what his son requested. And he did not know if he believed him. Even now, hours after their departure, his skin still burned where

Marcus had touched him. The momentary grip on his arm had been like fire, and he knew that the spell the Alusian had cast still blazed within the young man's body.

My touch does nothing. Boerak-El speaks to him.

What had Marcus heard?

All he could think of was his son's easy smile. The ready affection and the lightness of his heart. What would the god of sorrow do to these things?

Abalel, spare the heart and life of my son. Please...Abalel, I am desperate. He is all I have left.

Shaking, Hileshand went to find Antonie. He needed comfort and companionship, something familiar—something that had nothing to do with the School of the Prophets and those who had condoned the Alusian's actions this day.

But he discovered the Alusian had taken Antonie, too.

$\mathcal{J}$onathan Manda, abbot of the School of the Prophets, mourned deep in his heart for his good friend Myles Hileshand.

Hileshand responded to pain as he had as a child; he found a task and poured himself into it. Jonathan had seen him do this when he had learned of his father's death. He had seen him respond this way when Constance Perebole had called him a spoiled child who would never produce anything of worth. The former abbot had said these words before the entire school, but even then, there had not been tears with Hileshand; there had been only work.

So Jonathan made certain to fill that need for him, until the man could think with a level of peace once more. A field required clearing in the northern district—he sent Hileshand to it and gave him men to work alongside him, quiet men who would not affect him negatively.

"Don't let him out of your sight," he told Isule, as well as the foreman. "Restrain him if you have to. Set much work before him and allow him to exhaust himself with it."

"Aye," the sea captain answered quietly. He shifted his weight in his boots, stood there hesitatingly, then asked, "What happens when the god of sorrow touches a man?"

The wound was still fresh, the evening barely upon them. Young Marcus had been escorted out of Ausham less than three hours ago.

Jonathan's heart felt like it broke a little more. "What you saw," he replied, "has not been done in many years. Boerak-El does not speak to men. I cannot answer your question, for I do not know. The Alusian would likely tell you that because of the touch—or the voice, as she said—the man's fortune is changed. It is rewritten. The old is gone. What would have been no longer exists." He shrugged. "I do not know."

He glanced at the foreman. His name was Nels. He was large and used to labor; he would have no trouble with most men should it come to blows, but with Hileshand—a capable man when he was at peace and a ravaged father when he was not? Who could say?

"Do you fear for Marcus?" Isule asked.

"That he travels with an Alusian? No, I do not fear that." The abbot paused. "That the god of sorrow has spoken into his soul?" Jonathan let his breath out slowly. He frowned. "Yes, that concerns me."

Antonie Brunner did not like this. He did not like this at all.

The Alusian led them beneath the trees until the heavy green mass parted, and the North Road lay before them, winding like a river, gray as the sunlight faded. Two hours later, just before dusk, she dismounted and announced they were making camp. She made no move to leave the road.

"Here?" Marcus stood there awkwardly. "You desire to camp in the middle of the road?"

These were the first words either man had said to her. Antonie, sensing a great deal of trauma in his heart, expected to be punished for Marcus' question. But the Alusian responded calmly.

"Yes. Here, in the middle of the road. You will see why."

Spreading out her bedroll, she lay down and was asleep before the fire was built. It was a complete and sudden unconsciousness. She did not raise her head or stir as Marcus moved beside her, bringing the fire to life.

Antonie tended to the horses and tethered them on the eastern side of the road, and all the while, he kept his gaze on Hileshand's son. His heart pounded with a quick thought— what if they were to leave right now? Escaping prisoners. They could go back to Ausham.

Then, with an inward groan, he considered their circumstances more thoroughly. *She is Alusian.* The abbot's men had essentially forced them out the gate with her. She had requested both of them—Marcus and Antonie—and Antonie knew that all she would have to do to regain them was request them a second time.

He had read all that he could about this race—entities that looked like men and yet were not men. Many historians considered them to be the conveyers of the dead, for everywhere they appeared, a life was lost. This happened over and over again, in every country. Antonie wondered what it meant if a man actually *traveled* with one, and he suspected that in a short time, his life would be nothing more than one of these trees here, standing by the road. He would be nothing, and only young Derek would mourn his absence.

Antonie frowned. He could have told the boy such stories. An entire series of books could be devoted to this day alone.

The school had sent them with provisions. Antonie sat on the ground near the fire, putting his hands toward the flames, as Marcus made supper. "What do you think she meant?"

Marcus glanced at him.

"About…finding out why we sleep in the road?"

A call sounded through the gathering dark. At first, Antonie thought it sounded like a deep-throated wolf, but it carried on, a series of notes, stretching out into the dark. Every pitch was discordant and harsh. Bumps rose on his skin beneath the heavy sleeves of his cloak. He shrank closer to the ground.

The horses snickered and tossed their heads, prancing nervously.

"What is that?" he asked. It sounded close by.

"Are you a woman?" Marcus asked unexpectedly.

"What? No."

"Come, come, Antonie—you who claim to be well read. What lives in the northern woods? What calls like that? What would require our gracious hostess—" Marcus looked down at her sleeping form. "—a female, to sleep now, now that she is not alone?"

Antonie shuffled through the information in his head and let his breath out as he found the answer he desired. The northern woods near the Redaman River. Something interested in women. He swallowed. "The miron."

Marcus smiled darkly. "Very good."

"I was not expecting that. It is the…the right season, but

we did not see them in the woods between Ausham and the beach." Antonie groaned softly. "But we wouldn't have seen them, would we? We did not have a woman with us."

Marcus looked down at her again. "Likely, she has not slept in days, if she was traveling this road alone."

Antonie pulled his cloak tightly about him and whispered, "Why the effort, Marcus? If the road was dangerous and we were embedded in Ausham…why the effort? What does she want?"

Another braying cry rolled through the evening.

As if he hadn't heard it, Marcus answered Antonie's question with a fascinating level of calm. "Tell me about Alusian quests."

"They are considered holy journeys," Antonie said, his voice not much above a whisper. He turned his gaze from the fire and scanned the trees on either side of the road. They stretched long, dark arms toward them, as if attempting to meet over their campsite and cover it in shadow. *In the middle of the road,* she had said. *You will see why.*

Antonie shuddered. "They are called holy journeys because Abalel responds positively to them. His prophets, who hear his voice and know his ways, allowed the Alusian to do whatever she desired. They supplied her needs. Her journey is considered their journey."

He paused, desiring to ask a certain question and feeling unsure whether or not he should.

When Antonie had realized it was *Marcus* the Alusian had chosen, the force of the shock had momentarily relieved all his fears. He remembered Hileshand's behavior after the niessith's attack, and he could only imagine how the father would respond now, suddenly bereft.

Antonie wet his lips and whispered, "Did you hear

Boerak-El's voice?"

Marcus' answer was quiet. He was staring into the fire. "Yes."

Antonie enjoyed studying things that were difficult to know, and Alusian quests had fascinated him for years. He had read everything available to him about Boerak-El and why the god of sorrow sent his chosen race, the Alusian, on different quests. After years of research, the only element he knew with certainty was that Boerak-El did not operate in any sort of pattern. On one quest, he sent an Alusian female and her human companion to fight against the Galatian military, who subsequently lost the war and paid tribute to Ruthane for two hundred years after that. On another quest, the Alusian chose a boy, a small boy, and took him with her into the red Paxan deserts for three months. When they returned, the boy continued his studies, as if nothing had happened, and he eventually became a priest of Boerak-El. He was the only human priest this particular god of death ever had. The man lived among the Alusian and was buried among their dead, as one of them. That was seven hundred years ago.

It was all very interesting to Antonie because he understood none of it. Least of all did he understand why the Alusian quests were tolerated by Abalel—and Issen-El as well. The god of the sun and the god of the sea—these were not gods of death or sorrow. They had nothing in common with Boerak-El. Why pay him homage like this?

When Marcus said nothing more, Antonie tried to help him along. "There are some who say Boerak-El is feared by all the other gods of death, but no one knows why—he is least known among man. Man fears him from a distance, because they fear his Alusian. But now that..."

He realized what he was about to say. *Now that he has*

chosen you. Marcus looked at him, and for the first time, Antonie found himself feeling intimidated by him. He had felt this way often enough around Myles, who pushed and shoved his way forward when he wanted something. He had also found Hileshand fairly concerning at different times. But Marcus had been different. There was a reason Antonie had approached him first on the ship, when the niessith attacked. Marcus had not scared him. Until now.

"What's your question?" Marcus asked.

Antonie shivered and considered moving to the other side of the fire, but the Alusian was over there.

"Do you know why Boerak-El is feared by the other gods of death?"

There was no hesitation in his reply. "Yes."

But again, he said nothing more. Antonie built up his courage and had to prod him. "What is the reason?"

Marcus lowered his head. A long period of quiet ensued. Then Antonie heard words he never would have anticipated.

"Because there is only one god of death," Marcus answered quietly. He picked up a broken piece of branch from the road between his boots and tossed it into the flames. "And all the others are smoke."

Antonie stared at him. *What?* The words made no sense whatsoever.

Abruptly, Marcus stood to his feet and pulled a knife from his belt. For a moment, Antonie was thoroughly and completely terrified. He saw visions of the Alusian's companion slaying him in ten different ways.

Then Marcus flipped the blade and held the handle toward him.

"Here," he said gruffly. "You may need this."

A man stepped out onto the road.

chapter 47

The man who came out of the trees was not too much older than Antonie and Marcus. His clothes were inexpensive and simple but clean and appeared to have been recently pressed. He wore no weapons that Antonie saw.

A chill stole up the scribe's spine. The image was wrong. These woods, dangerous and damp, could not produce a man who looked as fresh as this, as if he had just stepped from his master's house and was about to run an errand. Antonie remembered a passage he had read several times out of The King's History of Paxa: The miron appear as men, but they are creatures of magic. They can change their forms.

"Stay where you are," Marcus directed, sword drawn.

The miron bent forward slightly, bringing up its hands and toying with its fingers below its chin, like a greedy merchant with a nervous habit. "I have a proposition," it hissed in Ruthanian. It looked like a normal man, but the voice gave everything away in an instant.

Antonie shivered.

"We are not interested in your propositions. Leave. Now."

"Wait, wait! I will give you gold—for the Alusian. For the female." The creature gestured with one spindly, manicured hand toward the Alusian as she slept. "Let me have the Alusian, and I will leave, just as you say." It added, "Kind sirs."

For a moment, Antonie allowed himself to consider the ugly possibility. What if they sold her? The Alusian slept like one of the dead she carried. He wondered if it was a spelled sleep; she had not stirred even as the miron had called to one another through the trees. Those had been loud calls. *Let the miron have her. The quest will be over. Both of us will be free of this.*

This was perfect—horrific and shameful, but a perfect idea. Then he looked at Marcus, and his hopes trickled away.

Marcus bore the magic of Boerak-El. He was not going to make a wise decision here.

And he didn't.

Marcus raised his sword and leveled the point at the miron's face. The creature stood several paces away—on the road but under the cover of the tree branches. It hissed its displeasure at the sword's new position. The fingers twiddled beneath the chin.

"How many of you are there?"

"Many," the creature answered.

Antonie thought it sounded like a sneer.

Marcus glanced upward, toward the stars. Then he lowered his gaze, as well as his sword, and said, "I give you a proposition of my own. If you can lay a hand to her, perhaps I will consider this sale." He paused. "Perhaps."

The creature hissed again, but it did not venture out from beneath the trees. "I will give you much gold for her. I will break the spell for you. I will return to you your life."

Antonie had no idea if the miron actually possessed the power to do this, but he immediately knew what he would do, if he were Marcus. He clutched the knife in his hand and stared hard at the back of Marcus' head. Take it! Take it, Marcus.

Marcus said with sarcasm, "I don't want to put you to any trouble."

The creature clearly did not understand him. Neither did Antonie.

So Marcus explained: "There is no spell to remove."

"This quest will kill you!"

"No. No, it won't. If you want the girl, come and take her."

Girl, he called her. Antonie shuddered. The miron collected the bones of women. The younger the woman, the more precious the bone, and if the girl was pregnant, she was considered a prize. They thought life was in the bones. They ate them.

The miron threw its head back and roared. Startled, Antonie stumbled backward several steps and regained his footing just as a wave of cold air washed across him. The night was cold already, but what he felt now was like the breath of ice. He saw pale yellow light falling across the road at his feet and spun around, knife raised.

The forest on the left side of the road was filled with perusan. Dozens of them. All of them men. There were soldiers, merchants, pages, jesters. One of them even wore a crown. Antonie gasped. He had not seen perusan in years. Compared to the miron, they seemed eerie and oddly foreign in their silence. They watched Antonie and Marcus and did not pay any attention to the miron scattered through the trees on the opposite side.

What did I do to deserve this? Antonie groaned. The perusan killed with their hands. They ripped people apart and left black patches of frozen skin on their victims. He had seen it done. It was horrible.

"Marcus!" Antonie yelled.

Marcus turned. The yellow light illuminated his face, and Antonie saw his smile clearly. "Excellent," the companion said.

There was, Antonie thought with dismay, a level of genuine pleasure in his voice.

"Antonie, get over here."

Antonie scrambled to do his bidding.

Marcus bent down and grabbed the Alusian's sword off her bedroll. She had laid her weapon beside her.

"I don't think this is a good plan," Antonie said. He grabbed the scabbard as Marcus passed the weapon to him, but a moment later, he cried out in surprise and pain, letting go quickly. Marcus caught the sword before it hit the ground.

"I can't touch that!"

"Why? What's wrong?"

Antonie knew there wasn't time to ask. There wasn't time to explain. He just looked at him quickly, horrified for so many reasons, and blurted, "Heat. It's hot. Give me yours."

They traded weapons.

Marcus pointed at the Alusian. "Don't let the perusan near her."

"What about the miron?!" Their enemies came from both sides.

Marcus grinned. "Don't go under the trees—and don't get too close, scribe. And remember to keep your fingers away from them."

"Fingers? What?"

Without explanation, Marcus turned toward the western side of the woods and the yellow horde that awaited him.

chapter 48

Antonie crouched beside the Alusian, gripping Marcus' sword. Sweat poured off his body. He sucked air through his open mouth.

The miron screamed somewhere in the trees before him. The original man had faded back into the shadows—Antonie had not noticed how or when—and the trees now shook as a large number of the creatures sprang between the branches, back and forth. The air filled with their jarring screams. Leaves fell like chunks of black snow.

"This is a very bad idea," he muttered again. There was but one way to kill a perusan—the head had to be separated from the body. But he did not know how one was supposed to kill the miron, if there was a specific way. They were creatures of magic. *Don't go under the trees,* Marcus had said.

The night was full upon them now, the sky cold and harsh. Antonie shivered and looked back toward Marcus.

There were so many perusan crowded along that side of the road, peeking out from around the trees, that Antonie could see the immediate area clearly, almost as if it were mid-day. Marcus cast a shadow as he stood there, sword drawn. The yellow perusan had cleared away as he had walked toward them.

Why didn't the perusan attack? Instead, they watched. They waited in the woods. And they watched.

Marcus straightened. The sword lowered. He considered the glowing entities before him for another long moment, then he lifted the scabbard from the road and sheathed the blade.

Antonie gulped, wide eyes.

Still the perusan did not attack.

"Antonie," Marcus called over his shoulder.

The scribe trembled. Surely he did not actually expect him to respond out loud.

"Tell me about the Alusian's interaction with the perusan. Will the perusan attack them?"

He *did* expect a response. Antonie didn't know the answer to his question. The perusan were common creatures—they had never interested him, because of that. He had not studied them. He swallowed and forced his mouth to work. His voice trembled as he said, "I don't know, my lord." He called him that without thinking but quickly determined it accurate. For as long as Boerak-El's magic persisted in Marcus, Antonie would call him nothing else. *My lord.*

Marcus took a few steps toward the trees, and the perusan avoided him, pulling deeper into the woods.

Eventually, the man put his back to the creatures and returned to the fire. He stood there facing the flames, waiting. The orange light reflected on his face. "Do they come, Antonie?" His voice was quiet.

"No, my lord."

The miron screamed periodically in the trees. The leaves continued to rain down all across the road, the branches shaking.

On the other side of the road, the perusan came no closer.

His back to the yellow glow, Marcus squatted down and reached for the wooden handle of the pot he had left on the fire. He pulled it off the embers, setting it in the soil of the road to cool. He did not appear alarmed. He questioned nothing.

Antonie stared at him. What had Boerak-El done to Hileshand's son? What sort of darkness was this, that even the perusan avoided him?

Antonie felt incredibly unsafe.

Marcus scowled at the leaves that had fallen into his stew. He dug them out with his fingers and frowned toward the shaking trees, as if to chide the miron for these unwanted gifts.

The original creature slid out of the forest and stepped toward the fire. Stopping where the branches began to taper overhead, it twiddled its fingers beneath its chin.

The trees behind it slowly grew still. The screaming stopped.

"Gold," the creature rasped. "For the female."

Marcus ignored its words and its approach. Antonie had no idea what was going on here, but trembling all the way to his bones, he compelled himself to sit down beside Marcus, near the fire, his back to the road they had just traveled. So now the miron stood on his left. The perusan stood on his right. This way he could watch them both, just in case. He kept the sword across his lap.

"Gold! Much, much gold!"

With a long sigh, as if he were addressed now by a bothersome child who strained his patience, Marcus set the wooden spoon down into the pot and stood to his feet, walking forward until the fire was at his back. The miron stood only a few paces away.

"No gold," he said. "You will not have this girl."

The miron hissed in a throbbing up-and-down pattern, and Antonie realized it was trying to laugh. "I can see your fortune, too." It pointed toward the Alusian. "She will not speak it, but I will speak it. This is no spell, yes." The beast cackled again. "It is a curse."

Antonie tried not to react. He tried to keep breathing. *Too late*, he thought. *It is too late for Marcus.* He would not be persuaded to believe every word this creature spoke, yet there was enough truth in its statements now to increase his concern. What else could make the perusan fearful like this? They brought death, so only something that possessed a greater threat of death could cause them to restrain themselves. *Too late.* He could see the curse already taking hold.

Marcus did not answer.

The creature continued. "The god of sorrow would have your soul, and when he takes it, there will be nothing left. The curse will consume you. His desires will become your desires. Your thoughts, his thoughts. He will come to possess you fully, and when he is through using you, you will be tossed aside like a pair of broken boots. You will surely die."

Boerak-El has nothing to do with man; he does not touch them except in times of death. Antonie had read that phrase many times. It fascinated him and scared him. He felt the last strips of his hope waving in the breeze, about to tear from their moorings.

"There will be nothing left of you," the creature sneered.

Marcus put his hand to the hilt of his sword. "You," he said slowly, "had best hope you are mistaken. You had best hope you speak the fool right now, for if my desires have become the desires of the god of sorrow, you will be dead in a matter of moments."

For a long time, the night was silent. The miron did not speak.

A call sounded far away—a long braying, muffled blast in the darkness.

The creature looked south, staring up the road. Then the head swung back around. "Beware my words, companion. There will be nothing left."

It turned and walked back into the trees.

Antonie heard commotion. The trees groaned as they bent forward. Leaves dropped in a mad flurry. He winced, preparing his ears, but the screaming did not start again. The motions and sounds began to move away, the bobbing of the trees flowing in a southerly direction, following the road.

What was this? They left? Then Antonie understood. *There is another party on the road tonight. Another woman.* He made a face and wondered if these other travelers were prepared for what came toward them now. He hoped they were.

In a few moments, everything was calm except his heart. The perusan remained in the trees on the opposite side of the road. They watched, and that was all.

Shaking, Antonie stared at Marcus' back. What would he do now?

The man returned to the fire and squatted down before it, taking up the spoon and stirring the pot. His face appeared blank in the moving light. Antonie had no comprehension of his thoughts.

"Hungry?" the companion asked. "I'm famished. Hand me my bag, would you?" He held out his hand, waited for Antonie to move.

Antonie met his gaze. He could hold it for only a moment and quickly looked away, doing as requested. He put the bag in Marcus' grip, and as his fingers brushed those of Hileshand's son, he felt extreme heat. The brief touch burned him. Touching Marcus was like touching glowing coals.

There will be nothing left of you.

Marcus did not speak a word concerning the miron's prophecy. It was almost as if he had not heard it. Antonie was too afraid to ask all the questions that stormed through his mind. He could not stop shaking.

Something was dreadfully wrong here. He could feel it all the way through his heart. He wondered if Hileshand would be able to recognize his son when they returned to Ausham. Then he grimaced, thinking in dismay, *If we return to Ausham. If we return from this quest at all.*

Marcus handed him a bowl of stew and started whistling as he spooned up a second for himself.

chapter 49

*M*arcus, the man who heard Boerak-El's voice, took the first watch.

Not that it mattered. Antonie knew he was not going to be able to sleep tonight. He still made the attempt, for he had no idea what the next day's journey would look like, but most of the night was spent flat on his back, his hands beneath his head, eyes wide open. He tried to focus on the stars winking against the black panel of night sky, yet his gaze was repeatedly drawn to the perusan that stood along the side of the road. Every time one of them twitched, Antonie looked.

At some point, exhaustion overtook him. When he opened his eyes the next time, the sky was pale, the stars invisible. Dawn had come and gone perhaps an hour before. He sat up quickly as he realized that Marcus had not awakened him for his watch.

From his current position on the road, the woods appeared to be clear. He saw no perusan, no yellow glow. But, of course, he wouldn't see them. It was day now. They came with the stars and the night dew, and they disappeared just as quickly. He breathed a sigh.

He looked toward the fire.

Marcus was no longer on the road. Instead, the Alusian had multiplied during the night. Antonie jerked at the discovery of one he did not recognize.

The creature sat facing him on the other side of the fire. There was a long shaft across his lap and a knife in his left hand. He ran the blade over the tip of the shaft, sharpening the wood into a point. Antonie shivered as he understood what the creature was doing—he was making a spear.

No doubt, the creature had heard Antonie's intake of breath and had seen his dramatic rise from the earth. But the Alusian did not look up, not right away. He ran the blade across the wood several more times, and only when he was ready did he raise his head.

Antonie gaped at him.

This Alusian had blue eyes. The hair was the standard dark color, the skin as white as milk, as if the touch of death had already occurred. All necessary signs were present. He was certainly Alusian—but the eyes were blue.

The moment this creature had wandered into camp, he had likely known the totality of Antonie's history, along with his present and future. The Alusian race knew much more than they should. In this moment, Antonie wished for a return in favor—for immediate information. An Alusian with blue eyes? There were different races of Alusian? He had never heard of blue eyes among them.

As if all these thoughts had been said aloud, the creature pulled back and studied him. The mouth rolled up on the left side. The blue eyes narrowed in something resembling humor. Antonie stared at him.

"Antonie Brunner."

Every muscle froze in Antonie's body.

"You are a scribe. You are employed by Lord Persus Claven. You are twenty-four years old and fluent in seven languages. You can read and write in ten languages. You are more than capable in many situations, yet you insist on others taking your steps for you. Upon occasion, you have stabbed men with writing utensils in an attempt to save them from niessith."

Antonie was uncertain how to respond to this. The female certainly had not been this prolific with her words yesterday. Antonie sat there and felt like one of the king's books. Everything about him was exposed to this creature.

The Alusian shook his head once and said simply, "Marcus told me."

He returned to sharpening the spear. After a few moments, he slid his hand across the point and seemed satisfied with it. He lifted his arm and tossed the spear onto a nearby pile that Antonie did not notice until the pieces of wood clattered against one another. There were at least a dozen roughly hewn shafts of wood lying there. What was this creature doing?

The Alusian reached for another whole, uncarved shaft from a different pile to his left. Two shafts remained.

Marcus told me. Those words were peculiar words for an Alusian. The curiosity finally overcame Antonie's common sense. "You...you did not see these things yourself?" Perhaps Antonie had misunderstood; he had only just awoken. He was not thinking clearly.

Calmly, the Alusian set to work on the new shaft. "Many things," he said, moving the knife. "I see many things." He nodded toward the road they had not traveled yet. "Marcus is with Bithania. They will return shortly."

Antonie followed his gaze but did not see them. The road curved to the left about half a mile away, and all he saw were trees.

Bithania. The name suited the elegance and the dark allure. It also suited the force and the tension. And the witchery.

"Why are you…doing that?" Antonie looked at the pile of pointed shafts.

The blue eyes appeared again as the creature met Antonie's gaze. The left side of the mouth rolled up. Was this a smile? Antonie did not know how to respond to this. This was not correct. It did not fit what Antonie understood about these creatures. The blue eyes weren't the only thing different about this fellow.

"You will see," the creature answered. "You will not like it, but you will see."

Wonderful, Antonie thought.

The Alusian looked at him steadily. For the first time, he pulled in a deep breath, full-lunged, nostrils flaring. Now here was behavior Antonie recognized—the odd manner of Alusian breathing.

"My name is Entan Gallowar." He set the spear and the knife aside. He folded his hands in his lap and gave Antonie his full blue-eyed attention. "Bithania has asked me to tell you your fortune."

Antonie had never heard of an Alusian volunteering such information. After a time, he remembered to breathe. His fortune must be truly dreadful if the Alusian meant him to know it. His heart ran. "Why? Why would she say that?"

"Because she is occupied and should not do it herself."

"But…why?"

Entan studied him a moment. "Bithania," he said, with the same level of calm, "is occupied. I am not. I will tell you your fortune. Do you understand why she asked this of me and not another?"

Antonie shook his head. His tension was so high that his stomach was hurting him. He leaned forward, swallowing down a groan.

"The only Alusian blood I bear is that of my grandfather. I will be gentle with you, when the others would not understand your thoughts." He watched the way Antonie squirmed, and his look softened. "You worry too much, Antonie Brunner. That is the issue of your heart, the vice that would see you lost and buried in the ground. You expect death and ultimate destruction, when it is life that awaits you instead. Be open to a different plan—for you will live. You will not experience death until you are an old man and far beyond the point of fear. Can you accept these words?"

Antonie could not bring himself to move. He wondered about the creature's thoughts. None of this made sense to him.

The Alusian inhaled again. "A man's fortune cannot be told in its entirety. There are not enough words in any language to convey the fullness of a life. What I give you today is only a glimpse of your fortune. Any fortune spoken by an Alusian, or any other, is ever only a glimpse.

"You are the keeper of prophecy. You are not the giver of this prophecy, but the word, spoken by another, will take place before your eyes. You will witness its birth, its death, and its life, and you will give testament to what you have seen."

Its birth, its death, and its life. Despite the roaring concern within him, Antonie took note of the order of those words. The Alusian never said anything they did not mean, and every word they did speak concealed deeper meaning.

"Your role here is important. Abalel chose you for this role, and he will see that you are able to fulfill it. Therefore, you have the opportunity to choose courage. Put the fear aside. You will find what you seek."

The fear momentarily abated. "Abalel?" the scribe whispered. "What of...what of the god of sorrow?"

Why would the Alusian speak of Abalel? It was Boerak-El who dictated his steps now—he was the god who had forced him out of Ausham. It had not been Abalel. Antonie did not understand. *The god of sorrow. God of death.*

Entan gave him a slow but genuine smile, and in this moment, he looked like any other man—a young man. He appeared no more than twenty. "You need the sun, O scribe. You need the light. This is not the time for sorrow, nor is it the time for fear. In every circumstance, you will be given only what you need, and what you need now is light for your path."

chapter 50

Shortly after the noon meal, Jonathan Manda went out to tend his garden. The snows approached; soon, he would not be able to work outside and would be forced to putter around with indoor pots instead. He did not like having plants indoors—it made him feel old. Tending plants inside the house was a pastime for those who could no longer bear the outdoor elements, so the winter months bothered him.

He was on his hands and knees in the cold soil when he felt a presence behind him, approaching on the road from the eastern gate. Leaning back on his knees, he sat up and looked.

A familiar face he saw. Very few times had this face brought him trouble, but this time he knew would be different.

The boy stepped forward and helped him to his feet. Jonathan never felt old on his hands and knees—only when he attempted to rise from them. The muscles trembled in his legs now. He gripped the boy's arms and looked him in the eyes.

"What do you do here?" he asked, forgoing their traditional greeting. He had no idea when Hileshand would return, and he did not wish for him to return and see this. The relationship between them was strained enough as it was.

The boy turned his arms so that he could put hands to Jonathan's elbows, a familiar grip, a gesture of fondness. Jonathan had great love for his nephew, but why had he come—now, of all days? Surely, he knew the situation. His presence here would be taken as laughter at a gravesite, should Hileshand discover him.

"Uncle, the clouds have come in, and they soon drop rain. We should go inside."

Rain? That would surely drive the men in from the fields. Hileshand would be somewhere on the premises, perhaps not searching Jonathan out, but the rain would still bring him much closer than Jonathan wanted. He sensed a plan in motion that he could not stop, and he winced at the thought of it.

"Why are you here?" he repeated, staring into his nephew's face.

A chill suddenly took him. What if the boy did not come now of his own accord? What if this unexpected visit was on behalf of someone else, an order from others of his kind that the boy could not waylay or control?

Abalel, what do you do here? We need peace. We must have peace. Jonathan grimaced at his memory of the Alusian yesterday.

His nephew replied, "It rains."

Water began to fall from the heavens.

Entan Gallowar propelled his uncle indoors.

The housekeeper, a middle-aged woman named Sabana, smiled when she saw Entan. Any other man she would have embraced. She enjoyed expressing her affection with her hands and her arms and a head upon her bosom. But she did not do these things with Entan. Her affection was there in all its fullness, but with Entan, she kept her distance. "Your uncle has missed you. You should come to us more often."

"I have been away," the boy said simply.

Away. That was all he ever said. Jonathan looked at him, but his nephew did not grace him with an in-depth answer. *Away.* That could mean anything.

Sabana was used to a constant stream of visitors at the abbot's house. She had tea on the sitting room table before Jonathan could settle himself. The chair felt uncomfortable. His legs still trembled.

"Sabana," Entan said, leaning back in his chair. "Would you bring in another cup? We expect someone."

The boy knew. He had planned this, had timed his approach with the rain.

Jonathan swallowed a groan.

As Sabana went back into the kitchen, Entan looked at his uncle. He adjusted his position in the chair and folded his arms, the left corner of his mouth curving upward. "If you have questions, you should ask them now."

Of course he had questions. He waited to ask them until after Sabana returned with the third cup. She made certain they had everything they needed and then vanished back into the kitchen.

"Why?" Jonathan asked. "You rub salt in an open wound by being here. Surely, you know this."

The boy nodded. "Yes."

Jonathan had dirt on his hands. He noticed this for the

first time and frowned, rubbing his palms together until the crumbs of the earth covered his lap. *Why, Abalel?* he wondered again. *This cannot be a good decision.* "Marcus Hileshand."

"Yes?" There was no hesitation. The boy knew this name.

"Tell me what has happened with him. What do you know?"

"I spoke with him this morning."

Jonathan stopped moving. He looked at him closely.

Calm, Entan continued, "He has accepted his fortune without complaint or fear. He is doing well."

His fortune? Jonathan could not believe it. "You actually gave him his fortune?"

"Not I. His fortune was told by another."

The female. Jonathan shuddered. Abalel's touch was a powerful thing. When a man entered through the gate and Abalel touched him, there was usually some sort of reaction within that man, some sort of change.

The touch of Boerak-El would also produce some sort of change.

Does Marcus Hileshand remain as Abalel made him? Does he think clearly, as himself, or does Boerak-El infuse him with foreign magic? Jonathan told himself to proceed with caution. Entan did not answer questions when they were forced upon him—Abalel's council had learned this years ago.

The boy had grown up behind these walls. His father, the son of Jonathan's brother's youngest daughter, had wanted to keep Entan safe, to withhold from him the bitterness of a world that would not be able to explain or accept him. The Alusian mother had been found dead at the bottom of a ravine outside of their small mountain town, and the matter was never resolved. No one knew how she died. The father had come to Jonathan's house in mourning, gripping his blue-eyed son and shaking.

Entan had been a quiet child, but he was more human than he was Alusian; that fact was visible in Jonathan's everyday interactions with him. His nephew was gentle. He was kind. He related well to Abalel.

But he was not immune to the god of sorrow any more than the rest of his mother's kind. Boerak-El had pursued him, even into Ausham. Four years ago in his thirteenth summer, Entan had simply walked out the western gate one day and had not returned for two years. He now made only sporadic visits. Jonathan did not know where he went or what he did. He did not know if he traveled with others or if he was consistently alone. Entan was not forthcoming about such things, even when pressed.

"Are you *certain* of Marcus' state of being?" Jonathan asked, searching the blue eyes for any sign of concern or threat of pain. Entan would feel these things, if they were there to be felt.

Entan frowned. "Uncle…your faith in Abalel seems to have wilted as of late. What has happened to cause you to fear?"

Jonathan pulled back from the table. "Excuse me?" he whispered. With any other, such words would have offended him. But he did not know how to respond to these words from an Alusian. "What do you mean?"

The door opened. Hileshand stepped into the room, water running off his cloak, droplets scattering as he turned to shut the door behind him. Apparently, the sky dropped rain with gusto.

Jonathan braced himself. He gripped the table edge with

both hands. "Myles," he said softly, silently commanding him to keep his peace.

The man turned. His gaze slammed into that of the Alusian.

The room seemed to jerk inward, growing smaller.

"If you are curious," Hileshand rasped, "I don't have anyone else to offer you. My son was the last I had."

He stood there, the dripping cloak heavy about his form, boots braced, arms slightly elevated. There was fire in his eyes. He was ready for the fight, driven for it.

Jonathan's nephew remained calm. He always remained calm, no matter what threatened him or stared at him like this with hatred. The boy pulled in a long, full breath, his chest rising then falling as he released the air through his nose.

He leaned back in his chair and said, "I bear a message from the one who wishes to carry your sorrow."

Odd words. And it was an odd choice, the choosing of those words. Jonathan desperately hoped Hileshand would not respond as he imagined him responding.

Hileshand reached beneath his cloak for his sword, and Jonathan stood to his feet. "Myles! Stop it! Wait."

"Your daughter lives."

Hileshand stopped, his hand frozen about the hilt of his sword, the blade still in the scabbard.

"But this you already know. You chose to believe the words Abalel spoke to you." His words relaxed and unhurried, Entan continued, "I will tell you now what you do not know. In two hours' time, the rain will stop. You and I, along with your friend Isule, will go south to the Redaman River and retrieve your daughter from a small mishap that has not yet taken place. It will not be difficult to retrieve her, for what will possess her has many fears and falls easily to a sword. In three days, she will be with you and safe."

Entan's eyes narrowed as he studied Hileshand, who stood there without words.

"Continue your courage. Accept Abalel's voice. Amilia will come to no harm. Nor will any harm come to the babe she carries."

Surprised, Jonathan stared at the boy. Amilia was pregnant? Hileshand had not mentioned this.

Immediately, an assumption formed in Jonathan's thoughts. He knew the girl was not married. With the exception of the twins, none in this family shared blood with the others. Perhaps there was a reason Hileshand had not mentioned the pregnancy. Perhaps the child was one of the son's. He frowned as he contemplated. *What if it is Marcus' child?* What if Boerak-El had so altered his fortune that he could no longer be trusted as the father?

Hileshand, a grandfather. The frown again moved in between Jonathan's brows. *A grandfather.* He felt as if Abalel reminded him of something with these words, but he could not take hold of what it was.

Entan pushed his chair back and stood. "Hileshand, I will ask you the same question I asked my uncle."

Hileshand's gaze snapped to Jonathan's.

Jonathan shrugged, both hands lifted. Yes. The boy was his nephew.

"What has happened to cause you to fear? You recently declared the universe to be unbalanced. But you do not remember these words now." Entan shook his head. "You should remember them, and find your peace in them—for *unbalanced* the universe remains."

The boy smiled with human-like warmth and gestured

toward the table. "Have a seat, Hileshand. We have two hours." He sat up and reached for the teapot, pulling away the floral covering from the spout. He looked at Hileshand. "Would you care for some tea?"

chapter 51

A strong wind blew down from the hills, flowing across the Redaman River. The cold almost felt as if it were a river itself, running on top of the land. It was forceful and determined to find its way to her bones. Amilia Hileshand wrapped her cloak more tightly about her and shivered, watching the darkening landscape as it slowly rolled past them.

The sun was setting now. By the time they reached the port, the stars would be watching them.

Myles had been right. Her fears of being on the water had slowly become manageable, yet they had not faded entirely. Far from that. She still had trouble sleeping. In truth, she had slept no more than a few hours combined in the last three days, and the two days before then, she had not slept at all. Her body ached and complained at her. Her head hurt.

But these things she kept to herself. Myles was stronger than she. He might not be Furmorean by birth, but he was Furmorean in his mind; the strength was apparent. She wished she had not been away from their homeland for so long. Perhaps then she would not be afraid.

This part of the Paxan countryside was mostly flat. She could see the rock-strewn, muddy banks about a stone's throw away on either side of the ship. The trees grew thick and heavy beyond the banks, like a blanket across the raised ground, and that was all she could see. The trees were like walls. Nothing was visible beyond them.

A hand touched her shoulder, and the warmth of Myles' arm slid around her as he stepped up to the rail. She glanced at him.

"Good?" he asked after a moment, watching her face.

She shivered again, and he turned her toward him, wrapping his arms around her. She saw his chest now and part of his sleeve, not the unending woods.

"Good," she answered against the front of his cloak. The chill in the air seemed to vanish. All he had to do was hold her.

She felt the rumble in his chest as he spoke. "We will reach Gressley's Point in an hour. One more hour, *aufane*, and you will be on solid ground again."

My love. She had heard this word before—it had been used many times by men who wished only to secure her favor for an evening, perhaps a few days. How was it that Myles could use it, the same word, and make it sound like gold? Every time he said it, her heart felt like it was sighing.

She tilted her head back and looked up at his face. "I wish Bithania was here."

Myles' brows came together. "Why?" he asked.

The one-word response contained much more vehemence than Amilia had been expecting. He sounded rather offended. Wiggling her arm free, she laid her hand on his chest. "Peace, Myles. I do not mean to offend you with this wish of mine."

He grimaced.

She smiled at his tension. "Relax," she whispered, spreading her fingers out and pushing her palm against him. "I do not question your judgment. I state an observation. It seems to be fairly wild country here."

She looked over at the trees. Early, early this morning, the night watchman had seen perusan on the banks, their yellow flesh glowing among the trunks. Amilia had been awake and had heard his shout.

With a sigh, she finished, "It would be nice to have a guide who could predict the road before it happened."

"We will find another guide in Gressley's Point."

But this new guide would not be one who could anticipate events before they happened. She could see the stone in Myles' gaze. He did not wish for an Alusian. He would not choose what he had chosen last time.

There was something he did not tell her in all of this. Several days ago, Amilia had concluded that the Alusian had said something to him, something that provoked him. But what could possibly alarm him to the extent that he regretted asking Bithania to be their guide?

She touched the scars on his jawline and began, "I would never doubt you…"

Something moved in her belly. It was fluttery and slight and thoroughly unexpected. She sucked in a quick breath.

Myles was holding her in his arms, his gaze steadily on her face. "What is it?" he asked. His hands went to her shoulders when she did not immediately answer him.

She was exhausted to the point of confusion and tears, and his question suddenly received both responses at the same time. Ignoring the curious looks of the sailors, he dropped a kiss on her lips, then another, and cradled her against him.

"Do you have something you wish to tell me?" he asked.

This was not the first time he had asked this question. Part of her suspected he asked it because he knew the answer, though *how* he knew it she could not even venture a guess. His father would not have told him. She had made him promise not to tell either son. *She* would be the one to tell them, when she was ready to do so.

She was not ready now. The familiar flood of concerns rushed through her mind. *I cannot be what he wants me to be, even if given the choice. What if he doesn't actually know? What if he thinks it is something else, and I tell him and I see the disgust in his eyes? Another man's child. It is nothing but a reminder of the past.* She would not be able to bear his rejection. She would not be able to bear a single dark look from him. If Myles Hileshand ever rejected her, she would die. There would be nothing left of her soul. *Unmentionable.* If he thought her that, she would be that, and there would be no hope for change.

The look in his eyes grew soft. "You can tell me," he said. His grip tightened on her shoulders. "Just tell me, Amilia."

She told him.

She watched his eyes. She had to see his thoughts. The fear made her heart run, but she had to know if she would live.

Yes. She would live.

He ran his hand over her hair. He touched her ears, her nose, her lips, and said, "I will show you every day that your trust in me is secure."

He forgot they were not alone. He kissed her as he had kissed her the first time, pulling away only when Finlan's distinct clearing of throat sounded across the deck. The old man had approached unnoticed.

Myles looked at him and smiled. Amilia thought Hileshand's son seemed perfectly at ease, and again she wondered how he could love her, yet nothing within her doubted his sincerity, especially not now.

Finlan shook his head at both of them. "You have to stop doing that," he said and pointed across the deck at the captain and first mate, who stood there and watched openly. "You told them she was your sister."

Myles corrected, "I believe *you* told them that."

"Yes, well…I was no wiser at the time. Thank you for that."

A huge weight was gone from her shoulders. Amilia felt like laughing uncontrollably. Instead, she contented herself with leaning over and kissing the old man's cheek. "Thank you, Finlan—for everything you have done."

He turned a beautiful shade of scarlet. "Well, now," he sputtered. "Well, now." A grin spilled across his lips. He seemed very pleased.

chapter 52

As the first lights of Gressley's Point came into view through the trees, Myles left Amilia with Finlan at the rail and disappeared below deck to retrieve the rest of their belongings from the main cabin. They traveled light; there was not much to carry.

He never returned.

The first mate sank a burly fist into Finlan's abdomen, doubling the old man over and leaving him in a groaning heap on the deck. Amilia pulled her breath in and stood there, unprepared for this.

Her gaze flicked to the first mate. She thought his name was Burtel, but she could not fully remember. The railing was at her back. Burtel had brought six or seven other members of the crew with him.

They all stared at her. One of them smiled.

Immediately after boarding, she had noticed that all of the men on this ship had the sort of faces that suggested plenty of rough times and hard circumstances. She was familiar with lines of hardship such as these; however, she had never suspected what the men who bore these lines could do when there was money involved. These were poor men, all of them. Desperate men.

The captain was not among them.

"What are you doing?" she asked quietly, knowing the answer to her question. "Don't do this. Please…"

Burtel shrugged, both hands lifted. "Wouldn't have done it," he answered simply. "We take on passengers all the time. A girl who is less than twenty years old? Plenty of gold in that, but not enough." His voice lowered. "But a girl who is with child? Well, that is a different story."

She wet her lips. "Please—"

He ignored her. "And she happens to be accompanied by a man who is not her brother *or* her husband—now, that is a different story altogether. I'm sorry, girl. For what it is worth, really, I am. But *you* are worth the king's purse."

He gestured toward Finlan, and two of his men took hold of the old man and heaved him over the railing into the river.

"Finlan!"

The old man cried out as he hit the water. One sailor picked up his knapsack and threw it into the water after him. Finlan carried little pieces of ash wood and that was all. Myles was the one with the gold.

Bithania's words the first night suddenly swarmed through Amilia's head, piling up. *You do not understand. There is a reason I will not speak your fortune.* This was her reason, wasn't it? This was what the Alusian had seen. *I will not speak your fortune.*

Myles.

She could not shout his name. The fear sealed her lungs.

She could not make a sound for him, because what if he didn't answer? What if these desperate men had killed him? *Myles.*

He did not come, and she could not call him.

Burtel stepped toward her. "Let me do this, girl, and I won't hurt you. Don't fight me. He ain't coming—that man who is not your husband. He's not going to save you, so there is no reason for you to try and fight me."

She remembered this part. She had been twelve the first time, when the evil men had killed her father and sold her in the North Square. She remembered this terror, the way it hurt her stomach.

They hauled her away from the railing, and the first mate bound her hands.

They did not take her into Gressley's Point.

Instead, they took her into the woods.

She grew unconscious of time. The moments seemed to slow, and every detail belonging to Burtel came to be carved deeply upon the fabric of her mind, as if she had the eye of a skilled painter or poet. The way he grunted when he walked. The turned-in feet. The rippled scars on his neck. The slight hunch in his back. His arms were covered with red and black tattoos, many of them words she did not recognize. Why would he have words written on his body? Why words? It did not fit him.

He favored his right hand. Except when it could not be avoided, he did not touch her with the other.

A harsh, braying scream reverberated through the trees. Burtel jerked, ducking down. The noise had surprised him.

She did not know how far into the woods they were. She did not know how long it had taken them to reach this place.

The night had fully come upon them along the way. Three of the men carried lanterns.

Five paces in front of them, a man stepped out of the trees. He looked like a servant. He was clean and young, his clothes well pressed. He looked at her and brought his hands up beneath his chin, twiddling his fingers together.

"Gold for the girl," he hissed, the voice a grating whisper.

Something was wrong with him. His voice was not right. He stared at her. She held his gaze a moment, the wonderings faint and disjointed in her head, and then she looked down.

"Gold for the girl," Burtel agreed. "Much, much gold. She is with child."

The man grinned, showing all his teeth. "I know." His fingers twirled. "You are kind sirs, yes. Very wise men. You care for us."

Burtel glanced through the darkness. All Amilia saw was the one man, but Burtel acted as if there were others, hidden just beyond the light.

"How many of you are there?"

The man grinned again. "Many. Give us the girl." He took a step forward.

Burtel jerked his hand up. "Wait. Just wait a moment. You must give us gold for her first. Much, much gold."

"Much, much gold," the man answered.

He motioned behind him. The trees shuddered. Amilia saw leaves and twigs fall like rose petals thrown during one of the king's processions through the streets of Helsman. It rained them.

The shaking stopped, and five or six other men joined the first. Each of these carried four bags tied with black string in pairs and looped over the shoulders. They placed the bags at Burtel's feet and backed away.

When they were finished, a small mountain lay there. If gold truly filled these bags, it was enough to buy a small town. It would be a fortune for men like these. Amilia released her breath slowly.

The sailors congratulated themselves, slapping one another on the back.

Burtel turned Amilia around to face him with his hand wrapped around her bonds. With his other hand, he took her by the hair and yanked her forward, putting his mouth to hers roughly. Everything in her recoiled from him.

Angry squawking filled the night. The first man from the woods ran up and shoved Burtel away.

"She is ours! Not yours! You leave now. Go." He took hold of Amilia's arm. His skin was warm, as if he had just released a teacup.

Burtel laughed, his eyes gleaming in the lantern light. "Fine. Whatever you say." He bowed low before Amilia. "Thank you, my lady. You have made me a king."

There was not enough gold in all of Paxa to make this filthy commoner a king. *What have you done?* she thought as the creature's strange grip dug into her skin. *This is not a man.*

"Go!" the creature demanded the second time.

Burtel's men gathered the bags from the ground, laughing among themselves and happy. The first mate turned to go.

"Wait," Amilia whispered.

He did not hear her.

She sucked in her breath. "Wait! Burtel!"

He turned back. His gaze rolled over her, and he said,

"Keep your peace, girl. I'm sure they'll treat you well."

His men snickered.

The fear still had her by the throat, but this was her last chance to ask this question. She had to know. Willing herself to be stronger than she was, she asked, "What did you do to Myles?"

The man shrugged. "Oh, don't worry about him. We didn't kill him, if that's what concerns you. He'll live, if he's lucky. We're going to sell him to Lord Jasenel."

Her heart stumbled. Amilia knew that name. More than that, she knew his face. Her former master had referred to him as an associate. Jasenel went to Bledeshure twice a year, and Olah always wanted to be sure he was well treated. *A business associate.* He was considered this because he had money, much money, and could afford to meet all of Olah's demands. Her words garbled as she whispered, "You are going to sell him to a gamer?"

Burtel lifted his hands to either side. "Like I said, girl— he'll live if he's lucky."

Myles had better luck than anyone Amilia had ever heard of. Her heart repeated its former stumble. "Why do you need more gold?" She motioned toward the sailors who sagged beneath the weight of the bags they bore. "You claim to be a king. What else do you need? Just let him go."

"Goodbye, girl. Enjoy yourself with the miron."

"Burtel!"

Burtel and his men disappeared into the night. They took the lanterns with them, and one by one, the trees all around her were consumed in darkness. Amilia saw nothing but a solid black mass. The branches and leaves blocked the moonlight.

She did not know what the miron were. There had not

been *miron* in the woods of Tarek, or in the woods of Fur-morea.

A scream sounded through the darkness. Amilia startled, and the creature pulled on her arm, turning her. She stumbled to keep her balance. It put a hand on her belly.

She had been sold to something that was not a man. This was not like being sold in the North Square; this was being lost beneath the sea. This was the niessith. The image of that hideous face slammed into her head, and she fought the hands on her body.

"Stop," the creature said.

A hand went over her face. She smelled something sweet like honey and stale like wax. She screamed against the palm and dragged in a deep breath as other hands grabbed her, squeezing her, holding her in place. *No! Myles!* She could not get out of all these grips, and even if she could, she wouldn't be able to see where she was going.

"Stop," the creature said again.

She trembled fiercely.

"There, there," it said and patted her head in the darkness. "Sleep. Go to sleep."

Sleep? She would never be able to sleep.

The hand returned to her face and stayed there. The smells of honey and wax. Heaviness rushed through her head, down her neck, her torso, her legs. *No,* she thought again and tried to move limbs that no longer responded to her. *Not like this! Not in the dark!*

The night filled with a deeper darkness. She felt the hands on her arms, additional hands on her stomach, then she felt nothing.

chapter 53

Firelight flickered along the rippling ceiling of branches. The trees swayed. The shadows danced. Leaves fell like snow in a wild storm.

Captain Isule had never seen anything like this. He crouched in the brush with Hileshand and the blue-eyed Alusian and tried to calm his sprinting heart. They had come upon the miron's camp about an hour ago, and this frenzied tree shaking had started shortly afterward. It had not ceased or grown weaker a single time. Isule's ears were ringing. His palms were sweating.

Killed by the miron, he thought again. It remained an unpleasant prospect.

He had no way of counting these things. *There are several,* Entan had told them. Isule now knew the boy had fed them an extreme understatement. *Several* applied to something that possessed the possibility of being counted. Who could count creatures that stayed aloft more than they walked the ground? There were, possibly, a hundred of the ape-like creatures jumping and swaying on the ground. The firelight caught in their fur and made it seem to glow in a ghostly way. A hundred Isule could see—but there were many more he could not see, except in the movement of the trees.

During the wait, he prayed to every god he had ever heard of, begging for mercy. He even prayed to Boerak-El.

The Alusian leaned close to him and raised his voice to be heard above the ruckus. "Tell me what you see."

The question was confusing. "What?" the captain shouted back.

"What do you see?" Entan pointed toward the dancing and jumping hairy bodies crowded under the trees.

What do I see?

Isule swallowed hard. "Ape-men completely covered with black hair, even the faces. Why? Why would you ask that?"

The Alusian smiled at him. He muttered words Isule didn't understand and, before Isule knew what the creature intended, he reached over and put fingers to Isule's temple. Instantly, the captain's eyes began to burn. He jerked his head away, shook it, rubbed his eyes, his cheeks, his forehead. What had the Alusian done to him?

"What do you see now?" Entan asked.

Isule looked again. A rush of chill bumps rolled across his skin. "By the gods," he whispered.

"The miron carry a peculiar magic that can affect the eyes. Now you see them as they are. Do you remember what I told you? Should this little adventure tonight not adhere to my expectations…don't let them close to your hands. Don't be fearful of them, but don't be close either."

"I will remember."

Entan turned to Hileshand. "What do you see?"

he asked.

"Twelve arms," Hileshand answered. "Some more, some less."

Entan nodded. "Good."

He set his hand on the man's shoulder. Hileshand looked at him sharply.

The boy turned his wrist, positioning his hand palm up in something that resembled a shrug. "See? Nothing. The Alusian touch does nothing, Hileshand. You worry for no reason. I told you." He turned his wrist again and resettled his hand on the man's shoulder. "Soon. It will be soon."

They waited.

The screaming choked off. The trees stopped shaking. Isule shook his head, trying to toss his thoughts in order, for the unexpected silence seemed to displace every piece of logic he possessed. *Soon. It will be soon.*

The crowd parted, stumbling over themselves to make way before a late arrival.

The miron that entered carried the girl. She lay across its upper shoulders, looped around the neck. Isule could not see her face, but he immediately saw the pale skin and blonde hair, and he gritted his teeth, knowing it was Amilia. She appeared unconscious, and he wondered how Hileshand would respond.

Entan leaned close to Hileshand. "Wait," he breathed.

Hileshand waited. Isule saw sweat on his forehead, despite the cold air. Their breath left their mouths in evaporating clouds.

"All right," Entan whispered, pulling his hand away. "Go now."

Hileshand stood to his feet. Without hesitation, he left the concealing wall of brush and walked into the firelight.

As the creatures saw him, they scrambled away on their feet and a few of their hands. There were cries of alarm.

Hileshand walked all the way into the center of the group. He pulled his sword and leveled it at the beast holding his daughter.

"That," he said, "is mine."

In reply, it seemed as if the entire woods screamed at him. The trees shook. The leaves fell. Isule pulled closer to the ground. Entan glanced at him, but Isule didn't care if the Alusian saw his concern. This "little adventure," as Entan had put it, was unlike anything any man had done before.

Hileshand took a step forward and roared, "You cannot have what does not belong to you!"

The miron gripping his daughter came forward as well. "She is *ours*. We traded gold for her! You cannot have her!"

"She was sold by a man who had no right to sell her."

The creature snarled, "We do not follow the rights of blood. We buy from those who sell."

The screams quieted. The woods grew still to listen.

"The rights of blood are not yours to protest. You have no authority to change them. Her blood is mine. You cannot have her without my permission, and I do not give it."

"Already ours!"

Hileshand lowered his sword. He stood there for a long moment in silence.

Fear rolled across Isule's body. A deep fear.

"Then," Hileshand said, his voice carrying through the trees, "I will kill you first and take what belongs to me."

For a moment, the woods were quiet. The miron standing before him started laughing. The wheezing hiss rolled up and down, warbling like the call of a bird.

"I do not fear your sword," the creature wheezed.

"Oh, no?" Hileshand smiled as if the creature had given him an invitation. "But you should." Drawing his arm back, he put his left hand on his blade and called loudly, "Abalel, are you with me?"

He held his hand on the metal. The smile returned to him and he moved his hand away. The blade began to glow.

Isule's eyes widened. Abalel had responded to Hileshand's request. *Are you with me?* Those were not the words of a spell. That was nothing more than a question; it could not even be called a request. Why would Abalel respond to *that*?

Concern flickered through the group.

"What?" Hileshand asked. He lifted the sword above his head. The light flowed slowly down the blade, getting on the hilt, which began to glow as well. Isule watched in fascination as even Hileshand's hand began to glow, then his wrist, his arm, a portion visible beneath his sleeve. The light spread down his skin toward his torso.

Hileshand lowered his arm. The light remained. His sleeve dropped down into place, but his hand remained visible, Abalel's light gleaming and overpowering even the glow of the fire. His hand was almost too bright to look at. Isule subconsciously pulled back as the light became visible at the collar of Hileshand's tunic. Abalel's mark moved, all on its own, sliding across the man's body.

It was, Isule thought, one of the most alarming things he had seen in his life. He had not known the god of the sun did things like this.

The father pointed the sword at his daughter. "That girl belongs to me. You will return her to me. You fear the god of the sun for good reason. You hide from even the shadow of his light. If you touch what is mine, Abalel will destroy you. If you do not believe me, believe Abalel. Believe his light.

You know his words are true."

Even the shadow of his light? What did that mean?

The answer came to Isule. *The moon,* he realized. The *shadow* of Abalel's light. The miron would not leave their trees, even at night. They would not step foot on the ground unless that ground was covered from the light of both sun and moon. He had traveled this part of the country many times and had learned much about the miron, but he had never considered that their fear of the sky had to do with Abalel.

You fear the god of the sun for good reason.

"Touch my daughter...and the god of the sun will destroy you. Every one of you." Hileshand made a slow circle, holding his sword out at eye level, repeating, "Every one of you."

The sword glowed. His hand glowed. The light moved up his throat, reached his jaw, spread through his cheek, entered his right eye. He didn't seem to notice. He completed his circle and stared at the miron holding his daughter.

The woods were quiet as the miron decided their course.

Later that night, they camped on the bank of the Redaman River, far from the reach of the trees. The night was clear, the moonlight spilling across them. The silver light seemed to ripple on the water like a blanket spread across the surface.

Hileshand sat by the fire and held his daughter in his arms. She did not awake for an hour, and when she opened her eyes, she did not know where she was. She hit him on the jaw. Hileshand blocked her struggles, rocked her, and spoke soothingly to her.

"*Goshane*," he whispered. *Little beloved.* "It is I, your father. It's all right. You're all right now."

She stopped moving and stared at him. Then she fell to tears, and he rocked her again, back and forth.

"It's all right, little one. You're safe now. You're safe."

chapter 54

Myles resurfaced beneath the grating sounds of laughter and rough voices. The words did not make sense to him. But he did not need to understand the language in order to recognize the excitement these voices contained. On the other side of his eyelids, happiness swirled like a snowstorm.

He pulled his eyes open and grimaced as the light brought him a new awareness of pain. His skull throbbed. Where was he, and why did he hurt like this?

Full consciousness crept back to him slowly. Someone had struck him from behind. He ran his tongue across his lips and tasted blood. *Behind and before*, he thought. He remembered the first hit, not the second.

The light wobbled as he tried to focus his vision on the action taking place before him.

He was still on the ship. The ceiling was low. Lanterns hung on iron hooks every few paces along the walls. Two more sat on the table, which was liberally covered with leather bags, stuffed to overflowing. Black string held many of them closed, but several of them had been opened, and gold flowed like blood. On the floor. In men's hands. Across the bags that remained untouched on the table. It was a fortune.

None of the crew stood upright. Two or three were flat on their backs, sprawled across the floor with black bottles, wineskins, and gold pieces lying scattered around them.

Myles became aware that he was seeing all of this through iron bars. He was in a cell.

At the realization, cold stillness swept through his bones. *Amilia.* He raised his head, his stomach complaining at the swift movement, and searched the room for her. She was not there. Something very similar to panic filled his gut.

The captain noticed his movements.

The man's name was Fherigan. He had been quiet for much of this voyage—Myles had seen very little of him. The first mate, Burtel, was the one who appeared to actually captain the vessel.

Burtel, calling out and swinging his hands, barely managed to remain standing. Myles had seen him drink heavily many times; every night, the man's steps had been a little slow, his speech slurred. He winced with the sunlight in the mornings. Tonight, however, he seemed to have lost all reason.

Fherigan caught the man's gaze and nodded toward the cell. Burtel wandered over, gripping the bars to keep himself upright.

Myles pushed himself into a sitting position. The light seemed to spin around him. He lowered his head, breathed deeply, waited for the rotations to slow. Long before they stopped entirely, he grabbed the bars and used them for support as he pulled himself to his feet. He almost went down again.

"Good morning, princess," Burtel said, and the room erupted with laughter.

Myles leaned close to him. Burtel was not yet drunk enough to be immune to fear. Blinking once, he took a step back, putting distance between himself and the bars.

"What have you done?" Myles demanded.

"Doesn't matter to you now, does it? We'll be in Port Soren by nightfall. You and me—we'll be parting ways there." He thrust a wobbling hand behind him, toward the table laden with gold. "You'll be adding to that for us. But, clearly, that doesn't really matter either. You remember I don't need you. You do anything I don't like, and you'll wish you hadn't, because I don't need you. I will kill you if you give me trouble."

Amilia. Myles felt cold fingers of fear press against his stomach and spine. He looked at the table again. This was more gold than he had ever seen in his life. *What does this have to do with Amilia?*

He gripped the bars. "What have you done?" he repeated.

Burtel grinned. "Made a greater sale than I have ever made before."

The room cheered. The captain sat quietly. He had been drinking as well—his position on the barrel rocked slowly back and forth. He adjusted his weight, turning his boots to better brace himself, and did not acknowledge Myles' pointed stare.

"What sale?"

Leaning back, Burtel put a hand over his heart in dramatic fashion and exclaimed, "What? You wish to know what happened?"

The man was a fool. Myles forced himself to calm. He could not allow the wild fear he sensed to build a foundation within him. He pushed out of his head the image of strangling this man with his bare hands. "Yes."

"There be things that live in these woods, princess. Things that are not men, but they pay as men. Your little girl was worth a fortune. Thank you for yesterday—for pressing her so hard to tell you about the pregnancy. Your child made all of this possible." The first mate raised his voice. "Let it never be said that Antor Burtel misses opportunity."

"Opportunity!" one of the men sang out.

They resemble men. They live in the trees.

Myles whispered, "You gave her to the miron?"

Burtel squeezed one eye shut and pointed at him. "Sold her. *Sold her* to the miron. I gave them nothing. I wouldn't do that."

They will know she is with child. You want the northern road. The northern road is the easier road. Myles gripped the bars until his hands turned white. The Alusian had known what would happen and had warned him, and he had ignored that warning. *What have I done?* This was his fault. His doing.

This journey carries a high price—and a higher price for her.

The miron were creatures that practiced strange rituals involving fire. Bithania had said it was now their mating season. He was uncertain what that meant for a woman, why Bithania would be concerned about it. He did not wish to know.

Myles fought nausea. It seemed to begin in the bottoms of his feet and consume his whole form.

"How far are we from Gressley's Point?" he asked, desperate. He heard the weakness in his voice and swallowed it down.

You cannot save her.

He remembered Bithania's words and shuddered severely.

The accursed first mate shrugged. The movement almost felled him. He staggered to keep his balance, and his crew chuckled at his antics. "Oh, I don't know. Fifteen hours, perhaps? Why would you ask? Weren't you listening? The blood games begin in the spring. They're training now." The man smiled. "You're big. They'll pay well for you. You will be worth all of my effort."

Burtel watched him with a pleasant expression on his face. He adjusted his position as necessary, with the wine steadily attempting to drag him toward the floor.

"What of Finlan?"

"The old man?" Burtel waved his hand in a dismissive gesture. "Doesn't matter about him either. Why do you care? We wouldn't have made anything with him."

Myles spoke slowly. "Did you kill him?"

"What else would we have done with him? Put him to work on the sails? Sold him as a stable boy?"

Laughter swept the room.

Burtel slid forward and patted one of the bars—a bar far away from Myles' hands. Then he pointed at the cell floor. "Sit. Go back to the floor and close your eyes now, while you can. You won't be sleeping tonight."

chapter 55

As they docked in Port Soren, Burtel proved to be more intelligent than Myles had considered him. Myles did not realize what the first mate had done until the strength drained from his limbs and he lost the ability to move. He collapsed on his back, his head slamming into the wooden floorboards.

"For safe keeping," Burtel told him through the bars.

He motioned to the guard, and the man opened the cell door. The first mate came in, and squatting down beside Myles' rebelling form, he patted his shoulder. "Something to keep you occupied, should you be considering thoughts you shouldn't be considering. You can't save her, you know. It's impossible to find the miron deep in the woods like that. You have to have a girl with you. The miron come only when they want something. And they definitely wanted her."

Myles wanted to kill him.

"What you feel now," Burtel said, squeezing the skin of Myles' forearm, "is nathsan powder. I put it in your food tonight, only enough to keep you…calm." His voice hardened. "You are not the imperious god you think you are. You can be brought down like any other."

"You'd best kill me, Burtel. I will kill you. I will kill you in a way you would not wish to die."

"Now, there's the strength his lordship will expect." Burtel looked down at him and smirked. "Try," he answered in challenge, leaning close. "If you kill me, my men will give you your life."

Myles couldn't even lift his hands off the floor.

The first mate's smirk became a grin. "That is what I thought."

They stripped him of everything but his trousers, chained him hand and foot, and carried him off the ship.

Within the hour, Myles could move his head slightly, but he did not begin to recover the use of his hands until the wagon stopped at Port Soren's eastern gate three hours later. He felt a faint pull in his fingers and realized they were moving on the other side of the shackles. He worked them, willing his hands to obey his urges.

The guards at the gate came near with torches, inspecting Myles as he lay there, strapped on his back to the wagon bed.

"What did you give him?" asked the first, peering down at him. He was a Ruthanian, Myles noted with some surprise. He had asked the question in his native tongue, and for a short moment, the others responded in kind.

Burtel knew these men. He was quite friendly with them. "Nathsan powder."

The guard glanced at him in the torchlight. "Wears off fairly quickly."

"Right. Did that on purpose. I don't want him slobbering and half-dead when I present him to his lordship."

"He's bigger than the last one."

Burtel grinned. "Oh, I know."

The second guard, the Paxan, bent over the edge of the wagon and held the torch near Myles' torso. He switched languages to jabber in Paxan, putting his hand down and feeling the lines of the half-moon scar on Myles' chest.

Burtel shoved him away from the wagon and snapped at him.

The Ruthanian suddenly developed an interest in the scar as well. "Wait a moment," he said, coming closer. "What is that?" He met Myles' gaze. "How did you come by this?"

"I don't care how he got the scar!" Burtel yelled. He ran his hands through his hair in frustration. "Does he meet with your approval? Can we continue?"

He grabbed Myles' cloak that lay in a wad in the corner of the wagon and stretched it over Myles' body. The night was cold, and the cloak simply draped over him like this didn't do much good. It did, however, what Burtel intended—the Ruthanian pulled away.

"Be warned. Lord Jasenel is much more familiar with the gods of death than I. He may not consider this man a blessing to his house."

"Or he will consider him a great blessing and pay more than he's worth."

Burtel was what he claimed to be—a man who did not miss an opportunity.

"Fine," said the Ruthanian, waving his hand. "Get him out of here. But don't forget our cut this time."

Burtel bowed low before them. "My lords. 'Tis always an honor."

The wagon jerked forward, the matching gray mares pulling into the darkness on the other side of the gate. Myles worked his hands. *Come on,* he thought.

The first time he had been beaten down like this and strapped to the bottom of a wagon, he had had no hope with which to fight back. His family had been scattered, the farm destroyed; nothing of his home remained. There were so many pieces that he hadn't known how to begin to sort them. In a way, Deregus had ruined him. He had removed Myles' reason for hope.

But this time was different. This time, Myles had a purpose, and he was willing to do whatever was necessary to achieve it. *Abalel,* he offered silently, *if you would help me, I would accept your help.*

For the next hour, he worked his hands and, when he could, pulled up on the chains, drawing on his arms, feeling the hold of the nathsan powder weakening through his shoulders and back. Slowly, he also began to be able to move his legs.

Beneath the cloak's covering, he aligned the sound of the shifting chains with the wagon's movements. He saw Burtel look at him only once.

Two hours after their passage through the gate, the quiet of the night shattered with a deafening roar.

The horses tossed their heads and sounded their fright. The wagon slowed, then stopped.

Myles had enough control of his upper body now to lift his head and peer through the shadows. He had heard a bellow like this before. There was a signature quality to it, something he recognized.

"What is that?" Burtel demanded of his men. He unsheathed his sword.

"Is that the miron?"

"Couldn't be. We have nothing they would want."

Goe'lah.

The word appeared in Myles' mind, a single thought that rose out above all the other possibilities. He knew what approached, and, along with that understanding, he knew what was about to happen.

These beasts were attracted to flame, to the light; they were not afraid of it. Upon human flesh, the oils of their skin had the same effect as boiling water, and their blood ate away what it touched—a large amount of it could even dissolve bone. This made them very dangerous to kill. Myles remembered Hileshand shouting at him when they had run into the goe'lah outside Tarek: *Into the woods! Away from the light!*

Myles turned his gaze to the lanterns hanging suspended above the front corners of the wagon's frame. The city had stopped at the wall. With the exception of the road itself, he had seen nothing resembling civilization beyond the gate. The trees were heavy and wild here. The night was fully dark—there was no light other than these lanterns. They hung there like targets painted on the side of a barn. And, unfortunately, he was chained to the wagon.

The beast appeared slowly, the light falling across hair-covered massive thighs and hips, a broad torso, shoulders and arms like the trunks of large oak trees. It was huge—several feet taller than the ones Myles had seen near the Terikbah border. The muscled shoulders were bowed forward. Lantern light reflecting off the slits of its eyes glittered like pinpricks in the darkness. The air escaped from its lungs in a hot hiss, rivulets of steam rising from the nostrils.

As one, every man around Myles scattered. They disappeared off the road into the trees. They did not yell. They did not hesitate—they ran, leaving the wagon behind.

The beast did not pursue them. It stayed with the light.

Myles jerked against the shackles on his wrists and ankles. He broke the skin and the shackles began to feel slick beneath the cloak.

The goe'lah put its head back and roared. The horses jerked forward and began to sprint, the wagon bouncing behind them. Myles pulled hard against the shackles, tried to sit up, but the chains restrained him, and the effects of the nathsan powder, though fading, made all movement sluggish.

The goe'lah roared again and gave pursuit.

This is not going to be pleasant, Myles thought, hearing the creature's feet pound the road behind him.

chapter 56

The horses galloped down the road for half a mile before the goe'lah caught them. It killed the first mare by grabbing it below the head and snapping its neck. The body stumbled, and the wagon slammed into it, flinging Myles forward. The shackles dug deep into his skin. He felt like his arms were being ripped from his body.

The rear wheels came up off the road. For an instant, the world seemed to float. Then the wagon dropped back down, and Myles' head slammed against the wagon bed. He never saw what happened to the second mare. He heard frantic screams, the crushing of bones. When his vision righted itself and he could see again, the second mare was missing.

The goe'lah flipped the wagon with a single attack. The wagon rolled and landed upside down in the grass on the other side of the road. Myles grunted as the chains bounced him in the air, holding him suspended above the soil. The wagon boxed him in. The only light was a flickering line near his feet, between two boards.

Roaring, the goe'lah splintered the wagon with its fists, pounding down against the rear wheels. Myles' legs released. Half of his body swung down and hit the ground. Grabbing the chains near his head, he hauled his weight forward and pulled away from the creature's hands as it groped for him under the wood. He could hear the six-inch claws ripping through the boards, far too close to his body.

That noise stopped.

Myles heard a hard heave of breath, and then the wagon lifted off the ground. Light washed across him. One of the lanterns had spilled oil and flame in the grass, throwing a golden glow across the road and trees.

The goe'lah elevated the wagon above its head, and Myles, dangling there, grimaced as the beast drew him close, growling. The breath was foul. Myles saw that the creature had been injured recently—there was a long, dark scar running down its pointed face, from the forehead to the jawline. The goe'lah roared. Myles gripped the chains with both hands to keep the pressure off his bleeding wrists.

The goe'lah shook the wagon violently and expressed its displeasure when Myles did not drop. It made as if to grab him, but as it released its grip and the wagon started to slide on the left side, the creature stopped. A second attempt was made, and when the wagon lowered again, the goe'lah screamed.

Pulling up on the chains, Myles propelled his legs forward and hooked one of his feet under the goe'lah's jaw. His toes responded as if he had kicked a tree. Pain jolted all the way up his leg, but his blow was solid and snapped the head back. The wagon hovered in the air then slid out of the creature's grip. Myles dropped twelve feet to land on his back.

Flashes of light filled his vision. Pain jagged through his

torso. His lungs did not want to function. He didn't see the wagon falling on top of him; he felt it only. Wood collapsed. Pressure on his chest, his legs, arms. Heat angrily jabbed into his right thigh.

The goe'lah grabbed the chains around his feet and dragged him out of the wreckage. Screaming at him, it slapped him with a clawed hand, and the force of the strike rolled him across the road. He was still bound by the wrists to the front of the wagon. The chains jerked taut, and he choked on the pain as his arms wrenched in their sockets.

The goe'lah started to drag him toward the fire in the grass. What remained of the wagon bounced along behind him, the shackles digging against his bones and tendons, the chains straight and rigid. Feeling the extra weight, the creature spun around, hand raised. It hissed when it saw the wagon following and walked around Myles to smash it to pieces.

As the chains slackened around his wrists, Myles lifted his head, wincing. A two-foot board stuck out of his thigh. The visible end was broken and jagged, covered with claw marks. Blood soaked into his trousers and spread slowly across the soil. He was bleeding badly. His vision clouded. He shook his head once, a swift jerk, to focus his mind.

He remembered the sight of Hileshand's sword after Abalel had put a hand to it. The blade had glowed with internal light. No sane man would do what Hileshand had done that night—he had killed these creatures in close proximity and had emerged from the fight with very minor wounds. He fought this way because he had asked the god of the sun to guide his sword, and the god of the sun had responded favorably to his request.

Myles did not have a sword, nor was he certain of the

exact words needed for the spell. Hileshand had not given details, and Myles had no idea if anything could save him.

But Bithania had told him that what he sought was in Ausham. Why tell him that if she knew he was not going to reach that city? Why agree to be their guide at all if the entirety of his fortune was this—being killed and eaten by a goe'lah outside Port Soren?

"Abalel," he groaned.

The goe'lah grunted in dominion over the shattered pieces of the wagon and began to walk around him, again headed toward the fire. Myles ran out of time.

"Abalel..." All intelligent words bled from his mind and he finished weakly, "I don't know the words."

He dragged in a breath and pushed himself up. His stomach rolled. The darkness rushed to close in around him. Dragging his arms forward, the chains taut, he reached for the board in his leg and pulled it from the muscle. The pain and the blood rolled freely.

Focusing his weight on his left leg, he climbed to his feet. A slight wind could have knocked him to the ground again. He staggered. The pain in his leg was excruciating.

The goe'lah still gripped the chains in one hand. Seeing him on his feet, it snarled at him, one fist lifting.

Closer, Myles thought, stumbling. *Come closer.*

The creature yanked on the chains. Myles' feet were ripped out from beneath him, and he slammed onto the road. Again, the flashes of light. Again, the difficulty breathing.

The goe'lah leaned over him, wrapping a hand around his left arm. The claws punctured him and dug in deep along his ribs. He felt tremendous heat as the creature's skin came in contact with his. Then the sensation vanished.

Closer, he commanded silently, grimacing.

It lifted him off the ground, brought him up near its face.

With his remaining strength, Myles slammed the broken board into the creature's throat.

Burning liquid hit him hard. It washed over his face, into his mouth, down his body. The goe'lah released him, and he dropped. He barely registered his impact on the road. His skin felt like it was on fire. He sucked in his breath against the agony he knew was coming.

The creature made a gurgling sound. It staggered around and then collapsed on its belly near him. It moved, trying to rise, but the shadow of its black blood spread out beneath it, flowing across the compacted soil like water from an overturned bucket. Much blood. The creature's struggles slowed. It set itself down quietly and ceased to move.

Myles lay there on his back, gasping for breath. He had seen what the goe'lah's blood had done to Hileshand's thighs. The top layers of skin had been eaten away, the muscles stripped bare. This amount of blood should have killed him. How was he still breathing?

With shuddering caution, he reached up and touched his face, his nose, his lips, his eyelids. Blood drenched him. It was sticky and reeked like cow manure. Everything he touched was still there and felt as he remembered it feeling—whole—but his skin was painful, bruised from the wagon falling on top of him. Everything hurt.

He sat up slowly. The pain pulled at his injured leg. A fantastic headache built up behind his eyes and stretched cleanly and clearly through his skull. He could even feel it in his ears.

He wasn't dead.

He rubbed the blood out of his eyes and looked around

the road. The goe'lah dead beside him. The chunks of wagon. The fire blazing in the grass.

He wasn't dead.

This was good.

His thigh throbbed. After a brief inspection, he discovered the goe'lah's blood had sealed the wound. Thoroughly disgusted, Myles released the jagged hole in his trousers and wondered how blood that did not burn him could somehow cauterize an open wound. *That doesn't make sense.*

But then, nothing about this made sense. He had been hearing stories about the goe'lah since he was a child; he had never heard *this* story before—a goe'lah that lacked heat, where the blood was hot on contact and then became cool.

His head was throbbing and felt heavy, as if something had been strapped around his skull. The links of the chains clinked together as he limped over to the wagon pieces that lay in the grass beside the fire and retrieved his cloak from beneath a broken wheel.

He was freezing and starting to shake. But he paused there, cloak in hand, and looked down at the black blood all over him. It was wet and glistened in the firelight. He was filthy. And chained. He was, obviously, going to have to do something about both of these things.

But not now. Right now, all he wanted to do was lie down. Somewhere far from this place.

Pulling the crumpled fabric across his frame, he reached into the interior pocket and, with relief, discovered that Burtel had not been thorough. The Alusian's letter was still there, as was the little stick of ash wood—a gift from Issen-El, god of the sea.

"Well, now," he muttered and made a list in his head. The entirety of his possessions consisted of a cloak and a bow without arrows. His lips twisted with mirth. "Better than last time."

He put the fire out by kicking dirt over the top of it. Then he limped into the woods. He didn't know where he was going.

You cannot save her.

Close to thirty hours had passed since Amilia had been sold to the miron. *Thirty hours.* He could not consider what had potentially transpired during that time. He couldn't. *Thirty hours.*

He could not think. How much blood had he lost? He no longer bled, but what sealed his wounds did not seal or assist his mind. He did not know where he was or where he was going. The ground seemed to pull at him, draining his remaining strength. As he stumbled forward, Bithania's words echoed in his head: *You cannot save her.*

Eight hours later, Marcus found his brother solidly asleep under a heresen tree. He had made it about two miles beyond the road. His cloak was pulled around him tightly. The chains from the ship stretched out beneath the bottom hem. There were multiple chains, many more than necessary. His attackers had been scared of him.

Myles was utterly filthy, coated in black blood from the top of his head to the bottoms of his feet. It had soaked through his cloak in several places. Marcus could not tell what was human blood and what was not in the fabric. His brother's face had been battered. His eyes were swollen.

Antonie swung the bag of wooden stakes off his back and kneeled down next to Myles, examining him closely. "He killed a goe'lah," he said over his shoulder.

They had found the body on the road. So had twenty oth-

ers—servants and soldiers from Lord Jasenel's estate about
a mile south. The lord was a well-known gamer. Marcus,
Bithania, and Antonie heard that he himself had come to see
the dead goe'lah and now offered two hundred pieces of gold
to anyone who could lead him to the man who had slain it, if
that man yet lived, which his soldiers declared to be unlikely.
Not if he cut the vein like this. A very foolish move.

It was rumored the slayer had a scar on his chest. A half-
moon carved into the skin. Apparently, guards at the city gate
had seen him yesterday—a slave being taken to Lord Jasenel's
estate. His lordship now greatly mourned the loss.

Marcus smiled down at his brother. Myles was extraordinary in the arena, no matter where that arena was found.

Antonie lifted a hand, fingers spread.

"You won't enjoy that," Bithania warned him.

But Antonie was being Antonie now. He had to ask the
question. He had to know what others did not know. Slowly,
he slid his hand forward and put a finger lightly to Myles'
cheek.

The blood had dried long ago, but that didn't matter.
Antonie held his finger there a moment too long, then he
jerked back. He inhaled quickly and shook his hand up and
down.

"By the gods," he declared and swore viciously. Swinging
his arm about, he lost his balance and landed on his back-
side.

Marcus chuckled beneath his breath. Even Bithania
seemed to lighten. The tightness eased around her lips.

The commotion awakened his brother. Myles opened his
eyes slowly, blinking in confusion when he saw he was not
alone.

"Do you yet require a guide to Ausham?" Bithania asked.

chapter 57

The Alusian knew the location of a wellspring that ran warm. The walk required less than an hour. The small pool was sheltered neatly beneath a rocky overhang covered with flowering moss. Myles stood there a moment, looking down into the clear water and then at the blood all over his body.

He glanced at Bithania and knew he did not need to state his concern aloud. He was going to ruin the pool, and it was obvious someone attended the area regularly. The brush had been cleared away. The area was swept and cleaned of cobwebs. A cabinet sat nestled against the back stones.

"It is necessary," Bithania said and walked away into the woods, giving him privacy.

With anyone else, Myles would have tested the water first and ensured himself of its reliability. The air smelled heavily of sulfur. The stones close to the water appeared coated with some sort of hard white mold. He had never seen anything like this before and did not fully know what to expect.

But he had determined he would not question Bithania's wisdom again. So he stripped off his trousers and without hesitation, dropped into the water, groaning as the precious heat rolled up through his body.

The blood washed off of him. There was more of it than he had realized. In a few moments, the water had turned black.

Marcus squatted down on the pool's rocky edge. He extended a hand toward his brother, palm up.

Myles was not certain why Marcus had been waiting to do this. He had been annoyed at the careful, measured distance his brother had displayed toward him. It was not like him. But now Marcus appeared ready for close proximity. Myles shook the black droplets off his fingers and grabbed the hand.

His brother held on to him, gripped him tightly. For a long time, he didn't say a word, and when he did eventually speak, his voice bore the dark vibrancy of strong emotion. "I do not wish to be put aside from you again."

Myles looked him in the eyes. "Nor I you." He eased his breath out in a sigh and strengthened his grip on his brother's hand. "Nor I you."

The first words Marcus had given him this morning concerned Amilia—she was safe. He had not greeted him before that; instead, Marcus had possessed but one concern: giving Myles relief. *She was never in any danger, Myles. Another guarded her steps.* Strange words they were. Myles did not yet understand all that his brother had said.

Marcus had also told him of the blue-eyed Alusian named Entan and his knowledge of the miron. Myles, in turn, had told Marcus of Finlan and Issen-El, the god of the sea, who gave gifts to men, unexpected gifts, three hundred miles from the waves.

A trapdoor set in the stone?

Aye. Finlan has checked the cave every week for thirty years. Issen-El always delivers something—but this was the first time he had delivered people.

"You killed a goe'lah," Antonie randomly called from several paces away. He was sitting on a squat, moss-covered stone, his legs crossed beneath him. He had done nothing but stare at Myles for the last hour. "You killed him with your bare hands."

Myles grinned and shrugged. Marcus released his hand and sat back as Myles answered, "It is not as thrilling as it sounds. This goe'lah wasn't like the goe'lah of the south. It bore no heat in its blood."

He returned his attention to the blackened water.

Antonie made a strangling noise in the back of his throat.

Marcus started laughing.

Looking at them both, Myles demanded, "What?"

Marcus shook his head. "Time to think a little larger, brother."

A stone's throw from the pool, Bithania Elemara Amary leaned back against a tall pine and watched the woods before her. She heard the men's steps and eventually saw their faces as the trees thinned.

A guard saw her. His eyes widened, and he warned his master quickly, "My lord."

Jasenel stopped walking. He saw the Alusian and a series of different emotions flickered through his eyes. Bithania had seen similar responses before. Jasenel, however, was much more purposeful with his emotions than some—his gaze was like iron. As a gamer, his standards concerning the sensation of fear were different than those of others.

"What you seek awaits you at the pool," Bithania told him. "His name is Myles Hileshand." She paused, her gaze intense. "He is more than you expect him to be. He is the fighter who killed the dragon in Blue Mountain."

She knew the gamer had heard that story, had discussed it at length with his associates, and she watched now as his interest peaked. "He fought a meusone in Tarek, and he is the one who cut the head from the *atham-laine*." She waited until the words could do nothing but strike him severely. "The preserved head you now possess in your keeping."

Again, Bithania watched the interest flare. It was very obvious, like flames in the night, rising toward the stars. The moment he had learned of it, Jasenel had put forth a substantial effort to obtain that head. He had purchased it for much gold and killed an associate who wished to take it from him. These gamers considered it a prize. The lore alone made it worthy of a vast fortune. This particular creature had never been seen by man before. None of them knew what it was.

"Myles Hileshand escaped the niessith on the coast. Last night, he slew the goe'lah with a piece of wood."

She eased her weight off the tree and walked toward Jasenel. His men tensed. Jasenel did not. She stopped her approach when less than a pace separated them.

Looking him in the eyes, she said, "Myles Hileshand is preserved by Boerak-El. Your gods of death will not have him, no matter the sacrifices you make for him."

Jasenel's look hardened. She could hear his thoughts and allowed them to run their course.

"See that you treat him appropriately," she warned. "You will not touch him in violence. You will not attempt to manipulate him. You will not use him for your own purposes. He does not belong to you. Do you understand?"

The man glared at her for a long moment. "Yes, my lady. I understand."

"Good," she replied and returned her back to the tree, folding her arms.

"Think *larger*?" Myles repeated, his arms folded and hooked over the oddly white stones of the pool's edge. The motion pulled at the claw cuts across his ribs, as well as the punctures in his left arm. He eased his weight back. "What do you mean?"

With a half smile, Marcus leaned on his heels and looked over at Antonie.

That was the only movement Marcus made; he did not call to him, but immediately, Antonie rose to his feet. "Yes, my lord?"

"Come put your hand in the water."

Antonie's eyes widened a bit, and he shook his head, saying firmly, "No."

"Why not?"

"Because that would be stupid."

Marcus' grin widened. "But *why* would that be stupid, Antonie?"

"The goe'lah's blood has blackened the water. The pool is ruined."

Myles looked at them both suspiciously. *What are you doing, brother?* he wondered. Clearly, Marcus was doing something.

The wound on his thigh was stinging; the hot water had reopened it. Even though he had reduced the pressure along his ribs and on his left arm, he remained very aware of those wounds as well. They were all beginning to sing to him. They would require a greater level of attention than he had given them so far.

He frowned down at the black water. And that attention would need to be given them somewhere else. But this soak was worth the pain. He felt awake now. Better. More like himself. The tension had eased in his back, and the goe'lah's blood had been stripped away from his skin.

He deliberately chose to ignore the conversation Marcus applied to him now. "I will need clothes." He glanced at his torn and bloody garments, lying where he had thrown them. "New clothes. Don't make me put those on again."

"Clothes are coming," Marcus answered secretively. His mouth curved upward at the corners, and a severe sort of twinkle jumped through his eyes. "But brace yourself, brother. This is not the story you assume it to be. It bears many surprises."

Myles frowned at him. The words sounded eerily famil-iar. "Why would *you* say that?" he asked.

He sensed movement beneath the trees.

Marcus stood to his feet as armed men walked into the clearing.

chapter 58

Burtel was with these newcomers, and he did not seem pleased to be so.

The first mate staggered forward, his arms gripped by two men much larger than he, who clearly did not look upon him with any level of favor. Sweat beaded his forehead. His right eye was swollen shut, the skin darkening. Blood coated his lips. He had been injured by rough hands.

Myles felt a brief rush of satisfaction.

Antonie moved out of the way, backing up slowly as the men approached.

"Yes, my lord," Burtel said, gasping for breath. He spoke hurriedly. "This is the man. This is the one I was bringing to you. I meant every word I told you! I meant them."

The lord gave Myles a thorough contemplation. His dark gaze was piercing.

"The one in the water?" he asked with cool precision, not adjusting his focus. His brows rose slowly. "Or the one beside the water?"

Burtel's left eye widened as he looked back and forth between Myles and Marcus. He groaned deeply, sagging in his captors' hands, and said, "The one in the water. The one with the scars."

But the lord had known which was which. Myles had not seen him look at his brother a single time.

Right now, Myles could wish he were not standing naked in a pool. He could also wish he had some option for getting out of that pool without an audience. Standing here like this, he looked like a slave again. The obvious presence of the shackles on his wrists did not alleviate his displeasure. Marcus had removed the chains and thrown them away into the woods, but the shackles themselves yet remained.

"You are Myles Hileshand."

With a disgruntled sigh, Myles nodded toward the first mate. "I am pleased to see you again, Burtel."

The man whimpered. Apparently, he remembered Myles' promise to kill him as clearly as Myles did.

"The Alusian speaks for you." The lord rolled his tongue about in his mouth and repeated with satisfaction, "The Alusian." He stared at Myles hard.

He held out his hand, and one of his men came forward and set a large silver cup on his palm. His fingers closed around the bottom of it and he walked toward the pool cautiously. Crouching beside it on the stones, the lord took the cup by the handle and carefully dipped the bowl into the black water.

Then he withdrew and walked to Burtel.

The sailor's working eye widened. "Lord Jasenel, no. Please no, my lord! Forgive me! I'll do—I'll do anything—"

Myles straightened at the man's panic. Drawing his arms off the pool's stone rim, he put his hands there instead and leaned his weight against them, watching and feeling little pity. In Amilia's absence, he had known a bitter type of fear. The force of it had taken him by surprise, and he wondered how he would respond when he saw her again. Burtel deserved death for his actions. Myles did not know what Jasenel intended now and told himself he wouldn't care, that he would feel nothing, even if Jasenel murdered this man for no reason other than to prove something.

"Stand still," Jasenel commanded.

"No, my lord—"

The guards obliged their master. Burtel struggled violently, but he was a sailor and, at times, a slaver, and he could not compete with men who appeared to have been trained for the arena. He could not escape their grips.

He shrieked as Jasenel lifted the silver cup above his head. "My lord! No, my lord!" Burtel started screaming incoherently and fought to free himself.

Jasenel looked at one of the men standing a few steps away, and that man came forward and took hold of Burtel's hair, forcing his head back.

The cup tipped slowly. At first, the angle was slight, as if Jasenel wished only to test the water. A very small amount struck the first mate's cheek and ran down his skin toward his ear. His screams grew more frantic.

The water left a bubbling, blistered trail on everything it touched. Jasenel tipped the cup a little more, and Burtel's cheek dissolved into a wide, jagged hole. His teeth and jawbone appeared on the other side. A horrific stench filled the air.

Antonie turned and stumbled in his attempt to get away. Landing on his hands and knees, he began to wretch repeatedly, his body jerking.

Burtel lost consciousness and became limp, hanging suspended in the soldiers' hands.

Myles had never before seen punishment of this magnitude. His anger toward the first mate dissipated, and he grimaced at the repulsive scene before him.

He fully expected that to be the end of it. But Jasenel, after completing his study of the hole in the man's face, lifted the cup and poured the rest of the liquid across Burtel's exposed throat. The sailor's flesh flowed into his clothes with the water. Jasenel watched in fascination as the man melted in front of him. His neck became bones and chunks of muscle. The clothes dissolved around the collar and down the chest.

Myles, disgusted, looked at Marcus. Marcus was not watching Burtel. He was watching Myles.

Myles suddenly remembered where he stood. He realized what he was standing in.

That was why Antonie had responded so vehemently to the suggestion of touching the water. And it was also why Marcus had not touched him, not right away.

That faint smile, rueful, reappeared on his brother's mouth. He held up his hand, the one Myles had touched. Marcus' skin was covered with blisters, as if he had held it near a fire. It was his left hand, not his sword hand. Marcus had *known* what the touch, still damp, would do to him, and he had persisted in it anyway.

Abalel.

The name seared through Myles' thoughts. He had asked for help, and help had been given him. He looked down at the black water, swirling against his skin. It was help beyond his expectations.

You bear the mark of God. He desires your life more

than the others desire your death.

As Ethan Strelleck's words returned to Myles, his heart raced. He fought a quick urge to jump from the water and run.

Drawing a deep breath, Myles remembered a ledge he had seen jutting out beneath the surface, positioned almost like a chair attached to the pool's back wall. He turned and sat upon it. The waters rose up his chest, coming just below the base of his arms. Leaning back, he spread his arms out to either side along the pool's rim and heard the clink of the shackles as they met the stone.

His left arm was bleeding. Crimson ran down his skin. The pool's heat was beginning to churn his senses a bit, or perhaps his leg was bleeding more than he thought. He couldn't tell in all this black water.

Jasenel's men dropped what remained of Burtel's body. After one more curious inspection of the man's chest and throat, Jasenel tossed the silver cup aside. It landed on a stone and rolled away.

He turned toward the pool. He saw Myles sitting there, observed *how* he was sitting there, and released a terrific groan, lifting his hands near his face with sudden emotion.

"Oh!" he cried. "What you could *do* for me! If that fool had only been an hour earlier! If there were no Alusian who spoke for you! An *Alusian* who spoke for you—consider the circumstances!"

He spun around toward Burtel's immobile body, and for a brief moment, Myles wondered if he would stalk over and start kicking it. But the man refrained. He forced himself to a level of calm that remained terse and awkward.

"Who has ever heard of a man *preserved* by a god of death? Does that not cause the mind to shake free of its moorings? Look at you." He groaned again and held out his hands to Myles in a beseeching manner. "*Look* at you."

Myles wished he wouldn't.

"A fighter who will not die." The man gestured toward the half-moon scar on Myles' chest. The black waters lapped at the bottom of it. "A twin of Ruthane. The chosen son, the son marked for sacrifice. Yet here you are, preserved—*preserved*—by the god of death."

Abalel was not a god of death. Myles considered Jasenel's words. The god of the sun who did preserve him; clearly, he did that. There could be no doubt of that. But Myles had never heard him referred to as a god of death before now. As he considered this, a frown grew between his brows, and he glanced at his brother, wondering what Marcus knew about all of this.

Arms folded, Marcus stood there silently. He scowled, but Myles knew this particular scowl—his brother was pleased with something secret.

"Tell me what you need, and I will do it. Anything. If I cannot have you…" The man shuddered. "Curse that Alusian! Tell me your requests. Please—give me a task before I drive myself mad."

Too late, Myles thought.

Calmly, Marcus pointed at one of the guards, one of the large ones who had been holding Burtel captive, and answered Jasenel's question. "We will need his clothes," he said.

chapter 59

They reached the gate of Ausham four days later.

Myles eased back on the reins and drew his mount to a stop before the imposing wall. It was not imposing due to its size. The wall of Bledeshure leaned into the sky and made this wall look like nothing—a small fence, something for goats or cows.

The iron was pulled back. The guards stood there, waiting for them to enter. They obviously recognized Marcus, the Alusian, and Antonie from their previous journey here. Myles felt their stares and the mild, curious comparisons between him and his brother.

He slid out of the saddle.

Marcus joined him on the ground. "What is it?" he asked, pulling his horse forward until he stood next to him.

Myles wasn't certain. But something shook within him, and that shaking had something to do with this gate.

Abalel. The School of the Prophets. The place where he dwells.

This gate was not a gate. He knew somewhere inside of him—somewhere deep and near his spine, he thought—that this next step was important. It was a commitment of some sort, though he could not put words to it; he didn't know what the commitment was, nor did he know who was making the commitment. If this was the place where Abalel dwelled—if what Old Finlan had told him was true about Ausham and the god of the sun spoke to his people here—did Myles want to hear his voice?

He considered that a moment. Was it to be expected that he would hear Abalel's voice? If so, what would it be like to hear the voice of a god? He could not imagine it being very enjoyable, especially with Abalel, who made the goe'lah appear as kindling for a much greater fire.

"What?" his brother pressed.

Myles shook his head. "I am thinking," he answered and looked at him sideways.

Marcus' brows rose. "Of…?"

"Of what is going to happen when I step through this gate."

"You told him?" Antonie whispered behind them.

Bithania hushed him.

The place where Abalel dwells.

If he put his mind to doing so, Myles thought he could *feel* the gate. He could almost feel some sort of current on his skin, like a breath of wind, except the trees stood quietly all around him. Not a leaf moved.

He heard his name. He shuddered as cold raced up his spine and bumps rose on his arms.

Myles. The sound carried to him on the wind he could not see. *Why do you wait, Myles? Come through the gate.*

He laughed beneath his breath at the uncommonness of

this experience.

Marcus frowned at him. "What?"

His brother had heard that voice enough not to be shaken by the sound of it now. Indeed, he appeared as if he had heard nothing. *Imagine that.* The chill that had seized Myles did not readily release him.

"That's an odd thing," he answered finally, shaking his head again. "Simply odd."

Marcus looked at him blankly. "What is odd?"

Gripping the reins, Myles walked his horse through the gate. He braced himself for what he would encounter on the other side.

But he encountered nothing. Nothing touched him. Nothing smote him from above. He wasn't ripped off his feet and thrown down the road, as he had half expected. *Calm,* he told his heart. What made him so nervous about this? He was not used to this jittery reaction within him, to the cold shaking that moved through his system.

Marcus fell into step beside him. "You all right?" he asked, looking at him closely.

"Yes."

"You are certain?"

Myles smiled. "Yes. Why do you ask?"

His brother shrugged with his hand, gesturing through the air. He seemed rather surprised. "Well…Abalel's touch affects men in different ways. Some of them walk through the gate and feel fear. Some laugh. Some don't respond at all." He glanced back at Bithania. "We thought you would… experience something. That's all." He took a shallow breath. "But it doesn't matter. Nothing is mandatory."

"So what happened when you came through the gate?"

Marcus hesitated. The eventual response he gave was

simple, but Myles sensed the depth his brother intended with these words. "I realized that everything Father had told me about Abalel was true."

A moment passed in quiet, then Marcus added softly, "It remains true. I carry it with me every day. My thoughts about my life changed when I felt his touch the first time."

The wind picked up and replaced the shivers across Myles' neck. Again, the trees did not respond to the increase. It felt like a wind, but it was not a wind. *So strange,* he thought. But no one else gave any attention to it.

Myles. His name. Spoken by Abalel.

A man would surely grow used to strange things within these walls. Who knew what could happen in the place where Abalel dwelt?

Half a mile away from the gate, Jonathan Manda's book grew heavy in his hands, and he set it down on his lap. Something had caught his attention, an item not on these pages, but he was uncertain what it was.

He waited.

Gradually, he felt a familiar wind on his skin, and in response to the invitation issued, he turned his head and listened for Abalel's voice. He heard words he had been expecting for days and breathed a sigh of hope, of relief. *Finally.*

"Myles," he said. "Amilia, my dear."

The man was sitting with his daughter a few paces away beneath a spreading oak tree. There was a large book lying open before them. They had been discussing a map of Paxa, spending a particular amount of time along the west shore and the Redaman River. Hileshand had detailed Port Soren to her—he had been there many times.

Both of them looked up at Jonathan's call.

~390~

He grinned. "They are here," he said and nodded toward the south. The smile filled his eyes. "Marcus and Myles. At the gate."

They ran. Both of them. Jonathan watched them go. Amilia, before she vanished behind the trees, whirled about and gave him the loveliest smile he had seen in quite some time. Then she whirled about again and was gone.

He sat there in his chair and considered the weighty glory of their hope.

"Entan," Jonathan called.

But his nephew did not appear. *Odd,* the man thought. Entan had been here only a few moments ago. He scanned the woods around him, but the boy remained elusive.

A frown eased between Jonathan's brows. *So again you leave me unexpectedly.* Again, he did not have a chance to say goodbye to him. It always brought a level of sadness to his heart when the boy showed how little he required human affection. There may be more *man* in his blood than Alusian, but his departures were always abrupt, always harsh.

Jonathan pushed himself to his feet and began the short walk to the gate.

Myles saw Amilia and Hileshand coming up the road and discovered he did not care about what he had cared for in the past. There was no propriety. There was no reason for distance. He dropped the reins and he ran toward them.

Hileshand slammed into him. It was like catching a twenty-year-old oak tree as it toppled from ax strokes. A solid hit. Myles had never been held as tightly as he was held now. In this moment, it seemed that not even the niessith had been as complete and determined as this. At the power of Hileshand's embrace, the caution slid out of Myles' hands;

he suddenly no longer possessed any doubts concerning this man.

Hileshand did not release him for a long time.

Myles' eyes burned. It was a peculiar sensation—he was not used to it. None of the words that came to his mind were adequate. None of them deserved to be said. So he did not say anything.

Hileshand pulled away, put a hand to the side of Myles' head, held it there, let him go.

"Good to see you, son," he whispered. Tears stained the shoulder of Myles' cloak. Hileshand noticed them and repented with a smile, wiping his face with the back of his hand. "It is..." The words trailed into a deep place in his throat. He tried again. "Thank you for coming home."

For the first time, Myles looked in Hileshand's eyes and felt no concern regarding the future. It was not that his concerns were suddenly removed from him, but he knew Hileshand would be there, no matter what happened, and that meant everything would be all right. *Oh,* he thought, the realization breathing to life within him. *So this is what Marcus knows. This is the reason he calls him "Father."*

chapter **60**

$\mathcal{T}$his was the first time Amilia had seen Marcus since the niessith's attack. She delighted in the sight of him now. He held her and kissed the top of her head, and it was a perfect meeting. She was so happy to see his face again. This was her family. This was hers, and it had returned to its state of completion. The world could be a good place again.

She reached up and put her hand to Marcus' forehead. "Are you all right?" she asked. "You feel rather feverish."

He smiled down at her. Her words drew laughter in his eyes, and she wasn't certain why. "I am fine." He hugged her close one last time and then pulled his arms away, saying as he did so, "I love you."

The words were softly spoken. She barely heard them. With a smile, she touched his shoulder and willed all the warmth she felt for this man to be visible in her eyes.

Furmorea was as different from Ruthane as black is different from gray—there were similarities but many distinctions. She had not said, "I love you," and meant it before in her life. True to their Furmorean blood, no one in her family had sought these words or said them. The words had been sought in Tarek, and she had given what was sought, but it had not been true then. It had been a lie.

But Marcus was worthy of these words, and she found she could say them and mean them without fear. "I love you, too, Marcus."

Her brother looked at her for a long moment. Eventually, he nodded. In the same quiet voice, he said, "I know." The smile returned slowly, though it did not seem as simple and honest as it had.

Before she could discover what troubled him, a hand dropped on her shoulder. She turned to see Myles, and every other thought disappeared out of her mind.

His face was covered with bruises and scrapes. *What has happened to you, aufane? What did that evil man do to you?*

Somewhere just below her jawline, all her breath came to a stop. She looked at him with caution, uncertain how he was going to respond to her now that he had his father and brother again—men who were his support. Antonie stood just a few paces away. Bithania was here as well, her presence cool and aloof and characteristically distant. Myles was not alone anymore.

Amilia had been five days without him. She looked at him and thought, *Five days. Do not make me go through that again.* She had wondered about this meeting, what he would do now, when his support was reinstated. Would he need her still? Or would he try to go back to what he had been before—tender and affectionate but nothing more?

By the gods, she thought. That would be a painful sort of death. She had not told their father anything that had occurred between them. She had wanted first to see what

Myles would do.

He pulled her against him and held her as his brother had held her. "I am glad you are all right," he said.

I am glad you are all right. Words that were truly callous. She took a deep breath, let it out. This was going to hurt, wasn't it? Already, he displayed distance.

Leaning into his embrace, she set her head against him, her ear to his chest. She would remind him of all the things he had told her when they had been alone, but she would allow him time, if he needed time. For the moment, she would simply hold on to this and remember what it had been like to be his only comfort.

I am glad you are all right.

She was glad he was all right, too.

Her ear to his heart, she felt the jump occur. She heard the unexpected tension, the sudden rampage. His grip tightened around her, and all at once, something seemed to give way within him and he broke. He shuddered, and she realized he was crying.

He kept repeating, over and over again, "I wouldn't survive if something happened to you. I love you. I never want to endure that again. Amilia…"

That was the scene Jonathan came upon as he rounded the bend. Myles was weeping, his arms around the girl. The abbot had seen few men cry like this in his lifetime, and his brows rose, for Hileshand had told him about Myles. The chosen son had been raised in Furmorea and was Furmorean in his thinking. He did not seek help. He did not understand why someone would want to help him. He knew nothing resembling softness.

These groans coming from him now, however—Jonathan shook his head. In a way, these were also true to his Furmorean upbringing. Nothing about this sound was soft.

This reaction had begun only a few moments ago. Jonathan had heard it from a distance; it had not started when Myles had come through the gate. So this response was not Abalel's unique and often unexpected touch upon entry. The poor boy was simply overcome.

Jonathan's brows rose a second time. *It is not Marcus' child,* he realized, looking at Amilia. It was the child of the chosen son.

Myles was the son of the prophecy—the man who, one day, would hold the Ruthanian throne in his hand. Watching the boy weep, Jonathan wondered how these things would come about. He should call a council to discuss this prophecy. It had not been discussed in fifteen years; perhaps Abalel had new things to say about it—additions to make.

Hileshand had retreated a little ways to speak with Marcus. Choosing to give Myles and Amilia privacy, Jonathan shuffled off the road and turned his attention to Hileshand and the son he called his firstborn.

Hileshand spoke easily with his son. His son spoke easily in reply. But Jonathan took note that neither of them touched the other. There was a respectful distance between them, something they had not employed before. Hileshand often communicated with his hands; he touched those he loved. Jonathan had seen him dote on his daughter. His hands were constantly upon her hands, her arms, the top of her head. He liked to speak without words.

Something violent had happened to his son Marcus, and this was Hileshand's first sight of him in the aftermath. There did not appear to be anything condemning or fearful in Hileshand's gaze, yet this son the father did not touch.

Oh, Abalel, Jonathan thought. *Your ways confuse me, and I am supposed to know them. Others depend on me for guidance. But what guidance and comfort can I offer here?*

The Alusian met his gaze. He wondered if the creature could hear his thoughts. Numerous times in the past, his nephew had responded to questions Jonathan had not asked, yet there were other times when Jonathan had asked the question and Entan had not understood it—further explanation had been required. So in the end, he was not certain what the Alusian knew and what they did not.

The female turned and walked down the road, making for the gate.

Marcus glanced at his father. It was a brief, searching look. Then he followed her.

Hileshand watched him go. Jonathan saw the concern flush through his friend's face and again felt a wave of pity for him. The Alusian had taken his son from him. She could direct the young man's steps even without words.

Bithania came within fifty paces of the gate and turned to face him, waiting for him to catch up with her.

Marcus approached slowly. He glanced at the guards along the wall and determined they would not be able to hear any words at this distance, if the words were spoken softly. The trees blocked this part of the road from the position of his father and siblings—it was relatively private.

Bithania studied him. He returned her gaze steadily, folding his arms and standing there for her inspection. He had become used to this now. She was more thorough than Hileshand. Her gaze was a rake through long grass. It overturned everything and saw everything, even if the process required effort and time.

"I warned you," she said.

He had anticipated these words from her, yet they still carried a sting. He shrugged, refusing to falter. "I will tell you what I told you before." His voice quieted. "You did not need to warn me. I knew. I've known for a long time."

"You will recover from her rejection."

As usual, Bithania was helpful, abrasive, and overtly sharp. "I know," he said.

"No," she answered. "You do not *know* this. But you should know it, and so I tell you."

"You are more convinced of my heart than I am." He met her gaze. "And you are mistaken. Stop it."

The guards watched them. Even across the distance, the focus of their attention was obvious. Bithania's horse seemed to agree with them. The creature tossed its head and looked at Marcus as if his every action was intended for its gaze alone.

He decided a swift shift in conversation was necessary. "Thank you for what you have done for my brother. Thank you for…restoring my father's heart. You have allowed him to feel peace again."

The Alusian's face hardened at his faint, well-deserved praise. In a way, she was like Myles, who, until this day, had not suffered much resembling blatant human warmth.

Marcus pressed her. "I mean these words, Bithania. My gratitude, my thanks, is worth your discomfort." He added dryly, "You should know it, and so I tell you."

She left him now, but she would return, and he was expected to travel with her when she did. Fulfilling her pledge to Myles and escorting him to Ausham—this was not the Alusian's quest. She intended something far different.

Marcus asked, "When should I expect you?"

"You," Bithania answered smoothly, "will never be able to *expect* me. You are a man." There was arrogance. There was snobbery. But then her tone softened. "Still, you should continue in your attempts. Your attempts amuse me."

He wasn't certain if these words should merely disturb him—or make him feel mildly horrified. He felt the wince flicker across his face.

She saw it, and humor drew thin lines around her eyes. "You needn't look for me. I will find you when it is time."

She put her back to him and swung into the saddle. The guards opened the iron for her hurriedly.

Marcus watched her departure. She rode out the gate at a strong canter, and the iron was pulled shut after her.

His steps weighted, he walked back the way he had come. He would remain with his father, with Myles and his sister, for as long as he could. In the meantime, he needed to come up with a way to tell them the reunion would be but short lived.

The plans and intentions of Boerak-El had not been difficult for Marcus to accept. The moment he had heard them, he had wanted them to be his plans—his intentions. He wanted this more than he had ever wanted anything.

But he could not yet explain that to his father. He did not know the right words.

chapter 61

Two days later, in the evening, Hileshand sat on the back porch of the little guesthouse Jonathan had assigned to them during their stay in Ausham. There was no railing, so he had dragged a second chair in front of him and propped his feet on the seat. Pipe in hand, he sat there and listened to something he had not heard very often: the hearty sound of Myles' laughter. *Myles.* The stern one. He was laughing.

Hileshand had three children, and all three were gathered now around the table in the kitchen. Since their reunion, they had told stories about Lord Jasenel, the goe'lah, and the Alusian. They had talked about Abalel and Issen-El and Finlan. They had also discussed the miron and the niessith, but with some constraint, because Amilia did not stomach either of those topics well. For two days, they had done nothing but talk.

A dramatic transition had occurred after Myles and Amilia had been ripped off the ship by the niessith. Myles was not at peace if Amilia was not beside him. If she stepped out, he twitched and was restless. He did not sit down unless she was somewhere in his line of sight, and he did not relax unless she was close enough for him to touch. A corner of Hileshand's mouth rose. All of this amused him in ways he had not anticipated.

Myles and Amilia. Hileshand had not seen the road markers along the way, but he thought he could, perhaps, see them now in the aftermath. There had always been something tender in Myles' treatment of her, even when he was upset. She argued with him upon occasion, yet he had never responded to her as he had with Hileshand and Marcus. Myles was gentle with Amilia. She was his gentleness.

Marcus had spent much time with her—but Myles was the one she had chosen.

Hileshand heard footsteps behind him. The door pushed open, and Marcus walked out onto the porch. He pulled up another chair, sat down, and propped his boots on the chair that held up his father's feet.

A moment passed in quiet. Hileshand could hear an owl calling in the trees. The kitchen had dropped into a suspicious silence, now that Marcus had left it.

This was the first time Hileshand had been alone with Marcus in what felt to be a long period. He wanted his son's voice. He wanted words. It did not fully matter to him what those words were, as long as he heard them. "Tell me your thoughts," he said, glancing at his son in the gathering dusk.

Marcus answered immediately. It would seem he had known what he was going to say in advance. "Unbalanced."

"Meaning?"

"The universe is unbalanced."

Hileshand lowered the pipe to his lap. He studied his son.

He did not know what to expect from him now. He felt he no longer knew how to anticipate his movements. But Marcus had just supplied him with a stepping stone.

"Tell me more," Hileshand said.

Marcus grinned. "I will always believe in that imbalance, Father, because it is true. There is only one, only one above the others. And all the others are smoke."

Finlan was very grateful for what Issen-El had given him.

The fisherman's lodge was less than a stone's throw from the harsh, stony bank of the Redaman River. Immediately after dragging himself out of the water, he had spied the building and headed toward it.

The one-roomed house had obviously been resting vacant for several years; the dust was like an early winter snow, covering everything with a thin white paste. But there was a table with chairs, a bed in the corner, pots for cooking, cabinets full of supplies, and more fishing rods than Finlan had seen in a lifetime.

Issen-El, he thought, *you give good gifts.*

For eight days, he rose early, fished until dusk, and released most of what he caught because he did not need it. The intent was simply to fish. He ate well at every meal. Fish stew. Fried fish. Fish with spices he had uncovered in a cabinet. He created new recipes. He used ones he had used many times before. And he felt in his old heart a high level of comfort. *Years, Issen-El. It has been years since I have had this enjoyment.*

He could imagine himself a young boy on the shore with his grandfather. At night, when the temperatures lowered, he would build a huge fire in the hearth and sit in front of it, a cup of tea in his hand and his ankles crossed before him.

And to think that all of this was the finishing result of a fist to his stomach and a forced swim. He did not worry about Myles and Amilia—he did not see a reason for concern. Issen-El had saved them once. He could save them again. Finlan knew they were all right—because he was all right. *Look at me,* he thought and waved his arms around his little house. *Issen-El gives good gifts!*

Early on the morning of the ninth day, there was a knock on his door. Dawn had just appeared over the earth. The sky was still filled with stars to the west. He was about to leave for the riverside.

His forehead wrinkling, Finlan went to see who it was. Perhaps it was the owner of the house, and he desired his house back. If that were the case, then extra courtesy was due.

He pulled open the door, a ready greeting on his lips. He paused.

An Alusian stood there—a young man barely beyond boyhood. The creature inhaled a long, deep-chested breath, and then, to Finlan's utter amazement, the Alusian smiled.

He did not say anything. He appeared to be waiting for something.

Finlan struggled within himself a moment and finally mumbled, "Good morning, I guess."

"My name is Entan Gallowar," the boy said. "I understand you seek passage to Ausham. If you still desire to make this journey, I will show you the way."

The smile persisted. It seemed genuine, though Finlan did not understand how it could be. *An Alusian who smiles? And he has blue eyes?* Where had this creature come from?

He had not asked these questions aloud, but Entan answered them all the same. "Issen-El sent me to you. He asks that you trust him one more time."

end of book I